CHILD BEHIND THE WALL

An absolutely gripping killer thriller with a huge twist

STEVE PARKER

Detective Ray Paterson Book 6

Joffe Books, London
www.joffebooks.com

First published in Great Britain 2020

This book is a work of fiction. Names, characters, businesses, organisations, places and events are either the product of the author's imagination or are used fictitiously. Any resemblance to actual persons, living or dead, events or locales is entirely coincidental.
The spelling used is British English except where fidelity to the author's rendering of accent or dialect supersedes this.

ISBN 978-1-78931-513-4

For Rod.
The best copper I ever worked with.
Good to have you back, my friend.

DAY 1

CHAPTER ONE

Monday 4 a.m.

'Mike One, Mike One from Mike Delta Control. We have a suspect at 1365 Lynton Road. Informant claims she saw a man carrying a holdall enter the rear of the premises through a window. Mike One, can you deal?' The CAD room went silent as Susan Limes, the dispatch operator at Southwark police station, waited for the reply.

'*Control from Mike One . . . all received. Show us attending.*'

'Thank you, Mike One. Any other takers?'

'*Mike Delta Four Five.*'

'*Mike Delta Two.*'

'Mike Delta Four Five and Mike Delta Two, thank you. Suspect is described as a male, approximately six foot, dressed in dark clothing. Suspect was seen to break a window at the rear of the property with an object, possibly a hammer. Units attending. House is said to be in darkness. Suggest a silent and careful approach.' Susan checked the monitor in front of her. The person calling in the break-in was shown to be living on the other side of an alley that looked in the direction of No. 1365. It was solid information.

'*Mike One, all received,*' said the unit's radio operator, PC Alun Evans. Susan could hear his partner, PC Peter Sackville, gunning the car into life.

'All units attending Lynton Road, be advised the duty officer has just left the station and is on his way,' said Susan. 'He instructs that the perimeter be secured and everybody stands by until his arrival.'

No one answered this time. The duty inspector, Stuart Norris — call sign Mike Delta One — was a desk hugger by nature. For him to turn out for anything at all, let alone a potential 'suspect-on' shout, seemed to render everyone speechless.

'*Control from Mike Delta Four Five, receiving?*' The normally dulcet tones of PC Andy Weimer sounded reedy over the radio.

'Go ahead, Mike Delta Four Five.'

'*We're about two minutes out. Show us to the rear of the premises.*'

'Mike Delta Four Five. Thank you. Let me know when you're on scene and await further instruction.'

'*All received, Mike Delta Control.*'

'*Control from Mike One . . . Less than a minute out.*'

'And thank you, Mike One. Mike Delta Two, your ETA?'

'*About three minutes.*'

Susan Limes looked back at her screen to see which of the vehicles attending contained two officers. Mike One, the area car, was always double crewed. As the main response vehicle and the fastest, the area car was also the borough's assigned pursuit vehicle. The driver was always teamed with an operator as a given. Budget and manpower cutbacks did not always afford the other vehicles the same level of security that was increasingly necessary. It was a good night tonight: Inspector Norris had decided to make sure his team were at least in with a chance if the shit hit the fan. All vehicles were double crewed.

The radio went silent as the cars descended on the scene.

* * *

As the suspected burglary scene loomed in front of her, PC Vicki Lane slowed the car. Her colleague Andy Weimer reached forward for the radio. 'Mike Delta Four Five . . . We're just entering the alleyway at the rear of the premises. We'll hold back about fifty feet in case anyone comes over the wall.'

Vicky killed the headlights and engine and they sat in the dark. Adrenaline pumped through her veins as she stared at a line of brick wall that was quickly swallowed up by the darkness of the alley. Both officers opened their doors slightly, ready to bail out and give chase to anyone who came over that wall. There was something about a 'suspects-on' shout that excited every copper up and down the country. The thought of catching Billy Burglar coming over the wall with a bag full of stolen goodies brought with it a rush that could not be had from any other means. Both officers knew from bitter experience that catching someone bang to rights was far more of a rarity than TV would have you believe and was more down to luck than judgement. Tonight was shaping up to be lucky.

'*Thank you, Four Five. Just to let you know we also have a dog unit on its way with a twenty-minute ETA.*'

The mention of a dog unit attending was both a source of comfort and fear. If there was someone inside, he wasn't getting away from the dog. Period. That was the good side. The not-so-good was that sometimes these dogs could be a tad erratic and had been known to bring down the odd copper if they were running after a suspect. Savvy coppers knew to stand and pull their arms in when the dogs came running. Still, there wasn't a copper on the ground that was going to wait twenty minutes for a dog unit to arrive. They wanted in and they all wanted to be the one to grab this burglar's collar.

* * *

PC Peter Sackville pulled up outside the house in Mike One. With the radio set to low, PC Alun Evans informed Susan

Limes of their arrival. Quietly, they exited the car and made their way toward the gate leading to the door of No. 1365.

PC Peter Sackville whispered into his radio. 'Mike Delta Four Five from Mike One. We're out the front and going in. Keep your eyes open for a runner out the back.'

'*All received, Mike One. Mind how you go.*'

'*Mike One from Mike Delta One . . .*' The thin, nasal voice of Inspector Norris cut across the airways. '*Stand by until I arrive.*'

The crew of the area car stopped in their tracks. Stuart Norris had earned himself the nickname of 'No Nuts Norris' among his team, on account of his preference for always hanging back until such time as he could assess the situation more thoroughly and decide whether more backup was needed.

PC Sackville heaved a sigh. There were enough units already on scene and more were on their way. There was no need to delay the inevitable. He clicked the transmit button on his radio. 'Mike Delta One . . . Your signal's breaking up. Could you repeat, please?' He grinned to himself and opened the gate.

'*Mike One, I said to stand by. Stand by! Do not enter those premises until I deem it safe to do so.*'

There was silence for a moment.

'Mike One to Mike Delta One . . . Sorry, guv. You're still breaking. Can you confirm you said, "enter those premises"? Over.'

It was the oldest trick in the book and everyone knew it. It just couldn't be proved — and everyone knew it. Sackville and Evans turned the volume on their radios down so that they couldn't hear Inspector Norris throwing a blue fit of temper over the airwaves.

Sackville flattened himself against the wall by the front door. He could see that it was very slightly ajar with no sign of damage. He knew the reason why. When an even slightly competent burglar intended to enter premises via the rear, he would try to open the front door first and to ensure another point of exit, should his original entry point be blocked.

Since the door was slightly ajar, there was every chance their burglar was still inside.

Carefully, PC Sackville pushed the door. It swung open silently — without squeaking. A good start: their arrival would be unannounced. The house was deathly quiet as Sackville poked his head inside and waited for his eyes to adjust to the dark. Nothing. He had to assume that the intruder was waiting for them in the shadows.

He pulled out his Maglite and shone it in front of him, his heart pounding through his shirt. He looked at Evans, nodded, stepped quickly into the dark and moved to the side to allow him in.

Evans found a light switch on the wall opposite and flicked on the hall light. 'Police!' he shouted. 'We know you're in here. Show yourself, now!'

Silence.

'Police!' yelled Sackville. 'Give it up, mate!'

Silence.

The two of them made their way deeper into the house, walking slowly, carefully, watching every door for any sign of a handle turning.

'Mike One now inside,' Sackville whispered into the radio. 'It's all quiet at the moment. Do we have an ETA for backup into the premises?'

'*Mike Delta Two pulling up now. Where d'you want us?*'

'We're in the hallway, Simon. Meet us in the hallway.'

'*All received.*'

'*Mike One!*' No Nuts Norris was shouting into his radio. '*I want you out, now! Wait until the dogs get there!*'

'Sorry, guv,' said Evans. 'We're already searching. Let us know when the dogs arrive and we'll leave.'

PC Sackville pressed his ear to a door just as PCs Stewart Greaves and Simon Hunt, the crew of Mike Delta Two, stepped into the hallway. Sackville raised a finger to his lips and the two newcomers stopped and nodded.

Sackville stepped away from the door and PC Evans replaced him. Evans's brow creased into a frown. Sackville looked toward PCs Greaves and Hunt and mouthed, 'Voice. Female.' He pressed his ear back against the door and listened again, straining to make out what the voice was saying. He felt the hairs on his arms stand up. He shook his head then stepped back, a finger to his lips.

'What?' Greaves whispered. 'Can you hear her?'

Sackville nodded.

'What's she saying?'

'Sounds like she's singing.'

Evans frowned. 'Singing what?'

Sackville shook his head. 'Sounds like some sort of nursery rhyme. Never heard it before. Sounds like *the childmaker . . . the childmaker . . . beware the childmaker.*'

'What the fuck's that all about?'

Sackville shrugged. His partner's frown deepened. He looked spooked for the first time Sackville could remember.

It didn't matter.

Sackville held up three fingers before miming a kicking motion. The four of them pulled out their tasers and took a deep breath as they waited out a countdown that would change their lives for ever.

On the count of three, Sackville made good on his instruction and kicked the door in. The beam from his Maglite sliced through the dark as he plunged into the room shouting, 'Police! Police!'

Evans, Greaves and Hunt followed behind, torches and tasers out. As the beams from their torches crisscrossed wildly through the dark, flashes of the room lit up, picking out bits of furniture, a sofa, a sideboard, some photos and a man lying on the floor.

'Oh, fuck!' Simon Hunt shouted. 'Body!'

The four officers all shone their torches at the man on the floor: six foot perhaps, a knife in his chest and a bloody mess where his face should have been.

'Fuck!' shouted Greaves as he jumped back.

All four stood rooted to the spot, their brains frozen and their legs not working.

‘Light!’ said Evans. ‘Put the bloody light on!’

PC Greaves swung his torch away, found the light switch and flicked it on. A sudden flash of bright, searing light flooded the room and caused each man to squint, heads down.

After a blinding second or two, PC Sackville managed to pick out Alun Evans and what he saw he struggled to comprehend. Standing behind Evans was a small, thin woman. With one hand, she held the dead man’s slick and bloody face to her own like a mask. In her other hand was a large kitchen knife.

CHAPTER TWO

As PC Sackville watched in horror, he heard a loud gasp. Evans's eyes were wide in shock and his legs were wobbling. Sackville heard a manic female giggle as Evans sagged onto his knees. The woman let out a wild screech and surged forward in a frenzy of stabbing and slashing at the wounded man in front of her.

After a second, instinct kicked in and PC Sackville charged her, head down, driving her into the wall. The sound of her body thudding against it acted as some sort of trigger and the rest of the shocked group sparked back to life. They piled in on her as she slashed and stabbed at the three burly policemen intent on taking her down and out. Any thought of tasers and Mace sprays never entered their heads as a mixture of fear and blood-red anger coursed through their veins. She wasn't going to get up again for a while if they had their way.

PC Sackville grabbed her wrist and twisted it viciously until she dropped the knife. He kicked it across the floor out of harm's way. Under a heavy rain of blows, the woman finally gave up the fight and fell onto her back. Three very shaken and very scared PCs stood over her, unsure of their next move. They backed away slightly as the tiny woman shook her head and painfully began to pull herself into an upright position. She scrabbled about as if looking for something. The woman picked up the gory mask and pressed it onto her face, the blood of the dead man mingling with her own.

Fascinated, Sackville watched the spindly frame of the woman turn onto its side and painfully, on shaky legs, begin to stand upright. As she got to a halfway, bent-double position, PC Simon Hunt took a Wembley-winning penalty shot to her face. The kick lifted the woman off her feet and sent her clattering to the floor like a puppet whose strings had been suddenly cut.

'What the fu . . .' Inspector Norris stood in the doorway. He had made it there just in time to see the Wembley winner.

Peter Sackville turned to Inspector Norris and snapped an order at him. This wasn't a time for rank; this was desperation driven by carnage. 'Get a fucking ambulance here, guv. Now!' PC Sackville looked toward his friend, Alun Evans, and all eyes followed his. A large pool of blood was flowing out from under him; his pallor was a deathly white and his eyes were glazed over.

'Jesus Christ . . .' Norris said. He took a second to gather his senses before grabbing his radio and demanding an ambulance as a matter of extreme urgency.

Greaves and Hunt began milling about, shaking their heads, unable to comprehend what they'd just witnessed and what they'd had to do to a small woman to stop her from killing them all. Sackville dropped to one knee and began to administer first aid to Evans. He lay on his side, blood seeping through his shirt and dripping onto the carpet. The wound itself was small but deep and it was pumping out small, rhythmic spurts of blood.

'Jesus,' Sackville said. 'Somebody get me a towel or something. Now! Move!' Someone turned and ran out of the room.

Sackville leaned into his friend's face and put on the calmest voice he could. 'Alun. It's me, Pete. You're gonna be all right, mate. Ambulance is coming.'

He could see that Evans's face was drained of colour, his lips thin and white. Blood bubbled at the corners of his mouth. His breathing was slowing down, too. Evans looked up at him with the eyes of a wounded dog. He gave a small, pained groan and took several sharp breaths.

'Where's that fucking towel?' Sackville shouted.

'Coming!' Simon Hunt rushed back into the room, bumping into Stewart Greaves standing by the door. Greaves lost his footing and staggered backward slightly, catching his balance on the fireplace. As Sackville turned and snatched the towel from Hunt, he saw Greaves totter and noticed that his hands were smothered in blood.

Greaves's hands began to shake violently and drops of blood flicked onto the wall. He grimaced, then staggered forward into the arms of Simon Hunt.

'Stewie! Jesus!' Hunt shouted.

Sackville saw it then. The patches of bright red that flooded Greaves's shirt. One on his right shoulder, another below his stab proof vest. 'Guv'nor! Get me that help. Quick! She's done Stewie too!'

In the distance, a faint wail of sirens — lots of sirens — told them that help was coming from all quarters. Other police units, ambulances, paramedics, CID — the works.

Sackville's mind swirled as he sat on the floor and cradled his friend's head. He was suddenly struck by an overwhelming sense of total helplessness. He felt a single tear trickle down his cheek as he watched Alun Evans die in his arms.

From somewhere in the back of the house, he heard a piercing scream. This house had more to give.

CHAPTER THREE

Fifteen minutes after PC Peter Sackville entered 1365 Lynton Road, the entire street had turned into a circus. Half a dozen ambulances, their blue lights still flashing, bathed the street in an alternating blue glow. Police cars that had rushed to their colleagues' aid were strewn across the road, left where their drivers and passengers abandoned them. At both ends of the street a cordon had been set up, a good three hundred yards away from the epicentre of the chaos that had claimed the life of one policeman and left the life of another hanging by a thread no thicker than a strand of DNA. Behind the cordons, the press had begun to arrive and broadcast their unverified stories to the masses. Facebook, Twitter and YouTube already had shaky, blurry video clips posted, courtesy of neighbours and passers-by who had got on with the important business of getting 'likes' for their blogs and pages.

Fifty-five minutes after Peter Sackville had entered the house, a dark Mercedes GLC SUV drew silently to a halt behind the barrage of press cameras. The first the wolves knew of Detective Superintendent Ray Paterson's arrival was the distinctive thunk of the door. Heads turned, followed by cameras and then a rush of reporters engulfed him.

'Superintendent Paterson . . . Jonathan Webster, Channel Four News . . . Can you tell us what's happened here, please?' A man in his early thirties shoved his microphone directly into Paterson's face. His cameraman followed suit.

Paterson ignored them both. Ignored them all, as he craned his neck to get a look through the crowd of reporters at the crime scene that awaited him.

'Mr Paterson. Can you tell us what's happened here this evening?' the newsman repeated.

Paterson turned his gaze away from the crime scene and stared at the newsman. 'Nope.'

The one-syllable response startled the newsman for a second but he quickly gained his composure and tried a different question. 'Why not?' It wasn't the best of questions.

'Because I don't bloody know, do I? I've just got here, you imbecile!'

That stopped the newsman in his tracks. That's just not the sort of response you expect from a senior detective in charge of a homicide investigation. Paterson strode past him and made his way through the crowd.

'Thanks very much, sir,' said the newsman, giving him the thumbs up and a cocky smile. 'That should play well later on.'

Without breaking his stride or turning back to look at the newsman, Paterson gave him a two-fingered salute then dug his hands into his pockets.

As he reached the cordon, the uniformed officer lifted the tape for him and he ducked under. 'Thanks, mate,' he said, walking on.

'You'll have to sign in, sir.' The young constable was a little unsure about challenging a man who was not much older than him but a good four ranks above him in the seniority stakes.

'Will do.' Paterson carried on walking. 'I'll do it in a minute. On the way back.'

As he made his way closer to the centre of events, he scanned the streets to see if he could see anyone he knew, anyone who might be able to tell him coherently what had happened in that house. In the distance, notebook in hand, was one of his team, DC Colin Yorkshire, talking to a uniformed PC. He'd catch up with him later. Paterson was also looking for the duty officer. He'd already been briefed that Inspector Norris was in charge. He'd met him a couple of times before at various briefings and hadn't been too impressed.

He glanced at his watch, took his phone out of his inside jacket pocket and scrolled through looking for missed calls or text messages. There were none. He slipped the phone back into his pocket and sighed. His breath made a little plume of condensation in the cold morning air.

He looked around the street again, keeping his back to the crowd of photographers who were busy trying to get shots of anything that might help sell more papers. What struck him most was the sheer number of people milling about his crime scene looking dazed and confused. He knew that whatever was inside that house was not going to be pretty.

He spotted an ambulance with its doors wide open. Sitting on the steps and silhouetted by the light from inside the vehicle was a uniformed police officer, running his fingers through his hair. He vaguely recognised PC Sackville from around the station and made a mental note making him number two on the list of people to see later.

'Gents!' he shouted. The ambulance crew stopped what they were doing. 'Do me a favour and shut the doors, please. Press are all over it.' He nodded his head backward to the crowd. 'Don't want to make it too easy for them.'

The ambulance men nodded, clambered inside and pulled the doors to.

Paterson stopped at the front gate for a second and looked at the outside of the house. The tiny front garden contained a broken fridge with no door lying on its side amid patchy clumps of unmown grass and small mounds of earth. Nothing remarkable about it. Mid-terrace, two-up two-down. Grubby. There were a few potted plants that hadn't seen a drop of water since they were planted and a water barrel that was probably a nod to being eco-friendly. The hole in the bottom of it ruined its chances. *So far, so standard*, Paterson thought to himself.

Standing at the front gate looking far too awake for five in the morning, another uniformed PC stood with an electronic tablet. His job was to log all comings and goings into the house. For him, this was going to be a long, tedious shift although, with a bit of luck, he might get to cane the overtime.

'Superintendent Paterson,' a nasal voice called to him from somewhere behind.

Paterson turned. 'Norris.' He gave a curt nod. 'What have we got here?'

Norris shook his head, a look of despair on his face as he recalled what he'd seen and what had happened to his team. 'Suspect-on shout. The area car was already on scene. The crew went inside . . . I told them not to — I told them to wait but they didn't. They found a man dead on the floor, knife in the chest and his face . . .' He struggled to compose himself. 'His face was missing.'

Paterson raised an eyebrow. 'And?'

Norris stopped for a moment and looked at Paterson as if surprised that what he'd just said hadn't seemed to faze Paterson at all. He took a deep breath.

'And a crazy woman attacked my officers. Stabbed one to death and hospitalised another.'

Paterson endeavoured to keep his face neutral.

'You also need to know . . . one of my officers, a female, made a horrific discovery inside. In the dining room.'

Paterson narrowed his eyes. 'Go on.'

Norris closed his eyes as if shielding himself from what he'd seen. 'There were human body parts scattered around.'

Paterson frowned. 'Body parts?'

Norris opened his eyes. 'Arms, legs, fingers. Some in jars, some in a large chest freezer. I think bits of the bodies were used to make decorations.'

'Decorations?'

'There was an ashtray made out of a skull. A small skull.'

Paterson felt his stomach lurch. 'How small we talking, Norris?'

'I think it's a child. All the bits were . . . small.' He dropped his head lower. 'And I think there's more than one.'

Paterson straightened his shoulders and drew a deep breath. He could deal with pretty much anything. But not kids. He hated the fact that people would harm children. Hated it.

'Where's the officer who found it all?'

'On her way to hospital. She was in deep shock. I'm afraid she wet herself and ran out in hysterics.'

'Can't say I blame her, poor girl.' Paterson looked at Norris. From what he'd said, he'd also been inside and seen the room. Maybe he wasn't as No Nuts as people thought. 'You all right?' he said, genuinely concerned. He'd seen his share of dismembered bodies and knew that it was a sight that never left a person.

'No. Not really. But what can I do?' Norris shrugged his skinny little shoulders. 'Part of the job, eh? I'll be fine.'

Paterson turned back to look at the house. 'Where's the suspect now?'

'She's on her way to hospital. She, er . . . resisted arrest, I'm afraid.'

Paterson shrugged. 'That's cheered me up a bit.'

Norris's eyes narrowed. No doubt his 'moral compass' was kicking in. From what Paterson knew of him he could be a prissy, self-righteous bastard.

The silence between them was broken abruptly.

'Oi, Oi, saveloy!'

Paterson recognised the voice and turned. 'Clocksy!' he said by way of greeting.

'Mornin' guv. Bit on the fresh side, innit?'

Paterson was sure he noticed Norris roll his eyes as Detective Inspector Johnny Clocks, large as life and twice as lairy, made his way toward them.

'All right there, No Nuts?' Clocks beamed a big smile at Norris and slapped him hard on the back.

Norris grimaced. '*Inspector Norris* if you please, Inspector Clocks.'

Clocks grinned at the man. 'I do not please, No Nuts. I do not please at all. Now stop gettin' all sniffy on me, y' big tart.' He turned to Paterson. 'You ain't started without me 'ave you, guv?'

'Wouldn't dream of it,' said Paterson. 'Just killing time with Inspector Norris until you got here.'

Clocks rubbed his hands together. 'Yeah. Sorry, I'm late, guv. I was a bit busy when you called.' He threw Paterson a wink and made a small thrusting movement with his hips. Inspector Norris shook his head.

Paterson looked at Clocks. 'Jesus. What are you? A dog or something? You never stop lately.'

'I know, right? Ever since I slapped a ring on Lyndsey's finger, I can't get 'er off of me. It's like magic. I should 'ave got engaged years ago.'

'Best you just stay engaged then, John. First bite of wedding cake and that all stops.'

'Yeah, I've heard that. S'why I told Lyndsey she's larding up a bit and to knock off the cake. She won't touch the stuff now.'

'Oh, she'll eat wedding cake, John. Trust me. But you really told Lyndsey she was "larding up"?'

Clocks nodded, a grin on his face.

'Bloody hell, man. That's brave. Dicing with death there.'

'Yeah, I know. Fun, though.'

Paterson smiled.

'So, as I understand it,' said Clocks, 'we've got some lunatic bird gone berserk with a knife, topped poor ol' Burglar Bill, killed one of us, fucked up another. That about right?'

Paterson nodded. 'More or less, yeah. A few things you've missed but I'll fill you in as we go.'

'Where is she now, then?'

'Gone to hospital. I'm led to believe she resisted arrest.'

Clocks smiled. 'Good. I love it when they resist arrest.'

Norris sighed loudly. Clocks turned on him.

'Rough ol' night for you, then, No Nuts. Sounds like you an' Teddy are gonna 'ave to sleep with the light on for the next six months, aintcha?'

Inspector Norris glared at him and bunched up his fists. He hardly had a reputation as a violent man, by any stretch of the imagination, but Clocks's continual lack of respect, especially tonight, might just tip him over. If Clocks had seen the man's change of posture, he didn't acknowledge it.

'You heard about the face?' said Paterson.

'Face? What face? Ain't 'eard nothin' about a face. Whose face?'

'After stabbing him to death, it seems our lunatic bird cut off our burglar's face and slapped it on over her own before she laid into our boys.'

Clocks wrinkled up his nose. He seemed to be thinking. 'What?'

Paterson looked over at Norris for confirmation. He nodded.

'That's a bit weird, innit? Never 'eard of anyone doin' that before.'

'I don't think it's a particularly common thing, John.'

Clocks cocked his head. 'Nah. Don't s'pose it is.'

'Hannibal Lecter did it in *Silence of the Lambs*,' Paterson said.

'Oh, yeah. I'd forgotten that. Bloody good film that was.'

'You didn't read the book then?'

Clocks crinkled his nose. 'Was it a book as well, then?'

'Yeah. Where'd you think the film . . . never mind. Doesn't matter.'

'Is there just the one, then? I 'ope so. It'll be a quick in an' out job.'

Paterson shook his head. 'Kids, Clocksy. Seems someone's been cutting them up.'

Clocks looked across at Paterson, then shook his head. 'Shit. That's never good.'

Paterson turned to Norris. 'Who's inside the house now?'

'Forensics are setting up.'

'I take it the place was searched thoroughly before they went in?'

Norris froze. In the panic and confusion, Norris had completely overlooked ordering an in-depth search of the house. Paterson and Clocks both glared at him.

'You better not be on a bleedin' wind-up, No Nuts,' said Clocks.

The look on Inspector Norris's face told Paterson that he wasn't.

'I . . . er, I . . .'

'Chrissakes! There might be another nutter in there.'

Paterson turned and ran toward the door, waving his arm at the PC on guard duty to get out of the way.

Clocks was two steps behind him.

Paterson burst into the hallway. 'Everybody out. Now! Premises are not secure.'

The two CSIs inside stopped what they were doing and looked at him, their expressions blank.

The elder of the two men said, 'Sorry? Who are you?'

'Never mind who we are,' Clocks said, his voice full of concern and authority. 'Grab yer 'andbags, make-up brushes and talcum powder and get the fuck out of here. C'mon, lively yerselves up.'

Clocks gave himself a satisfied nod as both CSIs took the hint and left.

'You got a plan then, Ray?'

'Yep. I'm thinking we get SCO19 here a bit quick.'

CHAPTER FOUR

The young PC on cordon duty broke the plastic tape that was strewn across the street to allow the first of two BMW X5s to enter the street. Inside each vehicle was a four-man team from SCO19, already part-briefed as to the nature of the job they were being asked to do.

Paterson guessed that the solid middle-aged man who got out first was Sergeant White. He fixed his eyes on Paterson, Clocks and Norris as he strode over. Paterson moved toward him, hand out. They shook.

'Sergeant Harry White, sir,' the sergeant said.

'Morning. I'm Detective Superintendent Paterson, the officer in charge here.'

Sergeant White eyed him up. 'I know who you are, sir.'

Paterson looked at him, a slight frown wrinkled his forehead as he tried to remember if he had seen Sergeant White before. He couldn't place him.

'From?'

'From the TV, sir. Seems you're quite the star these days.' Paterson felt somewhat embarrassed as Sergeant White looked past him to the other two officers. 'And this must be Inspector Clocks,' he said, locking eyes with Clocks.

'Correct,' said Paterson. Clocks and White had already gotten themselves into a staring contest. Paterson shook his head as the two men ignored the world around them.

'Do you two know each other?'

Neither man replied.

'Okay then. When you two lovebirds have stopped making googly eyes at each other, do you think we could do some police work? Just asking.'

Sergeant White was the first to break contact. 'Sir.' He turned his attention to Paterson.

'Thank you, Sergeant. I take it you've been briefed?'

'Minimal, sir. What you got?'

Paterson filled him in as to what had happened and that the house had not been properly searched due to an oversight. Sergeant White looked over at Inspector Norris and gave him a look that would have killed a puppy. Norris turned away, his embarrassment complete.

'So,' said White. 'You need a full house clearance, then?'

'Please,' said Paterson.

'I'll brief my team. Do you have a plan of the house? Helps if we know where we're going?'

Clocks saw his moment. 'You're goin' in there, skipper. It's a two-up two-down with a bog — probably on the top deck. I doubt you'll lose your way but if you're not out in half an hour, we'll come an' find yer.'

Sergeant White dished out another look and killed puppy number two. 'You shouldn't have waited for us, gents. I'm sure you're both brave enough to have handled it by yourself.'

Clocks grinned. 'Yeah. Coupla reasons we didn't. First, we know how you boys love a bit of strutting around like Jack the Peanut, puffing up yer chests in front of the press, so thought we'd do you a favour there — and, second, we're detectives and you're just hired help. The Commissioner's Commandos. Expendable.'

Now it was Sergeant White's turn to grin. 'That's good to know, sir. Now, if you'll excuse me, I'll go and brief my team.'

Paterson and Clocks watched the sergeant as he turned away and headed back toward his team.

'What's his bleedin' problem?'

Paterson shrugged. 'No idea, mate. But he doesn't like you, that's for sure.'

'Really? I dunno why. I'm a fuckin' delight. Ask anyone.'

'I have done. Believe me.'

'Sod him. What's the plan then?'

'We get out of the way while Nineteen go and do their thing, and while they're doing that, we're gonna go see if we can find out a bit more about what happened in there.'

Paterson went one way, Clocks the other and they spent the next twenty minutes trying to piece together what had gone on inside the house in more detail. It wasn't going to be easy. Those who went inside after hearing the scream from their colleague were now trying to wipe out what they had seen from their memory banks and one or two were trying not to be sick again. After ten minutes of getting nowhere, they decided to give up asking questions for now but each made a note of the respective officers' names. They'd come back to them later.

Fifteen minutes later, Sergeant White and his team emerged from inside the belly of this suburban beast. He looked shaken as he approached Paterson.

'House is clear, sir,' he said to Paterson. 'You still need us here?'

'Somewhere else to be, Sergeant?' Paterson broke eye contact and looked over his shoulder at the house. Something bothered the sergeant.

'I thought we'd all go and dip our eyes in a bucket of bleach to see if we can burn out what we've just seen.'

Paterson picked up on the tone but ignored it. He wasn't in the mood for a fight. 'Yeah. I'm sorry about that. I understand it's rough in there?'

'Something like that.'

'Round your team up, Sergeant, and wait in the van until I release you.'

Sergeant White said nothing.

Paterson turned his head to face the sergeant. 'You not hear me, sergeant?'

'Sir.' Sergeant White turned abruptly and headed back toward the van.

'It's not just me, is it?' said Clocks. 'Geezer's got a right attitude on 'im.'

'No, Clocksy. It's not just you, mate. We'll worry about him later. Come on.'

'Where we going?

'Inside. Something's not right.'

'How'd you mean?'

'Two murders in there tonight, yes?'

Clocks nodded.

'And they found, what?'

'Some right 'orrible shit.'

'Which was?'

'Bits of bodies an' tablecloths an' clothes made out of skin and some other nasty shit.'

'That's right. So if this is some sort of a murder house, aren't you curious to know where the owners of all that "'orrible shit," as you call it, are?'

'Now you mention it, yeah. But Nineteen said it was clear.'

'It is. Of live people. We're looking for the dead.'

'They'd have found the bodies, Ray. Surely?'

'Depends where they are, I suppose.'

'Then we get the gardeners in. They can start digging later.'

'Hmm.' Paterson wasn't listening.

'Still don't think we should g—'

Paterson was already marching off towards the open door of the house.

'Oh, okay,' said Clocks. 'Here we go then.'

'Oi!' a white-suited CSI shouted. 'Where you going? That's a bloody crime scene. We go in first.'

Clocks answered. 'Your crime scene's already fucked, mate. The world an' 'is missus have trampled all over it. We won't be long.' He turned to join Paterson, then stopped. 'Sarge!' he called to the small team of SCO19 officers milling around outside their van, all looking moody, one or two having a crafty ciggy and one or two sending up plumes of dragon-grade smoke from their vapes.

'Inspector. How can I help you now?'

'First of all by knockin' off the sarcasm and second, by getting two of your little firm to come back in with us.'

'Premises is secure, sir.'

'So you said. There's something else, though. Now get yer arses over 'ere an' in that 'ouse a bit lively or do I have to have you up on a discipline for refusing a lawful order?'

'Sorry, sir. Didn't know I was being ordered.'

'Play it back in yer 'ead then and listen to the subtext. And, just so we're clear, when I say anything to you in the future, it'll be an order. Gottit?'

'Sir,' said Sergeant White. He pointed to one of his team, a young black girl. 'You're up, Jen. With me. Let's go.'

Jen glowered at Clocks, dropped her cigarette and ground it out under her boot. 'Skip,' she said.

'That's the spirit.' Clocks turned sharply on his heel and headed for the house.

* * *

By the time all three entered the house, Paterson was standing inside the hall, hands in pockets to avoid touching anything, and looking around.

'What we after, guv?'

Paterson ignored him and looked over his shoulder at Sergeant White. 'What's behind this door, Sergeant?'

'Leads down to the basement, sir. We checked it out thoroughly. Clean as a whistle.'

Paterson nodded. 'Anything unusual about it?'

Sergeant White shrugged. 'Not particularly. There was another door down there leading to nowhere.'

Paterson frowned. 'Sorry? I don't understand. What does that mean?'

'Well, there was a door in the middle of the basement. We opened it but it was blank. Someone had bricked it up.'

Paterson shot his partner a look. 'And you didn't think that might be important enough to mention to us?'

Sergeant White shrugged again. 'Not overly. It's not like anyone was gonna bust out of there waving a weapon at us was it, sir?'

Paterson spun around and turned to face Harry White.

'All right, Sergeant. I've had about all of your lip I'm gonna take. Now I don't know what your problem is with us and frankly, I don't give a shit. But it stops right now. Understood? I don't know if you're new, experienced or just showing off but if you don't sort yourself out and start behaving civilly, me and you are going to have a real problem. Is that clear?'

Sergeant White took a deep breath and pulled his shoulders back. 'Sounds like a threat, sir.'

'Does it? Well, my apologies. It was meant to sound like a promise.'

The two men stared at each other.

White conceded. 'Fair enough, sir. I apologise.'

'Thank you, Sergeant.' He looked over at Johnny Clocks. 'And my inspector.'

Sergeant White baulked.

'That's the way it works with me, Sarge. You've been obnoxious to both of us since the second you turned up. So, apologise to him as well or we revert back to my earlier threat — sorry. Promise.'

Sergeant White turned toward Clocks who was standing with his hand out and a wide grin on his face. 'Bygones, eh, Sarge.'

The sergeant took his hand and shook it.

'Wow. Some grip you got there, skipper. Not gonna ask how you got it. None of my business. I can guess though.'

He winked at Sergeant White, who grinned at him through gritted teeth.

Paterson pushed the door open and peered into the darkness of the basement.

'Light switch on the left, sir.' said Sergeant White.

Paterson flicked on the switch. A dim light illuminated the basement from somewhere off to the right. He tested the first stair before putting his full weight on it. It seemed solid enough and he knew that Nineteen had been tramping around on it a few minutes before. He made his way down the wooden stairs and stood in a room larger than he had imagined. Sergeant White was correct. There wasn't much in the room save for a few bits of dust-covered furniture, a damp chill and the musty smell of old piss.

At the end of the room was the door. It had been white once upon a time. Now it was a yellowish colour with the paint peeling in little strips. Paterson noticed that the handle had no dust on it. No doubt the result of someone from White's team opening it. They wouldn't have been concerned about preserving evidence at that point.

He reached into his pocket and pulled out a handkerchief to cover the handle as he turned the doorknob. It swung back easily. Too easily for a room that looked as if it hadn't been used for quite a while.

He stared at the brick wall in front of him, which was just as White had said. He peered at it closely for a moment or two. 'The mortar looks new,' he murmured to himself.

Sergeant White and Johnny Clocks moved closer, both intrigued by Paterson's scrutiny of the wall.

Paterson rubbed at the mortar between the bricks. 'Jesus!' He jumped backwards, startling everyone.

'What the fffff . . . ?' Clocks instinctively cocked his fist ready for who-knew-what.

'Shh, shh, shh.' Paterson held his hand held up and pressed his ear to the wall.

'What?' Clocks whispered. 'What is it?'

'You hear it?' said Paterson, beckoning Clocks over and pushing him against the wall in his place. 'Listen.'

Clocks listened, but his face registered nothing.

'Keep listening.'

It seemed like an eternity before Clocks suddenly pulled his ear away from the wall. He looked straight at Paterson. 'Christ almighty. Is that moaning? I can hear moaning. Some poor sod's in there.'

Paterson turned to Sergeant White. 'Get a couple of sledgehammers or something. I want this open. Now.'

White got straight on his radio and less than two minutes later three officers from his team were taking their first big swings at the wall.

'Be careful!' Paterson snapped. 'If someone's in there I don't want them copping a faceful of sledge.'

A hole appeared and Paterson stopped them. 'Torch.'

Someone handed him a torch and he poked it, then his head inside the hole. 'For the love of God . . .' He pulled his head back and held the back of his hand to his nose. 'Fuckin' stink . . . There's something in there. Didn't see. Gimme a sec.' He took a deep breath, pressed his handkerchief to his mouth and looked back inside the hole.

'Christ!' He drew his head back and began to pull at the bricks. 'Get an ambulance! Get it now!'

Clocks and White tore at the bricks with him. The wall soon gave up its hidden cargo. A small child, a boy, wrapped from head to foot in cling film, was propped upright. There was a small hole in the plastic, where his mouth was, to allow him to breathe.

Johnny Clocks lifted the boy out and laid him gently on the floor. Sergeant White handed him a lock knife. Clocks cut away the cling film starting at the head, and after peeling back the first few layers of plastic abruptly turned away. He let out a deep breath followed by a dry heave.

Paterson looked down and saw why Clocks had reacted so violently. The child's face was missing. Clocks took a deep breath and went back to cutting away at the cling film, his hands shaking. He spoke gently to the boy as his eyes filled with tears and a fire ignited in his head. 'It's okay, son. I've gotcha now, mate. You're safe. You're safe. You'll be all right.'

Paterson poked his head inside the wall and shone the torch to the right. Nothing. He turned to his left and lit up another cling-filmed body.

By the time paramedics had removed as much cling film from the boy as they could and got tubes into him, the wall had given up another five bodies, three little girls and two boys. They were older — ten, maybe twelve. All were dead, all in various states of decay. Five minutes later, the young boy breathed his last.

Paterson stood in the middle of the room and closed his eyes. 'Tear this fucking house to pieces,' he said. That was an order.

CHAPTER FIVE

Paterson and Clocks stood outside the house as the first rays of the early morning sun crept over the rooftops. Paterson took a deep breath and tried to process what he'd seen and done in the basement.

This was going to be something to share with Eileen next Monday. Eileen Markham was his Met-appointed counsellor whose sole job was to ensure that Paterson was given a space to vent his feelings every fortnight. This served two purposes: the first, to alleviate the Met of some of their responsibilities to an employee, should he ever decide to sue for damages; the second, for Eileen to provide HR with accurate reports as to his state of mind and progress. From her point of view, she was concerned that he wasn't making proper progress. She'd long ago cottoned on that he wasn't being truthful with her and his sudden flashes of rage when she brought up certain things with him caused her some concern — though not enough to do anything about it. From his point of view, the whole thing was a waste of time.

Clocks began walking around in little circles. Every so often he would ball his fists, grimace and shake his head. Paterson knew his friend well enough to know that his anger was building and it was best just to stay out of the way and leave him alone to work it out himself. He just hoped no senior officer came along poking his nose in. Despite his profession, Clocks wasn't the biggest fan of authority and he most definitely wasn't the biggest fan of senior officers who thought they were better than anyone else.

A dark Jaguar pulled up at the end of the street and a uniformed police officer stepped out of the back. Paterson recognised Commander Peter Lewis. He'd had a run-in with him before, mostly around the time of the Adam Walker case when Lewis was a superintendent. He seemed a decent enough man, but Paterson couldn't warm to him. If you asked him why, he couldn't give an answer. Johnny Clocks had him down as a 'proper wrong 'un'. Not one to trust.

The look on Lewis's face told Paterson that he wasn't here for fun. He hoped the man was just looking for an update so that he could feed the reporters their titbits at the inevitable press conference.

'Mr Paterson!' he called. Commander Lewis made a bee-line for the pair of them.

'Sir,' said Paterson. Clocks gave him a weak nod and turned away. 'What brings you here?'

'Seriously? A dead police officer, another seriously wounded and a dead burglar with no face. Why would I not be here?'

Clocks turned back to face him. ''Cos it's early in the mornin' and it's a bit near the sharp end. Just sayin'.'

Lewis squinted at him from under the peak of his cap. 'I see you haven't changed, Inspector Clocks.'

'It's Detective Inspector Clocks, sir, and I try not to. I'm a big believer in continuity. Very important, don't you think?'

'Let me bring you up to speed, sir,' Paterson cut in before Clocks brought the conversation down a level. 'We searched the property and found six children behind the wall. Five were dead, had been for a while and one alive. Barely. We got to him first. Unfortunately, he didn't make it.'

Commander Lewis stared at him, then shook his head slowly. 'Dear God. Who gave you permission to conduct an invasive search? That's for specialists to do. You may have contaminated the whole scene.'

Paterson was stunned. Clocks glowered at Lewis. It was as if the man hadn't heard what they'd just said about the children. Paterson was the first to speak.

'I'm sorry? Are you really going to get sniffy about protocol and evidence when we dug out a dying child from behind a solid brick wall? What's the matter with you?'

'Don't take that tone with me, Paterson. You know there are set ways of dealing with things. If you've screwed up the crime scene, then we may lose any possibility of conviction.'

Clocks started to pace the floor, his lips set thin and his fingers balling and stretching.

'You know what?' Paterson said. 'Fuck the crime scene. The kid's life was more important and I'm not hanging about until some bloke in a white paper suit and a hammer does exactly what we did. We saved his life.'

'Evidently, you didn't. Didn't you say he died?'

Paterson took a step back and shook his head in disbelief. 'What? What'd you say?' He moved toward Lewis, his face taking on a hard look.

'Oi, Lewis!'

Commander Lewis snapped around to face a visibly angry Johnny Clocks.

'Do us all a favour an' fuck off back to the ivory tower you live in. Go on. Off you go an' tell Commissioner Anderson we've been naughty boys again. He'll cream his tighty-whities at the thought of putting us in front of another disciplinary panel.'

Lewis removed his cap and thrust it under his armpit. A little blue vein was pulsing on his forehead as he lunged forward. Clocks took a quick step back, a smile on his face.

'Woah, look out, Ray. The commander here thinks he's gonna 'ave a go.'

Lewis checked himself. There were far too many witnesses around for him to lose his temper, let alone give the impression of even thinking of assaulting a junior colleague.

'I swear to God, Clocks. One of these days . . .'

'Yeah, well. Today ain't it, is it?'

'No. Today isn't. But your day is coming.'

'Is that right?'

Commander Lewis glared at Clocks. 'Oh, yeah, that's right. Just a matter of time.'

'Ooh. Scary ol' stuff.'

'Sir,' said Paterson. 'We did what had to be done. What *needed* to be done. Now, if you want to make something of it, that's your prerogative. You go ahead. I'm happy to justify my actions to anyone. Now, we have to get on. As DI Clocks said, go back to your ivory tower. Thanks for coming.'

Lewis looked back and forth at each man, clearly fuming at his treatment from such junior officers. He jabbed his index finger at the air. 'Full updates, Paterson. You keep me posted every step of the way. Understand?'

'Yes, sir. I'm on it.'

With that, the fifth most senior rank in the Met turned away and stormed back to his car. Paterson and Clocks said nothing as they watched him slip into the back seat and slam the door.

'What now?' said Clocks.

'Now we go to the hospital. We see this woman and try to find out what the fuck's happened here.'

CHAPTER SIX

Back in the car, Paterson rubbed his eyes and face with both hands before reaching around and scratching the back of his neck. He was tired. Mentally weary. This day was just getting started.

'How long you had this, then?' said Clocks. Paterson guessed that he didn't want to talk about the house or its occupants. He needed to change the subject.

'What?' Paterson stopped scratching.

'This. How long you had it?'

Paterson twigged. 'The car, you mean?'

'Yes, the car. Where's the Aston gone?'

'Sold it.'

'What? Why? I loved that car. Why didn't you give me first refusal?'

'Sorry, John. I didn't know you had two hundred odd grand sitting around doing nothing? You should have said.'

Clocks shifted uncomfortably in his seat. 'You know I ain't. But we could've worked something out. We're mates.'

Paterson gave him a grin and a slow nod. 'What? Hundred pound a month for the rest of your life.'

Clocks gave him a feigned look of hurt. 'Yeah, all right. No need for that, was there? We've not all got squillion pound trust funds, 'ave we?'

'No,' Paterson said. 'That was out of order. My bad. Sorry.'

'S'all right, you knob. I'll let you off. Seriously, though, why the change? You goin' skint?'

'Skint? Not at all. It's just that you kept telling me I looked like a flash Herbert driving around in a showy motor and I got to thinking you may be right. So I flogged it.'

'I also said that blokes with big cars like your Aston 'ave all got little dicks. That got anything to do with it? Are you fed up advertisin' the fact?'

'What? No. What're you talkin' about?'

'You sure. I mean, you have got a little dick, aintcha?' He waggled his pinky finger at Paterson.

'I don't think so. Your Lyndsey seemed happy enough with it.'

Clocks's grin dropped. 'What?'

'You heard.'

'Don't joke about that. Out of order, that is. I love her.'

I know you do. Don't say I've got a little dick, then.'

'Fair enough then, donkey boy. You ain't got a little dick.'

'Good. Going back to what you said, I've actually got even more money now. I flogged the car and cancelled the order for the Aston Vanquish, so I'm quids in. And that's all thanks to you, matey. Sound advice.'

Clocks stared at him. 'Bastard!'

Paterson grinned and started up the car.

* * *

Two armed guards stood outside the private room of the woman guilty of at least two murders they knew of, and maybe many more. Paterson and Clocks held up their warrant cards to the first guard they came to. He studied them closely for any irregularities. Satisfied, he let them pass.

The room was cool, dimly lit and deathly quiet. Lying on the bed was a woman who looked no bigger than a starved rat. Both of her hands were secured to the bed rails by handcuffs. She appeared to be sleeping but stirred slightly as the two policemen approached her bed.

Paterson noticed that her face was swollen and she had a bruised and puffy right eye. There were a few specks of dry blood on her chin. Had this been any other woman, Paterson would have been outraged at her treatment. For this woman though, his bag of fucks was empty.

'Wake up,' he said. No politeness.

The woman stirred some more.

Clocks slapped her shoulder with the back of his hand. 'Oi! C'mon, princess. Wake up. Time to talk.'

The woman's eyes seemed to take ages as they flickered open. Paterson could see that the white of her right eye was fully bloodshot. Whoever hit her hadn't been playing around. He made a mental note to find out who did this to her. He owed him a drink.

'Did they sing to you?' The woman's voice was slurry, the result of a heavy dose of painkillers, swollen lips and a couple of loose teeth.

Clocks frowned and bent closer. 'What'd you say?' said Clocks.

She licked her lips as if thirsty. 'Did they sing to you?'

Paterson and Clocks looked at each other.

'They sing to me. Listen . . .'

'Who sings to you?' said Paterson.

The woman said nothing, listening to the sound only she could hear. Her face dropped and a look of sadness spread across it.

'My children. My babies. They sing to me.'

Paterson looked across at Clocks and shrugged.

'Bloke in a room down the corridor's got 'is radio on. Probably that.' Clocks shrugged back.

'My babies . . .'

'What do they sing to you, love?' said Paterson.

She fixed her eyes on him. 'Muuuuummmmyyy,' she moaned.

'What's she say?' said Clocks.

'Not sure. I think it was Mummy.'

Clocks wrinkled his nose. 'She's off her fuckin' nut, Ray.'

'And thank you, Doctor Clocks. Duly noted.'

The woman continued to moan, quieter this time, until the sound faded to nothing.

'He'll . . . come soooooon.'

'What?' said Clocks. 'Who's coming?'

'He'll . . . come . . .'

'Yeah, I know. You said that. Who's coming?'

'He's coming for you . . .'

'Is 'e? Is 'e as mad as you then, love?'

Paterson leaned in closer. 'C'mon. Tell us. Who's coming?'

'The . . . Childmaker, the Childmaker . . .' she whispered in a sing-song voice.

'The who?'

Suddenly the little woman sprang upward and forwards, her mouth gaping to show a row of broken yellow teeth mottled by blood and spit. Paterson jumped back just before the woman's teeth snapped down on nothing but air.

And then she kicked off. Her face twisted red with fury. 'He will come! He will come!' she screamed. The handcuffs clinked against the metal guardrail as she fought furiously to free herself from her restraints.

The two guards burst into the room. Paterson held his hand up to them. 'It's okay,' he said. 'We're okay. You can stand down.'

Outside, the sound of urgent footsteps came running toward them. Two nurses pushed their way past the two guards.

'What's going on?' said the older of the two.

'He will kill you! He'll fucking kill you all! Babies! You'll all be fucking babies. My babies! My babies!' She threw her head back and let out a gut-wrenching scream.

Everyone stood stock still, not sure how to play this.

Clocks looked at the young nurse standing next to him. She was clearly upset but too inexperienced to know quite what to do. Her more senior colleague was running for the medicine cabinet.

'Oh,' said Clocks to the young nurse. 'I was gonna tell you that on the way out.' He had to raise his voice over the still screaming woman.

The nurse looked at him. 'What? Tell me what?'

'I dunno what's 'appened, but for some reason, she woke up with the right 'ump.' He sauntered out of the room.

CHAPTER SEVEN

The office for today's meeting was on the seventh floor of New Scotland Yard. It was big, bright and air-conditioned. In the middle was a large laminated desk surrounded by twelve high-backed orthopaedic chairs, only six of which were occupied. They seated three very senior Metropolitan police officers: Assistant Commissioner Sam Morne; Deputy Commissioner Richard Johnson; Assistant Commissioner (Crime) Richard North. Two seats were given over to Lucinda Rosebery, the Chief Constable of the Greater Manchester Police, and Lauren Harris, Director of Public Prosecutions.

One chair still to be filled at the head of the table was for Sir Scott Anderson, the Metropolitan Police Commissioner. To the right of Anderson's chair was a less comfortable one in which sat Sacha Kirby, today's note-taker.

It was Anderson who had called the meeting for 11:30 a.m. sharp and it was he who was five minutes late, a deliberate tactic on his part. He loathed people who were tardy but he was the type of man who considered himself just that bit better than most and keeping important people waiting was a ploy to let them know he was in charge.

Lauren Harris looked up from her papers at the clock on the wall. Six minutes late now. That was his usual period of tardiness and woe betide anyone who came into the room later than him.

Sure enough, she heard his cracked-ice laugh coming from outside the room as he finished off a brief conversation with someone of no importance to him.

The door opened and Anderson strode into the room in full regalia — very smart, everything sharply pressed, not a double crease in sight — and carrying a black and aluminium attaché case. He flashed a crooked smile and said, 'Good morning, everyone. My apologies for the late appearance. Thank you all for coming this morning.'

He sat himself down at the head of the table and clicked open the briefcase. He pulled out a two-inch-thick pile of papers, dropped it onto the desk and untied the purple ribbon that held it all together.

'I take it everyone has got to know each other by now? Is there any need for us to do round-robin introductions?'

The room agreed there wasn't.

'Good. Let's get to it then, shall we?'

Everybody shifted in their seats, getting themselves comfortable, and fiddled about with their pens and paper, until Anderson began.

'I've called you all here today for reasons that will become apparent as we go along. As you all know, nearly four weeks ago, Detective Chief Inspector Lambert, the head of the Beckenham and Bromley murder squad, was gunned down in his office. His attacker then set about carving a single word into his chest . . . *Leave*. We don't know what was meant by it. Lambert survived. Unfortunately, he is in a bad way and he is not expected to recover. His family are making preparations for his departure.

'We put together a squad consisting of some of our very best detectives, which is quite literally working twenty-four-seven, and they have been making some headway but not enough.'

He pressed a button on his remote control and a fifty-two-inch screen at the back of the room snapped to life. The image of a figure, head down and wearing a baseball cap, filled the screen.

'The footage you're about to see has been taken in its entirety from the station's CCTV,' said Anderson. 'This is the person who carried out the attack.'

'What do we know about this person?' said Chief Constable Roseby.

Anderson seemed somewhat irritated at being interrupted so soon into his presentation as he paused the CCTV. 'So little, Lucinda, it's embarrassing. All the tech analysis department will put their names to is that she is white, five-eight to five-ten and of solid build. The CCTV doesn't show any visible marks or scars. As you can see, she is wearing a baseball cap and at no point do we ever see her face clearly enough to make a positive ID.'

He started the film again and played it through to the end.

'Unfortunately, there was no CCTV inside Lambert's office so we don't know with one hundred percent accuracy what went on in there. But we do know the outcome. I'd be interested in your thoughts. Over to you.'

'How did she get in?' said AC North.

'She posed as a police officer. We've spoken to the PC who let her into the building when she flashed her warrant card. Said she was a DCI Anna Leeming and that she was here to see DCI Lambert.'

'His description?' AC North, again.

'All he could say was that she was pretty with blonde hair. Other than that, nothing remarkable about her apart from the size of her chest which seemed to do a good job of blinding him to any other physical attributes. He did say she seemed to be in a hurry and kept her head down more than it was up.'

'As I said, we've analysed the CCTV meticulously, of course. All the relevant experts have come up with something that, put together, adds up to a whole pile of nothing.'

'What was Lambert working on, sir?' said Lucinda Roseby.

'Glad you asked that. He was investigating two Met detectives for the murder and mutilation of a number of young girls in the Beckenham area. Detective Superintendent Ray Paterson and Detective Inspector Johnny Clocks were his prime suspects.'

The room fell silent and one or two of those present frowned.

'Really? Those two?' Lucinda said.

Anderson held her gaze. 'Yes. *Those* two. Are you aware of them, then?'

'Only by reputation. Bad boys, I understand?'

Anderson snorted. 'So it would seem. They do have a certain propensity for the unorthodox.' He held up a sheaf of papers. 'These are summary reports on their mental health from the Met's psychiatrist who has been treating them both. According to her, John Clocks is a high-functioning psychopath who has turned his mental focus to what he believes is some form of justice.'

At least two of the officers present had screwed their noses up at the word *psychopath*.

'Seriously? Psychopaths?' said AC North.

'Sure. Why not? Nothing wrong with being a psychopath. I'm sure you all know, the majority of high achievers in this world display the signs of being one. In fact, they would all likely be classed as such if tested. Pick any world leader and match them up against the criteria used for determining psychopathic traits and you'll see it present in all of them, plain as day. The difference between a high-functioning psychopath and a criminal psychopath is how that psychopathy manifests itself. Very few world leaders go on to become serial killers.' Anderson paused. 'At least in the ordinary sense of the word.'

AC North nodded and scribbled something on his notepad.

'Paterson, according to our psychiatrist, is beginning to exhibit signs of a similar worldview to Clocks on how justice is meted out.' Anderson slid a single sheet of paper from the bottom of his stack. 'She has also noted that he is, in her view, a '*serial liar with a deep devotion to and almost a hero worship of John Clocks. He is showing the early signs of a mental rupture that, if left unchecked, could be harmful to himself and others.*'

'So, how come he's not on gardening leave if we're worried?' AC North piped up again.

'When pushed, the psychiatrist wasn't prepared to commit herself fully to her notes, stating that they were just observations.'

'So, what's the bloody point of that? Looks like we need to look at her abilities.'

'Indeed. The thing is, Paterson is a man of *very* substantial means and if we were to relieve him of duty on the basis of her report, his lawyers would take us apart. That's not a fight I want at this point. I want them nailed on evidence. Strong, solid evidence. I want them both at work where we can keep a close eye on them.'

'Fair enough. Circling back, how did that meeting go between them and Lambert?' said AC North.

'Not fruitful, I'm afraid. You may remember that Paterson's wife and a colleague fell prey to a serial killer — himself a serving officer, unfortunately — who was killing girls and carving words between their breasts. It seems that with the murders on his patch, Lambert was considering the possibility that a copycat serial killer was operating. Apparently, Paterson and Clocks claimed there wasn't enough in the actual kill method to convince them that it was a copycat.'

A set of images from Paterson's and Lambert's respective cases flashed onto the screen. Everybody grimaced at the sight.

'As you can see,' said Anderson, 'these pictures do seem to suggest a certain similarity between the two cases. Dissatisfied with the outcome of the meeting, Lambert went away with the distinct impression that both men knew more than they were letting on. Lambert eventually came to see me and I authorised his request for surveillance on the two of them.

'On the night of Lambert's shooting, a surveillance team was tasked with following Paterson and Clocks, but one of its undercover officers made the unfortunate mistake of entering a police-heavy pub. DI Clocks quickly identified him and outed him. The UC came out somewhat battered and bruised but swore blind that he'd fallen over in the toilets. We believe, but cannot prove, that he told them about Lambert's investigation.'

'So there's no way to tie them into the attack on Lambert?'

Anderson shook his head. 'No. The pub was packed full of witnesses and they made a point of staying until closing time. After that, they were followed home by the rest of the team. There were no untoward incidents from either of them. That evening, Lambert was gunned down.'

'So, are we thinking a paid assassin?' said Lucinda.

'Seems that way,' said Anderson. 'We've run checks on Paterson's and Clocks's phones — job, personal and house phones — but, again, there's nothing out of the ordinary. We obtained a judge's warrant for their computers and our tech boys remotely interrogated those computers, and apart from Johnny Clocks's somewhat excessive use of a porn site called *Enormous Norks*, there was nothing out of the ordinary. There is nothing to tie these two men to the crime.'

'Then why are we all here, sir?' said North.

'Because I strongly believe these two are as guilty as fuck and I want it proved. Because Paterson and Clocks are now surveillance aware, I want to bring in a whole new, larger team of officers. Lucinda is here to sanction the use of undercover officers from Greater Manchester. Lauren from the DPP has obtained all necessary permissions to carry out covert electronic surveillance on anyone we think may be associated with them in a criminal enterprise. You will be given folders containing full backgrounds on both officers and you will see that, without a doubt, these men are dangerous and, frankly, out of control.'

'Then why are they not on full suspension pending an investigation?' said Lucinda. 'I don't understand.'

Commissioner Anderson gave her a 'poor dear' look. 'Read their files and you'll understand why. It's been said that if these two bastards fell into a vat of industrial strength boiling tar, they'd find a way to slip out of it clean as a whistle. Nothing sticks to them. They even got a commendation from the President of the United States after they started a gun battle on American soil and killed a so-called terrorist. No, these two are clever. They will be called in and questioned as part of the ongoing investigation into Lambert. But, for now at least, I want them out there on the streets. Out there is our best chance of them getting too cocky and making a mistake.'

'Sir,' said AC North, 'with respect, it's no secret that you have no time for these two men and I understand your feeling, but it sounds like this could be construed as a bit of a witch hunt. Just saying.'

Commissioner Anderson gave an exaggerated nod. 'It could indeed, Richard. And believe me, I have no qualms about burning them at the stake.'

CHAPTER EIGHT

Paterson and Clocks walked back into Tower Bridge police station tired and distraught. Though neither of them would admit it, the scene inside 1365 Lynton Road had affected them both. On the surface, they took it in their stride. Both men had seen more of death than was good for anyone's mental health and they'd seen it arrive at the hands of some seriously wicked and deranged individuals. But this was a whole new level of crazy. They needed to get on top of this and both of them knew that wherever this case went, it was going to take them somewhere neither man wanted to be.

'Where to first, Ray?' said Clocks. He stepped aside to let a uniformed PC carrying a tray of teas pass him. As he did, Clocks swiped two mugs off the tray and gave the copper a wink. 'Don't mind, do ya, mate? We've just come from a fuckin' awful crime scene. Could slaughter a cuppa.'

The PC looked as if he did mind but wasn't going to object. He'd no doubt heard what had happened in Lynton Road and probably thanked Christ he was assigned to the CAD room and hadn't been required to set foot in there.

'D'you know if the suspect has been released from 'ospital yet?' Clocks asked him.

'Yes, sir, she has. About an hour or so after you left. According to the officers that brought her back, she's only got superficial wounds, bruising and a couple of wobbly teeth, but the doc said she could go. From what I understand, I think they were glad to see the back of her.'

Clocks grinned. 'I'll bet they were.'

With a nod, the PC disappeared back inside the CAD room.

'Let's go and have a word with the custody sergeant and see if she's been booked in yet,' said Paterson. 'I want Jackie Hartnett assigned to this one. She can carry out the initial interview.'

Jackie Hartnett, a no-nonsense detective constable, had been in Paterson's squad for a year now and had proved her worth on more than one occasion. He trusted her to do the right thing at the right time even if she needed to 'bend' things slightly to suit the situation.

'I can't see us 'anging on to this wacko for long, guv. She'll 'ave to be sectioned under the Mental Health Act.'

'I know. But let's give it a quick run first. The divisional surgeon can take a look at her. He's not a shrink, so hopefully he'll certify her physically fit for interview. If he does, we'll get it started as soon as possible after that. If we get questioned on it later, I'll say I considered her fit for interview at the time. *But*, if she goes off on one, we terminate the interview and I'll plead that I didn't realise she was *that* crazy. If he's not happy with her state of mind, though, the duty inspector can section her and we get her carted off to the Maudsley Hospital. She'll get banged up in a padded cell somewhere and we'll go again when we can. Let's see if she's given a name yet.'

'That sounds like a plan to me.' Clocks pushed open the door to the custody suite. 'Not a good one, but it's something.'

The custody sergeant in charge was clearly having a bad day.

'Sir.' The sergeant gave a curt nod of the head as Paterson and Clocks walked over to him. He knew what they were here for. 'She's in Cell No. 1 Quiet now but, fuck me, she was a handful when she came in. Three female officers had to get her into the cell and search her. That didn't go too well. Dirty bitch tried biting them and then she started gobbing at them.'

Johnny Clocks grimaced. He probably remembered old Albert Tanner senior doing that to him. Clocks gave Tanner a backhander that nearly took the old boy's head off. Spitting was just not acceptable.

'They stuck a spit hood on her, of course. Funny thing is, as soon as that went on, she quietened down. They lifted it off, she kicked up. They dropped it back on, she calmed down. I swear, it was like putting a towel over a budgie's cage.'

Paterson smiled at the thought. 'Is the divisional surgeon on his way? I need to know she's fit to be detained.'

'The doctors at the hospital seem to think she is, but, yes, I've called him. He's on his way. I think he'll ask the duty officer to section her.'

'I'm sure. Have we got a name for her?'

The custody sergeant gave him a look. 'No, sir. She wasn't inclined to give us one. But the voters' register shows a Miss Elizabeth May living there alone.'

Paterson turned to Clocks. 'We need to get upstairs and see what the troops have got for us so far.'

* * *

The office fell silent as they walked in. Everybody knew what they'd seen and done and, however they dressed it up, they were distressed.

'You okay, boys?' Jackie Hartnett was up on her feet the second she saw them. She had two kids of her own, both adults now, but, for some reason, Paterson and Clocks brought out the mothering instinct in her. Paterson wondered if she somehow knew that, for all of their bravado, they were both just a little bit scared of this world.

'Yes, Jack,' said Clocks. 'Just a bit . . . y'know.'

'Yeah. Wanna coffee?'

'I'd prefer a shag if there's one going? Need to calm meself down a bit.'

She grinned. 'All right. But have a word with your Lyndsey first and see what she says. Until you get the okay from her, coffee it will be. Ray? Want a drink?'

'Christ, yeah. I could murder a bottle of voddy.'

'Good idea, guv,' Clocks said. 'Bung half a pint of the clear stuff in me coffee, Jack. Good gel.'

'I'll put a *nip* of vodka in it, guv.' She walked off towards the kitchen.

Paterson walked into his office, plonked himself down in his chair and swung his feet up on his desk. With both hands, he forced his hair back and screwed his eyes tightly shut. He needed a minute to himself. He didn't get it. DC Ronnie 'Dusty' Doneghan tapped on the open door.

'Guv,' he said. 'You doing a briefing for the troops?' Paterson's eyes snapped open. 'Got some bits of info for you.'

Paterson swung his legs off the desk and opened his bottom drawer. 'Yeah, Dusty. Gimme a minute. Just need to clear my head a bit.'

'Sure. When you're ready.' Dusty walked back out into the main office and slid back behind his desk.

Paterson took out the bottle of Smirnoff he kept at the back of the drawer and two tumblers. He poured two large drinks for himself and Clocks and took them out into the main office. Jackie Hartnett was coming the other way with two big mugs of coffee. Her face dropped when she saw the two glasses Paterson was carrying.

'Cheers, Jack,' Paterson said. 'Bit too hot for me at the moment. I'll have it after this when it's cooled down a bit.'

Jackie shook her head.

Clocks looked up from his desk and saw Paterson heading toward the meeting area at the back of the room. 'Heads up, you lot. Let's 'ave yer then!' Clocks called to the detectives. 'Catch-up time.'

The team quickly finished up whatever they were doing and took up seats close to Paterson. Clocks switched on the large monitor hanging from the wall.

'Afternoon all,' said Paterson, checking his watch before taking a swig from the glass. 'Sorry about this but, as you know, bit of a rough day. Right then . . . this morning, at 1365 Lynton Road, a burglar entered the premises and left a lot deader than he went in, and without his face. Actually, I lie. He did come out with it but someone put it in an evidence bag first.' A few officers chuckled.

'Four police officers entered the house with the intention of nicking Burglar Bill but unfortunately ran into the occupant of the house. Turns out she was wearing the burglar's face after having sliced it off. We're not a hundred percent sure of what happened yet but, from what we know so far, this bitch then stabbed and killed PC Evans. As other officers fought to detain her, she stabbed another one, causing him significant injury to his abdomen. His condition is listed as critical. She was eventually detained and taken to hospital, where DI Clocks and myself had a little chat with her. After she tried to bite my face off, we came to the conclusion that she is off her trolley, big time.

'When we spoke to her, she kept asking if we could hear the singing and said that *he* was coming and that *he* would *make us into babies*. From what I can make of it, I think she looked upon these children as her babies. Their moans and cries . . . she considered them songs.'

Everyone's eyes widened.

'Yep,' said Clocks. 'Looks like she lost the plot a good few years ago.'

Paterson continued. 'An initial search of the property revealed a number of human body parts strewn around the premises. At the moment, these parts are believed to be those of several children. Due to an oversight on the part of a certain inspector, a second, more thorough search was carried out. This time it revealed the bodies of four children, wrapped in cling film of some sort. A fifth child, the first one found, was alive at the time. Unfortunately, he subsequently died.

'So my first question to you all is . . . what the fuck? My second question is . . . what have we found out so far?'

Dusty spoke. 'I've already done a quick check on a couple of databases. We have an initial name of Elizabeth May, English. Born 25 March 1988 — makes her thirty-two. I'll need to firm it up, of course, but it's a start.'

'Anythin' else?' said Clocks.

'Not much. Unemployed, council pays the rent, bills, etc.'

'Anyone livin' with her?'

'Not according to the council but I'll double-check. How far back you want me to go, guv?'

'As far back as you can. She couldn't 'ave done all this on her own. She kept bangin' on about someone coming. Called him the Childmaker.'

'Childmaker?' said Jackie. Her expression showed genuine confusion.

Clocks stared straight at her. 'That's what we thought. No idea what it means yet or who it is. Maybe she's pregnant and referring her 'usband? P'rhaps she's tryin' to 'ave a kid. We dunno.'

DC Michael 'Monkey' Harris said, 'I've had an initial inventory of the crime scene come through from DC Yorkshire. It really isn't good.'

'Is he still there, then?' said Paterson. He looked concerned.

'Yeah. He's acting as the exhibits officer. Checking things are correctly bagged and tagged and recording it all.'

Paterson sighed. 'This won't go well. He's a bit of a mummy's boy, that one.'

Everyone in the room nodded. Colin Yorkshire was not the most liked of men and was just passing through the murder squad on his way to a promotion.

'Ready for this?' Monkey Harris wrinkled his nose.

'Go on,' said Paterson.

Monkey took a deep breath. 'Right, here we go. So far they have found . . .' He cleared his throat. 'One pair of hands, small, believed to be those of a child, in a paper bag found in a kitchen drawer . . . A small head in the kitchen freezer — female. Frosted . . . Several skulls in the kitchen cupboard. Missing the jaws. One in the sink that had dried cereal in it. One on a coffee table that had dead flowers in it, *naturally*. A small penis used as a curtain drawstring.'

'That must be mine,' said Clocks. 'I wondered where it 'ad gone.'

Paterson snorted. It brought a bit of levity into the meeting.

'In that case, don't bother about clearing our leg-over with your Lyndsey, guv,' said Jackie Hartnett. 'Sounds like it's not gonna be worth the bother.'

Clocks pointed at her. Cheeky.

'To continue,' said Monkey. 'A hollowed-out torso that was being used to store a number of human bones . . . five face masks cut from young children . . . pair of crudely stitched trousers made out of human skin — child size . . . small jacket made out of the skin of a human child.'

'Jesus, God almighty,' said Dusty his voice slightly above a whisper. He shook his head in disbelief.

'There's still a bit more,' said Monkey. He looked back at his list. 'Human teeth — lots of 'em — hanging on strings like a door curtain to keep the flies out . . . four placemats made of human skin . . . a young girl's face stretched out to make a small cushion cover . . . six eyeballs — assorted colours . . . cornflakes packet containing human toenails — lots of them, too.' Monkey swallowed hard and looked back at the faces of his colleagues. Too stunned to say anything. 'And that's just the downstairs. They're starting upstairs later today.'

The room stayed silent for a moment, no more jokes, no more silly banter, no one sure what to say, everyone unsure if what they were hearing could really be true.

'Right . . .' Clocks snapped everyone back to reality. 'Shitloads to do. First up, Jackie and Dusty . . . you get to interview her. The div surgeon's on his way. I've no doubt he'll ask the duty officer to section her under the Mental Health Act and we also have a psychiatrist en route from the Maudsley. That should speed up the process of getting her sectioned. Monkey . . . find out as much as you can about this woman. Call social services and see if she's come to their attention and then do some digging about her background. Get the neighbours interviewed and see what they can tell you about her and that fuckin' house of death. Any blokes knocking about, any funny comin's an' goin's — anything. Anything at all. You ferret around deeper than a ferret in a Yorkshireman's trousers, gottit?'

Monkey got it.

'And while you're at it, Monkey,' said Paterson, 'make sure we get someone in here from Missing Persons and an expert on children that go missing. We need to find out how all these kids have gone on the missing list. Were they snatched? Were they given up? Trafficked? Whatever. I'll make sure the labs are working overtime on this. We need to find out who these poor little souls are.'

Monkey gave him the thumbs up.

Paterson turned to walk away and the detectives rose from their seats eager to go to work. All except for DC Hartnett. She sat still.

Paterson noticed her. 'Jack. What's the matter.'

She turned to him. 'What if she can't have a baby, sir.'

Paterson shrugged. 'And . . . ?'

'What if she wants a baby, can't have one, so her and her other half decide that if they can't have one of their own, they'll just make one. From other children.'

Clocks stared at her.

'A fucking childmaker,' whispered Paterson as he nodded to himself.

''Oi! Bellend!' Clocks called across the room. His nickname for Detective Constable Toni Bell was predictable.

'Sir?' DC Bell, a strikingly attractive black woman in her early thirties with a shock of tightly cropped pure white hair, was the team's resident whiz-kid who understood all things computers and could easily use and understand all of the Met's many databases. Her sense of humour and banter was almost on par with Clocks's. She would bite back with her own pet name for him: 'Fuckwit.'

'Check all the maternity wards of every 'ospital an' all the baby clinics in a twenty-mile radius of 'ere. I wanna know if anyone has lost a baby in the last five years and took it bad. And by *bad* I mean really, *really* fuckin' bad.'

'Every hospital? You've gotta be kidding? You know how many that's gonna be?'

'Do I look like I'm fuckin' kiddin'?'

DC Bell let out a deep sigh. 'No, guv.'

'And that's because I'm not. Now get on with it. Get help. Do what you need to, but get it done.'

She nodded.

Clocks shook his head. 'Their parents are gonna be devastated.'

Paterson turned to Jackie. 'If you're right, then we're also looking for something *really* fucking terrible.'

She nodded.

CHAPTER NINE

Elizabeth May's eyes fixated on DC Hartnett as she reminded her that she was still under caution. Her head tilted slightly to one side as Hartnett introduced everyone in the room.

'I'm Detective Constable Jackie Hartnett, this is Detective Constable Doneghan. Also present is . . .' She looked expectantly at the man seated in the corner of the interview room, pad and pencil balanced on his knee, scribbling notes. He stopped what he was doing and looked up.

'Sorry,' he said. 'Er, I'm Doctor Jeremy Geyt, senior psychiatrist at the Maudsley Hospital in London.'

'Thank you,' said DC Hartnett. 'Doctor Geyt is here in a professional capacity to observe and take notes on the prisoner. He will also be acting as an appropriate adult if the prisoner is deemed to be of unsound mind and is aware of his right to terminate this interview if he feels that it is inappropriate to continue.'

Jackie Hartnett nodded then turned to a smartly dressed woman she knew of old: Christine McKenna, a whip-smart solicitor who had featured in the defence of a number of high-profile murderers over the years. She was a tough, cold-hearted snide of a woman who delighted in making fools of the police whenever and wherever she could. Hartnett couldn't stand the smug, self-centred bitch. The lawyer introduced herself and, with the preliminaries out of the way, the interview began.

'Can you please confirm your name for me?' Jackie directed her question and smiled pleasantly at Elizabeth Mays.

Elizabeth said nothing but kept her eyes fixed on Jackie.

'Your name? I understand that your name is Elizabeth May, is that correct?'

'Heeeee is coming . . .' Elizabeth's voice was low, quiet. 'Listen.' She cocked her head to the side, listening.

'What? Who's coming? What can you hear?' Too many questions, all off-topic, but something about Elizabeth May unsettled DC Hartnett.

Elizabeth said nothing else. Her eyes and head moved slowly as she looked around the room. She stopped when she got to Dr Geyt.

'Elizabeth, can you hear me?' said Jackie.

Elizabeth ignored her and turned her deep gaze to the doctor. He looked down quickly and began scribbling.

'Heeee issss coooomiiiing.' The words, still small, still quiet, had an air of menace buried in the tone.

'Who is, love?' Dusty Doneghan said.

Elizabeth May peeled her eyes off Dr Geyt and turned her head slowly toward Dusty. She lifted her hand and shifted her gaze from Dusty. One by one, she began to move her fingers, watching them carefully, little spindly sticks like those of a witch, then, slowly, she stood up.

'Sit yourself back down,' DC Hartnett's voice carried an edge. Elizabeth ignored her instruction. Christine McKenna leaned away from her client and watched her with a wary eye.

'Hey,' said Hartnett. 'I said *siddown*. Do it or you'll be removed, forcibly if necessary.'

A smile crossed Elizabeth's face. She nodded. Without warning she hopped backwards and sat on her haunches on the chair.

Everybody in the room watched her closely. This was unusual.

Jackie Hartnett swallowed hard. Her mouth was dry. When asked at a later date to give her opinion of Elizabeth May during her first meeting with her, she would say that Elizabeth was the only person she had ever met in her career who truly unsettled her. And she felt it the second she set foot in the interview room.

* * *

In a small, airless room just ten feet away, Paterson and Clocks were watching the interview unfold on a group of small monitors. Both men were sitting, hands steepled on their knees, heads bent forward, intent on the screen.

'What's she up to, Ray?'

Paterson shook his head.

'She's right off 'er bleeding trolley, this one. Something's not right.'

'Shhhh,' said Paterson. 'Give it a second.'

'Miss McKenna,' DC Hartnett said, 'can you please get your client to sit down properly. We need to get on with this interview.'

Christine McKenna fixed Hartnett with a gaze that would cut ice. 'It would seem my client feels more comfortable in sitting this way, detective. As far as I'm aware there is no legal obligation that states a client cannot sit in this manner if this is what makes her comfortable.'

DC Hartnett slipped her a thin, washed-out grin. 'Thank you for your help, Miss McKenna.'

'I . . . can't . . .'

The room fell silent as heads turned toward Elizabeth again.

'Hear . . . them . . .'

Dusty Doneghan was getting agitated now. 'What? What can't you hear? Give us a clue and help us out, love. C'mon.'

Christine McKenna flashed him a look that said she would likely be able to make capital out of his attitude if he didn't shape up quickly.

Elizabeth sat quietly, fingers moving, head tilting from side to side, her face now pained. Her eyes darted around the room. 'I can't hear them.' Her voice startled everyone in the room. This wasn't the voice they'd heard moments before. This was a deep, bassy voice more akin to a man than a woman and it was agitated.

'I can't hear them. They've stopped singing.'

'Singing?' said Christine McKenna, looking more than a little confused by what was going on now.

Doctor Geyt sat transfixed. Paterson wondered for a moment if Sir David Attenborough might look like that if he found a real live mermaid or something.

'Who's stopped singing, Elizabeth? Who?' Jackie clearly felt that this might be the time to push.

'Tell me, Elizabeth. Who's stopped singing? Who's coming?'

Her voice changed again. A small, nasally little girl voice. 'Why have they stopped? Why aren't they singing anymore? Please . . . tell me?'

'If you tell me who they are, Elizabeth, I might be able to tell you why they've stopped singing. Help me and I'll help you.'

Elizabeth stopped abruptly — like a broken toy. Her head swivelled toward Jackie Hartnett.

'My children.' Her voice was now matter-of-fact.

Jackie looked confused.

'Where are my fucking children, bitch!'

Jackie looked stunned for a second but in that second, Elizabeth May sprang forward out of the chair and hurled herself across the table. Her claw-like fingers grabbed two chunks of Hartnett's hair and her momentum drove the detective backwards and onto the floor.

All in the room panicked. Chairs went backwards as McKenna and Doctor Geyt made sure they were out of the way. Elizabeth completely lost it. She held on to one tuft of Jackie Hartnett's hair and began punching her in the face while she screamed, 'Where are my children? My babies?

Bitch! Tell me! Tell me, whore!' Jackie began swinging wildly at the woman, but it made no difference. She clung on.

Dusty moved fast. He bent down and grabbed Elizabeth by the hair, yanking her head back hard. Her eyes stared up at him but she clung on, still screaming at Hartnett, still swinging with one hand.

Paterson and Clocks were up and running. They burst into the interview room and bundled their way into the scrum. Clocks grabbed Elizabeth's legs and pulled them out from under her, stretching her out flat and banging her face on the floor. Elizabeth clung on to Hartnett as if the life of her children depended on it. Clocks pulled her away, weakening her grip. Dusty moved aside as Paterson moved in. He grabbed hold of Elizabeth's wrist, twisted it toward him, then snapped it downward toward her elbow. Elizabeth screamed as her wrist broke clean in two and she lost her grip.

With DC Hartnett free, Clocks pulled Elizabeth face down across the room and away from the group. Elizabeth spun herself over and kicked out furiously at Clocks, calling him a combination of swear words that even he hadn't heard before.

Christine McKenna, outraged at seeing her client being manhandled, shouted at Clocks.

'Officer. That's enough! Let her go.'

Clocks half turned his head to look at her. 'What?'

'Let her go. You're hurting her.'

'Oh, fuck me!' said Clocks. He doubled over in pain as Elizabeth's foot connected with his left testicle. He let her go.

Elizabeth sprang up. Paterson moved forward but stopped as he felt Jackie Hartnett push to get past him.

'Get out my fucking way!' Jackie screamed at Paterson. He made sure she couldn't get past.

Elizabeth turned and headbutted Christine McKenna square on the nose, dropping her like a sack of wet cement. Primed and ready to fight, she turned, just as Jackie Hartnett's right cross came over the top of Paterson's shoulder and hit her on the chin. The punch sent Elizabeth backward into the wall. She slid down into a sitting position on the floor before falling onto her left side, banging her head on the floor.

Clocks looked impressed.

'Call me a whore . . .' said Jackie. She shook her fist out. Two bruised and fractured knuckles.

Christine McKenna was face up, spark out and had an obviously broken nose.

'Not a complete waste of time then.' Jackie said. She pulled out her mobile phone and took half a dozen photos of the woman to pin up on the canteen bulletin board. Clocks did the same.

CHAPTER TEN

It was late afternoon when Ray Paterson halted suddenly at the open door to the mortuary at Guy's Hospital. Clocks stopped short of bumping into him.

'Wassamatter?' Clocks said, irritated.

'Before we go in, lay off of him.'

'Who? Jock?'

Paterson nodded. 'Yeah. Give the old sod a break, John. He's got a problem and doesn't need you to keep digging at him.'

'Me? You mean *us*. You're just as bad.'

Paterson felt guilty for a second. 'Yeah I know, but that's only because you wind him up and drag me into it.'

Clocks smiled. 'He loves it. A bit of banter don't hurt 'im. Christ, he must go off 'is nut down here on his own all day — just the dead to talk to. No wonder 'e's drinkin' all the formaldehyde.'

'Whisky. Just whisky.'

Clocks shrugged. 'Don't really matter, does it?' He stepped forward as Paterson opened the door. 'Whatever 'e's drinking, it does a good job of lighting up 'is nose. You gotta admit it came in 'andy last time we were 'ere with the dead Muslims. Saw that taser mark on the back of the geezer's neck. Woulda missed them if his nose 'adn't doubled up as a torch.'

Paterson sighed as Clocks stepped inside and made his way down the stairs.

Jock Hudson had his back to them and was busy working on a small body on the table in front of him. On separate tables were the bodies of three other youngsters taken from Lynton Road. None of them were in good condition. All of them had bits of their bodies missing — limbs, fingers, toes and the odd ear — but all of them had one thing in common: most of the skin had been flayed from their bodies.

Paterson and Clocks already knew this, having taken them from inside the walls at the address, but this was different. Seeing these tiny bodies laid out under the harsh lights of the cutting table made it all seem worse somehow.

'Clocksy,' said Jock without turning to acknowledge them. Although he'd only said one word, his accent was easily distinguishable: thick Glaswegian.

Paterson and Clocks both stopped for a second and looked at each other, neither man sure of how he knew it was them that entered the room.

'Is Paterson with ye?'

'Wotcha, Jock. Yeah, 'e's 'ere with me. 'Ow'd you know it was us?'

'Wisnae hard. I heard ye talking at the doorway. Still a simpleton, I see?'

Clocks face broke into a big grin, which he turned toward Paterson. It said, *See? He started it. Loves a bit of banter this one. Loves it.*

'Nothing's changed there, Jock,' Paterson confirmed.

The sharp clang of metal echoed around the cavernous room as Hudson dropped his scalpel into a metallic bowl and began to turn around.

'Hold on!' Clocks shouted. 'Don't turn around yet. Ain't got me sunnies on. Ray, don't look at him!'

Hudson turned. His red nose, the object of Clocks's constant torment, was a normal colour although his cheeks were still slightly florid. Clocks peered at him as he crossed the room.

He held both arms out and wobbled his head in a gesture of mock surprise. 'Oi, oi. What's 'appened 'ere then? Why's the light gone out? Batteries gone dead on ya?'

Hudson glared at Clocks. 'Ye're no as funny as ye think ye are, Timex my laddie.'

Clocks turned to Paterson. 'What's he say? His mouth moved but . . .'

Paterson shrugged. 'No idea. I'll call a translator. See if we can get to the bottom of it.'

Clocks walked straight up to Hudson and gazed at his nose. Hudson made a grab for his nose before turning sharply away.

'Is that make-up, Jock? You wearin' bloody make-up now?'

'What? No. Dinnae be sae stupid.'

'You are, aintcha? Fuckin' hell, Ray. He's gone all Mary Quant on us.'

'It's no make-up, ye gobshite. It's special stuff from the doctors. Medication.'

'What's he say?' said Paterson, in too deep now to stop.

Clocks shrugged. 'Dunno. Something about he's wearing make-up now because he really wants to be a lady.'

'Oh,' said Paterson. 'Who knew?'

'We should have done, Ray. All the signs were there. He's always wearing an apron and cutting up meat. Pink jobs.'

'Will you two bastards stop taking the pish?' Jock spun back to face them, anger etched on his face.

Clocks held his hands up. 'Sorry, Jock? Too far?'

'Aye. Too far, laddie. Ye never ken when to give up, do ye?'

'No. Sorry. It's because I'm English. We don't know how to give up. An', who's this Ken you keep goin' on about? Is 'e givin' up?'

Paterson knew it was enough now. Business to attend to. 'Sorry, Jock. What do we have?'

Hudson nodded. It was over. Until the next time.

'So far, I've examined five o' them. Early indications are that all five suffered from some form of asphyxiation.'

'Is that what killed them? Strangulation?' said Paterson.

Hudson shook his head. 'No. See here.' He pointed to the child on his table. A faint pink mark could be seen around his throat, on what little skin he had left on his body. 'They all have it. I cannae be certain yet, but I dinnae think it's a cord or rope. Definitely not a wire. Too thick. But my feeling is that what this bastard did was put a bag over their heads afore she carried out her other depravities.'

Paterson and Clocks grimaced as they looked at the child.

'What? Why?' said Clocks, turning his head to the side.

'I've no idea. Number of reasons somebody part-strangles another. Sex games . . . power . . . control . . . excitement — sheer fun. Who the hell knows?'

'If you had to hazard a guess, which one would you go for?' said Paterson.

'I think . . . I dinnae ken what to think at this stage.'

Paterson nodded.

Clocks scowled as he looked back at the dead child. 'What sort of age are these kids, Jock? Any idea?'

'Not for sure but I'd doubt if any of them were over ten or twelve.'

'Jesus.' Clocks gripped the rail on the side of the table.

'Why has he skinned them, then? What's that all about?' said Paterson.

'Fuck knows,' said Hudson. 'I heard that the house was full o' bits an' pieces made out o' skin. Is that right?'

Clocks nodded. 'Whoever did this is one sausage short of a packet.' Jock looked at him, plainly puzzled. Paterson was used to Clocks's made-up sayings but for those not in the know, they sounded distinctly odd.

'I was saving the worst for last, boys.'

'Of course you were. Go on,' said Paterson.

'I cannae be certain — not yet — but I think these bairns were alive when she skinned them.'

Paterson closed his eyes and lifted his head before taking a deep breath. Clocks gripped the rail tighter.

'Why'd you say that?' Paterson's gaze focused directly on Hudson.

'In short, the blood. There's dried blood around the edges of the skin where the incisions were made. If they were dead, there widnae be blood. Well, a bit, depending on how long they had been dead, of course. Freshly dead . . . some blood. Long-time dead . . . little to none. That said, it depends on where they're cut. Blood stops circulating and settles at the lowest point in the body. It pools and mottles the skin. That aside, there's evidence of dried blood over all of the wounds that I've seen so far. So, until I know for certain, I'm saying they were alive.'

'What the fuck's wrong with people?' said Paterson. 'How the hell do you get so broken that you can do this sort of stuff? To anyone, let alone kids.'

'I hear rumours that she was trying to make a child out of bits and pieces,' said Hudson.

Clocks looked at him sharply. 'Where'd you hear that?'

'When they were brought in. Couple of policemen were just talking.'

'Were they?' Clocks was not impressed. 'Well, they fuckin' shouldn't be. Stupid rumours like that that cause all sorts of shit if they leak into the outside. That's exactly the sort of crap that'd blow up on Twotter or whatever they call it. People need to keep their fuckin' traps shut.'

'So, is it true?'

'No idea,' said Paterson. 'We haven't found a little Frankenstein in the basement if that's what you're asking but, who knows? Maybe.'

'Okay. To sum up,' said Clocks. 'We've banged up a fuckin' monster, who likes to torment her victims by some sort of suffocation and then skins 'em alive before making 'em into household ornaments. And maybe, somewhere, there's a good chance she's trying to make her very own boy just like Geppetto.'

‘Who?’ said Paterson.

Clocks looked at him, bewildered. ‘Geppetto. Pinocchio’s ol’ dad. The Disney film. A classic. He made a wooden puppet ’cos he couldn’t ’ave kids ’imself. I suspect that was because ’e didn’t ’ave a missus to be honest. He used to pray the puppet would come to life an’ one night it did. Turns out puppet boy was a right little bastard, always causing his dad grief. See? Careful what you wish for.’

‘Never heard of it,’ said Paterson.

‘What?’

‘Never heard of it. Didn’t watch stuff like that when I was a kid. Wasn’t allowed.’

Clocks frowned. ‘That’s not right. Child abuse, right there.’

‘It is what it is. C’mon, we got things to do. See you soon, Jock. Keep us posted.’

CHAPTER ELEVEN

Civilian station officer Michael Paladin's day wasn't going as well as he'd hoped when he reported for work that morning. He had worked for the Met for some eighteen years now, the last two as a control room operator in Southwark police station. Today, he was on the desk. He'd had his fair share of both quiet and busy days but this one was shaping up to be a humdinger.

Once news of Lynton Road broke, the station was under siege from reporters wanting to know more. Those who didn't show up in person were busy blocking up the phones, email and Twitter accounts of the station.

Already, a half dozen or so people had been in to the front desk to offer up theories and neighbours with whom they didn't get on as suspects. Chief among these visitors was a man known to everybody at the station as Daft Jack. Jack was harmless enough but had a habit of confessing to every crime that made it into the news. So far, he'd confessed to being Jack the Ripper, the Yorkshire Ripper and Reggie and Ronnie Kray, among a multitude of other criminals. No one took him seriously, but he was a pain in the arse. Every allegation made had to be logged and meticulously checked and, as Johnny Clocks once pointed out, 'Well, the geezer's a nutter but one day, 'e might actually come good an' kill someone. Then we'll have him for something.'

Michael Paladin's phone rang for what had to have been the fortieth time in the last two hours and he was feeling a little snappy when he answered it.

'Southwark Police.'

'Good afternoon.' Silence.

'Hello. Southwark police. How can I help you?'

'That's better,' said the voice on the other end of the line. 'Manners cost nothing.'

Paladin rolled his eyes. *Great. I need you.*

'My apologies. What can I help you with, sir?'

'I have some information with regards to the killings at Lynton Road.'

Paladin was typing it into his computer as the man spoke.

'I see, sir. Can you let me have the details please and I'll get someone to call you back as soon as they can.'

'I want to speak to Superintendent Paterson. I will give him the information.'

'Well, I'm sorry, but that's not possible at the moment, I'm afraid. Mr Paterson is extremely busy and is unable to take your call at the moment. But if you leave me your name and number I will get him to call you back when he can.'

'Thank you, officer. Most kind of you. But I must talk to him. Now. I insist.'

Paladin shook his head. Why did no one ever listen?

'Well, sir, I'm sorry but, as I said, Mr Paterson is extremely busy.'

'I might just email him then.'

'Er . . . you could do but he'd prefer to talk to you. You know how it is with emails. Sometimes they get lost or don't make it through. It's just not possible to talk to him right now, though.'

The line went silent for a moment.

'Sir?' said Paladin. 'You still there?'

'Yes,' said the man. 'You have a point about the emails. Thank you.'

'No problem.'

'I will leave him a message then, if you can assure me that he will receive it.'

'Yep. He will. I promise. Fire away when you're ready.'

'Thank you. Please tell him to let her go.'

Paladin frowned.

'Sorry? Let who go?'

'Elizabeth. She was arrested this morning at 1365 Lynton Road.'

Paladin felt himself jolt upright.

'Are you aware of today's events, officer?'

'Yes. Of course I am.'

'Good. Then tell him to let her go.'

'I don't think that's going to be possible at the moment, I'm afraid. She's in custody.'

'Tell him to let her go.'

'Sir, she's under arrest.'

'Tell him to let her go.'

'Look. Who are you, exactly? Mr Paterson will need to know.'

'He will know soon enough.'

'What does that mean?'

'It means that if he doesn't let her go I will peel the skin from his face.'

The phone went dead.

Paladin looked up at the whiteboard on the wall in front of him and dialled Paterson's mobile phone number.

CHAPTER TWELVE

Paterson was in his office when the call came through from station officer Michael Paladin. He listened carefully to what the man had to say, jotted down a few notes on a loose piece of paper, thanked him and then hung up.

Anger rose from the depth of his brain. If there was one thing that riled Paterson it was a coward and if anyone wanted to harm him, he'd rather they didn't leave threatening messages. He checked the clock on the wall. 7:34 p.m. Time for an end of day debrief soon.

'John!' he called out into the main office.

Clocks looked up from his two-finger typing. 'What?'

'Pop in here a minute, please.'

'I'm busy.'

'John. Get your arse in here, now!'

Clocks tutted and jerked his head in a small show of annoyance. He sauntered into Paterson's office. 'Yes, guv. What can I do you for?'

Paterson handed him the note he'd just scribbled.

'What's this?'

'Station officer just phoned it in to me.'

Clocks scanned it and handed it back. 'Well, that's not nice.'

'That's what I thought.'

'Is that all there is?'

'Yep.'

'Anything about the caller? Accent? Speech used? Impediment?'

'Seems not, other than that he spoke nicely.'

'Geezer's got the right nark with you by the sound of it?'

'Doesn't it?'

'Right, so, whoever this caller was could be the phantom Childmaker of Old London Town?'

'Possibly. Can't be sure.'

'But we fancy Elizabeth for it, don't we?'

'We did, but this throws it open a bit doesn't it?'

Clocks shrugged. 'Maybe. No mention of a relationship, then? Could be a brother, boyfriend or something.'

'Nothing apparently.'

Clocks sat himself down. 'That's chucked a spanner in the works, innit?'

Paterson scratched his head. 'Just a bit.' He glanced up at the clock again. 'Let's just have the debrief and see what comes out of it. Maybe someone on the team has something that might tie it together. I dunno.' He rose up out of his chair and the two men headed out into the main office.

'Listen up everyone,' he called. 'Debrief time. Let's see where we are. C'mon. Chop, chop.'

The team quickly settled themselves down as Paterson brought them up to speed with Jock Hudson's initial findings, careful to remind them that he was still working and had reached no definite conclusions. He then told them about the phone message that had been received.

'Anyone got any ideas about that?' he said. 'Anything you picked up today that might tie in?'

DC Bell spoke up. 'Can't tie it in yet, guv, but just to let you know that I've contacted all the hospitals you asked for and I'm waiting for the results to come back. It's a big ask, you've asked.'

'I know, but it has to be done.'

'And I've been doing a deep dive into Elizabeth's background. There's a few interesting things thrown up.'

'Do I need to sit me arse down for this?' Clocks asked.

'Up to you, guv. I might be a few minutes with it.'

Clocks dragged out a chair and sat.

'I've found out that Elizabeth has a long history of mental illness stemming back to her childhood. According to her notes lodged with social services, she was the product of an incestuous relationship. Her mum and dad were brother and sister.'

Bell must have spotted Paterson's confusion. 'I know, guv. You're gonna ask why she wasn't taken into care at a young age. Seems this only came to light later in life when she was assigned a new case worker. This one was right on the ball. Elizabeth was whipped away faster than a lightning bolt strikes. Mum and Dad were nicked, assessed and found to be severely mentally impaired. They both got banged up in a mental institution. Apparently, Dad topped himself while inside and Mum went even madder than she was before. She's still there.

'Shrinks says that by the time she was twelve, Elizabeth was showing signs of extreme aggression — fighting with neighbours' kids, kids at school, teachers, smashing cars and windows and — here we go . . .' Bell looked at her notes. '. . . set fire to a few cats, one dog and a house. Long-term bedwetter, the usual stuff that points toward serial killer traits. She made a number of allegations of sexual assault by her older brother.'

'Anything else?' said Clocks.

'Yep. Stay in your seat, guv. It seems she also has a sister. Both siblings are older than her. Both of them also the product of Mum and Dad's dodgy relationship. The brother lives in a nice house in the countryside somewhere in Waltham Abbey near Epping Forest and is an architect. Has his own firm in London and is doing all right. Notes on him said he was showing signs of a mental break too, but luckily the change of social worker was good for him as well.'

'Was he ever charged with abusing Elizabeth or spend any time in an institution?' said Paterson.

'Nothing I can find. He was a kid. Under the age of criminal responsibility for most of the abuse allegations and, of course, by the time the social worker was involved, Elizabeth was so damaged and insular, she clammed up and said nothing bad about him. She was devoted to him. So, if he did do anything to her, nothing came of it. With all that said, it might be that none of the allegations against him were true and that it was just some sort of fantasy on her part. Who knows?'

'That sounds about right,' said Clocks. 'So, what about the sister, then? Where's she these days?'

'No idea. She went missing after Mum and Dad were banged up. No known relatives to go to, so it seems that she just upped and ran away. Would have been about fifteen, sixteen by then.'

'Did she show signs of mental problems, at all?' asked Dusty.

'Oh yeah. Social worker said she was also abused by the parents. Notes don't say whether the brother abused her, too, but if he did, that might be why she ran when she could. Saw the chance and took it.'

'Do you have an address for the social worker who broke all this, Toni?' said Paterson. 'I want to go and visit her. Have a chat.'

'Last known address was Plot 457, Nunhead Cemetery. She died about five years back.'

'I'm not bleedin' surprised,' said Clocks. 'Shit she must have seen and gone through.'

'Okay,' said Paterson, 'the brother then? We'll go and see him. Got an address for him?'

'Yes. Give it to you in a sec. Description is . . . male, white, thirty-nine years old.'

'Okay,' said Paterson. 'Until we know otherwise, the brother and sister are now Persons of Interest. Got a name for him?'

'Yeah. Name of Marcus May.'

Paterson felt his stomach lurch. 'Oh, Christ, no.'

CHAPTER THIRTEEN

Johnny Clocks pulled onto his driveway and frowned when he saw the red Vauxhall convertible blocking his garage. Carrie Gedmine was visiting. Carrie was a long-time friend of Clocks's fiancée, Lyndsey Kitchener, and for a while Ray Paterson's sometime girlfriend. She was a good detective, solid and reliable, but she had an arrogance about her that wound him up.

He could see why Paterson had taken a shine to her. She was tall, very much in shape and had a terrific sense of humour. She also took no shit from anyone and, after Paterson's estranged wife had died, she took away just a smidgeon of the pain that drove him up and out of bed every day.

Paterson's reputation with women as the good-looking rich kid didn't seem to bother her and she would often tell her friends that she had 'calmed him down' and that they were talking about marriage. That was a shock to Paterson who swore blind to anyone who'd listen that he had no intention of getting married to Carrie or anyone else.

In the end, her downfall was her clinginess. It started with her constantly calling and texting him and sometimes turning up late at night on his doorstep. It changed up a gear when he came home from work every night to find her sitting in her car waiting for him. He'd spoken to her about it several times — that he wasn't looking for a relationship so soon, but she never took the hint. So, he decided the best thing to do was rip off the plaster and break up with her. It didn't go down too well.

For a while, the calls and texts intensified, as did the unexpected visits in the middle of the night. Things got so uncomfortable, he spilled it all to Lyndsey and asked her to have a word. She did, and things calmed down to the point where both Carrie and Paterson could speak to each other civilly and even, occasionally, go for an after-work drink, but only in the company of Lyndsey and Clocks.

Clocks knew why she was there: his September wedding to Lyndsey. Carrie was her maid of honour, which necessitated her being around Lyndsey a bit more than Clocks wanted and, in truth, a bit more than Lyndsey wanted, too. She was certainly one to latch on.

He jumped out of the car and let himself into the house. 'Lynds, it's me!' I'm home.' He stopped to listen for a second. 'I've 'ad a right shitty old day, girl.'

'Hi, John! In here!' Lyndsey called. 'Come and tell me about it.'

He dropped his keys into a small bowl on the hallway sideboard, quickly sifted through a small pile of letters and headed toward the living room.

'There's some ol' banger in the drive. Whose is that?'

He stepped into the living room and saw Carrie sitting opposite Lyndsey.

'Look out. There's one in 'ere an' all. All right, Carrie?' He winked at her.

'Hiya Timex. Always a pleasure to be insulted by you.'

He walked over to the chair Lyndsey was sitting in and kissed her on the forehead.

'All right sweetie?' he said to Lyndsey. 'Shoot anyone today?' Lyndsey was an inspector with SCO19, the Met's specialist firearms team.

'Nope. Quiet day today. Unless of course you piss me off in some way.'

She grinned up at him.

'Not me, love. I love you far too much for that.'

Carrie groaned. 'Ah, isn't that sweet? The rufty-tufty Detective Inspector is all gooey on the inside.'

He looked over to her and smiled. 'Probably not unlike yerself. That's why they all call you Cadburys.'

'Cadburys?' Carrie said.

'Yeah. Tasty on the outside and full of cream on the inside.'

She frowned.

Lyndsey scowled. 'Hold on, John. That's bang out of order. Apologise, now.'

'What? She knows I'm only muckin' about. Don't cha?' He winked at her again. 'I made that up, love. They don't really call you that. Honest.'

Carrie Gedmine gave him a drop-dead look. He knew that she'd never really approved of him and Lyndsey — probably thought that Lynds could do a lot better. She was probably right.

'Yeah, I know you're mucking about. Always mucking about. That's you. Don't worry about it.'

'I wasn't,' he said, as he headed back out to the hallway. He stopped in the doorway. 'I'm gonna make a brew and go upstairs. Anyone want one? It'll probably taste a bit different to what you're used to, Carrie. We call it tea.'

She shook her head.

'No?' said Clocks. He shrugged. 'Suit yerselves. See ya later.'

He turned and walked upstairs.

Carrie called after him. 'Mind your eyes watching all that porn, John. You'll go blind.'

'Good!' he shouted back. 'Brilliant. Let's 'ope it 'appens before I get to all the ones you're in 'cos I won't be able to look at you in the same way anymore.' He jogged up the stairs chuckling to himself.

CHAPTER FOURTEEN

Detective Inspector Caroline Tek from the Greater Manchester Police Service sat opposite Commissioner Anderson. He was busy reading the first daily report that she had compiled on the surveillance of both Paterson and Clocks and it didn't make for the kind of reading that Anderson enjoyed. He knew it was early days and wasn't expecting much. Anything would do.

Every minute or so he would flick over a page and occasionally nod, or not, at what he was reading. He never said a word and left DI Tek feeling somewhat uncomfortable and on her guard. She'd heard that he could be a bit of a handful — rude, surly, but mostly arrogant and she didn't relish being on the end of a bollocking for just doing her job.

Finally, Anderson put down the report and tapped the flat of his hand on it. He was done.

He sniffed and looked across his desk at her. 'That's disappointing.'

'Sir,' was all she could think of saying.

Anderson sat himself back in his chair and rubbed his face for a couple of seconds. 'Nothing at all? You're quite sure?'

'Yes, sir. I've examined all the reports, photos, and run through the CCTV myself. Of course, it's extremely early days, but there is nothing so far to suggest that Paterson and Clocks are other than clean. Not once have they been acting in a manner that could be described as suspicious. There is no suspicious movement on their accounts. All phone calls, emails, texts and such have been monitored and . . . nothing. They've been nowhere that is outside of their norm. Paterson is a loner as far as we can tell. Clocks went straight home to his girlfriend, Lyndsey Kitchener, and they're just, well . . . normal. There is nothing to suggest that they had any involvement in the shooting of DCI Lambert. Nothing.'

'As I said . . . disappointing.' He looked out of the window in silence for a while. 'So, what's next, Inspector?'

'We keep going, sir. This is just Day One.'

'Much as I don't want it to, I feel that we're just going to turn up more of the same. Nothing.'

'Possible. But sometimes targets slip up. One word . . . one call and it gives us a bite. The bite we need.'

Anderson pulled a face that suggested neither of these two would make that slip. They were too shrewd to make amateur mistakes. 'Pressure needs to be applied.'

'Pressure, sir?'

'As we have nothing to suggest a criminal offence has taken place, my next move would be to call them in for interview as part of the ongoing investigation into the attack on Lambert. Nothing out of the ordinary. They knew him. He came to them for advice and, although they felt there was nothing they could help him with, that contact is enough for us to speak to them on a more formal level.'

DI Tek said nothing. She could see Anderson was running a train of thought and she didn't want to derail him.

'Once they're being interviewed the pressure can be ramped up. More difficult questions. See how they respond and, more importantly, how they behave and what they say before and after the interview. See if they collude in their approach, on their projected answers. See what they say and do once they've been interviewed. That might give us the bite we need.' He fixed her with a stare.

'It's possible but . . .'

'What?'

'May I give you some advice before you proceed, sir?' She looked sheepish as she readied herself to throw a spanner in the works for the most senior police officer in London. This wasn't the best position for a detective inspector to be in.

Anderson's eyes narrowed slightly. 'Certainly.'

'You need to be careful how you proceed with this, sir. Paterson can certainly afford the best legal teams in the country and if they get a whiff that you've interviewed them with the intention of provoking a conversation they wouldn't otherwise have had or a remark they wouldn't otherwise have said, then it'll get tossed in court. Assuming of course, that it even gets there in the first place.'

'Nonsense. These two men are suspects in the attempted murder of a senior police officer and God only knows what else they've done. I can justify it if I have to.'

'No, sir. You can't. I'm sorry, but think about it. If these two are suspects then questions will be asked why they weren't arrested and, at the very least, why they weren't suspended pending investigation. Someone will ask why you allowed them to continue working knowing that they were suspects for murder. You'll be highly criticized for letting them carry on in the hope of catching them out.'

'I'm sure I can get around that, Inspector. That's really not for you to worry about.' He shot her a supercilious grin.

She looked straight at him. He really was an arrogant prick.

'Sir,' she said. That one word contained everything she thought about him.

'I'll have them pulled in tomorrow. I'll let you know when and where.' He pushed his chair back and stood up. Meeting over.

DAY 2

CHAPTER FIFTEEN

8 a.m.

Johnny Clocks looked very pleased with himself though he struggled to hide it as Paterson wandered into the squad room. He turned off his computer screen and followed Paterson as he headed toward the kitchen. A couple of detectives looked up from their desks and one of them, Dusty Doneghan, shook his head.

'Got a sec, guv?' Clocks called to Paterson.

Paterson shot him a glance but carried on walking toward the kitchen. 'Yep, what is it?' He flicked the kettle on as Clocks wandered in behind him.

'What's up?'

'Good news an' bad news. What'd you want first?'

Paterson eyed him. Clocks was looking a bit full of himself, so whatever the bad news was, it couldn't be that bad. 'I'm going first, John. I've got bad news and even more bad news. So, what do *you* want first?'

Clocks's shoulders dropped. 'I'll 'ave the bad news.'

'We've got two meetings this morning. One is with somebody from the missing persons unit.' He glanced at a sheet of paper on his desk. 'A DCI Henson. She's coming along with someone from some global missing kids thing.'

'That's not so bad. What's next?'

'We've got a profiler coming in first.'

'Oh, fuck that. No. Why? They're all a bunch of fairground fortune tellers pretending to have a real job. It's all made-up crap to justify their inability to get a proper job in Tesco's or something.'

Paterson shrugged. 'I don't disagree with you, but you know how this works. We have to be seen to be looking into every lead, every clue and we have to take every bit of help offered us. We'll get crucified if we don't.'

'An' we'll get led up the garden path if we do. Waste of soddin' time.'

'Why are you so against them?'

'Because, to my mind, you can't reduce a sick, crazed psychopath down to an A4 sheet of characteristics. Doesn't matter what the FBI or the bods up at NSY say . . . you can't. Telling us we're lookin' for a forty-year-old white man with mummy issues and a wank bank book of pictures of Celine Dion ain't gonna help us catch whoever's doing this.'

Paterson sneered. 'Really? Celine Dion?'

'Whoever. Doesn't matter. Point is, we'll catch him by good old-fashioned police work . . . door knocking . . . databases . . . punching people. Tried and trusted.'

'John,' said Paterson.

'What?'

'Play nice.'

A grin spread across Clocks's face.

'Before we start on your news, I've got something else to tell you.'

'Go on . . .' Clocks sounded hesitant.

'Our killer's brother, Marcus May. I think I may know him.'

Clocks wrinkled his nose. 'What? Why? How? Why didn't you say anything last night?'

'No point saying anything. I don't know if it's him or not until I put a face to the name. We're going to the address later to check him out. If it's the same person, we know each other from our teens. We used to belong to the same martial arts club. We fought each other on the mat a good few times. Twice in a tournament.' Paterson stared off into the distance. 'He kicked the living shit out of me every time.'

Clocks frowned.

'I had a black belt, as did he — and we were both a handful. But I tell you, John . . . he was brutal. No mercy. Vicious bastard.'

'Okay, so he used to beat you up for yer dinner money when you were kids together. So what?'

'So, if he *is* our killer's brother, he might be involved.'

'You think he could be the phone caller? The man from Gillette who's goin' to give you a right proper shave?'

'Could be.'

Clocks shrugged. 'Okay. An' again . . . so what?'

'So, if the two of us end up face to face and we're having to nick him, just stay out of it. Whatever happens, don't get involved, John, because he will fuck you up real bad, mate.'

Clocks shrugged again. 'Ooh. Sounds scary.'

'He is. If he's been keeping it up, the best advice I can give you is to run or, if you're in a car, knock him down and drive off a bit lively because unless you break both his legs and his back or kill him, he'll be seriously pissed at that.'

Clocks chuckled. 'Duly noted. Scary motherfucker with an attitude. There's a first.'

'Right . . . what's your news? Give me the bad news first.'

'Tetley's gone on the sick.' DC Colin Yorkshire wasn't the most liked man on Paterson's squad, but he was good at his job. Meticulous.

Paterson shook his head as he dunked a teabag in his cup. 'Wonderful. What's wrong with him?'

Clocks shrugged. 'Said he was strugglin' with what he saw inside Lynton Road. Hadn't slept all night and was goin' off to see his doctor later today.'

'Can't say I'm overly upset.'

Paterson leaned back on the counter, hand in one pocket, mug in the other. 'Still, he was a body. We're gonna need someone to stand in for him, do a bit of door knocking, admin and stuff.'

'I know. Which brings me onto the good news.' His grin grew wider. 'I got someone in.'

'Let's have it then. You look like you're gonna pop.'

Clocks nodded. 'Right . . . ready?

'Yeah. Go on then.'

'It's . . . Carrie.'

Paterson's face fell and his shoulders dropped. 'What?'

'Carrie.'

'Carrie. You serious?'

'Yeah.'

'I thought you said it was good news.'

'Yeah, I did, didn't I? No. I lied.'

'Fuck's sake. Couldn't you have got anyone else?'

'Yeah. Lots of people but where's the fun in that?

'You're a sick bastard, you know that?'

'Yes thanks.'

'When's she coming in?'

Clocks looked at his watch. 'About twenty minutes ago. She's been waiting in your office. Very keen to start working with you, Ray.'

Paterson put down his tea and walked toward his office giving Clocks a filthy look as he passed him. Clocks's grin was still plastered to his face.

'Don't worry, Ray. If you're not out in half an hour, I'll come rescue you.'

Paterson, about to step into his office, turned to Clocks. 'I won't forget this.'

Clocks gave him a quick thumbs up. 'Me neither, mate.'

Paterson walked into his office.

Carrie Gedmine was suited and booted, hair pulled back and looking every inch the professional. She was seated with her back to the door when Paterson walked in, but on hearing the door open, stood up. Respect for the rank, even though he was her ex-lover. She turned to face him, smiling.

'Good morning, Carrie. Sit down, please, no need for that.'

She nodded and re-seated herself opposite him.

Paterson took his seat, leaned forward and clasped his hands in front of him on top of the desk. 'So . . . Word is you're on the squad now. How'd that happen?'

For a second, he wondered if that question sounded as stupid to her as it did to him. He knew exactly why. DC Colin Yorkshire didn't have the stomach for the job and Johnny Clocks was a stitch-up merchant.

Carrie just looked at him.

'Yeah, scrub that. I know. We're a man down and you're filling in.'

'That's it, sir.'

'Okay. Good. Have you been brought up to speed?'

'DI Clocks gave me a quick briefing when he offered me the chance to fill in. This is unbelievable. I can't get my head around the thought of someone doing this. This is just . . . madness.'

Paterson's mind quickly jumped back to the house, to the cellar, to the walls and the children. 'Can you handle this, Carrie?'

'Sir?'

'Can you handle this?'

'Handle what?'

'Two things. First of all, this case. It is bloody horrific and we're going after someone who is a whole new level of crazy.'

'Yes, I can handle it. I'm not known for having a weak disposition.' She looked him directly in the eyes. 'And the second thing?'

Paterson met her gaze. 'Us.'

'Us? There is no us. Is there?'

He gave a curt nod of the head. 'No, Carrie. There isn't. But I need to know that us working together isn't going to be a problem. I need to know that you're going to be able to do your job properly and not let the past get in the way of the present. Can you do that?'

Carrie shifted in her seat. Moved forward and dropped the pleasantries.

'Can I speak freely? *Sir.*'

Paterson knew that tone of voice well, having been on the end of it a few times. 'Course you can.'

'How fucking arrogant are you?'

Paterson was taken aback. He hadn't expected that. 'Excuse me?'

'I said, how fucking arrogant are you — that you think you're going to be *a distraction* and that I can't or won't be able to do my job properly? I'm a police officer, not a fucking fourteen-year-old girl with a crush on a pop star. Get over yourself.'

'Carrie . . . I'm . . .'

'The next word out of your mouth, sir, better be *sorry*, because I don't need this shit. Yes, we were together . . . yes, I'd hoped we would stay together — maybe build a life — but you made it perfectly clear that you weren't interested — after you shagged me a few dozen times, that is. Yes, I was bloody upset but that was at the time. I'm *well* over you.'

'To be fair,' he ventured, 'that upset dragged on a bit, didn't it? All the calls and the turning up in the middle of the night. That wasn't good, was it?'

Carrie stood up. 'I took it badly, I admit that — but, as I said, I'm over you now. Way over it. But I can see you might find it a problem with me being here and if you're not professional enough to work with me then best we don't work together at all.' She turned abruptly and headed for the door.

Paterson rubbed his face. 'Carrie. Wait a minute.'

She stood at the door, her back to him.

'I'm sorry. I was out of order. I shouldn't have . . .'

She spun around. Her face was etched with anger. 'No, Ray. You shouldn't have.'

He nodded. 'I'm sorry. I shouldn't have doubted you. Stay. We can work together, I'm sure.'

She took a deep breath and looked at him. He felt like a little boy who'd been caught with his hands down his pants and got a bollocking from his mum. 'Okay,' she said. 'Let's hope so. I'll grab a desk. Sir.'

* * *

Carrie Gedmine was observed leaving the governor's office with a big smile spread across her face.

CHAPTER SIXTEEN

Paterson's small squad of detectives took their seats hurriedly as he stood at the front of the room. His quick two-minute briefing with Dusty Doneghan had put him out of sorts. He knew that his detectives weren't going to be overly happy either when they heard what he had to say. Johnny Clocks sat by the side of him handing out dirty looks to the last of the stragglers. Finally, everybody settled down, notebooks and pads at the ready.

'Morning all,' said Paterson. 'Rough day, yesterday.' There was a collective nodding of heads and the odd murmur in the room. 'First of all, congratulations are in order for our Jackie here, who yesterday dished out a right-hander to our suspect after she was attacked by her. Jackie successfully ironed her out but only after Miss McKenna had been head-butted into unconsciousness by said suspect.'

Clocks held his phone up and showed everyone a picture of Christine McKenna lying on the floor. The room broke into a round of spontaneous clapping and whistling.

Jackie held her hands up. The right one was strapped up from knuckles to wrist. 'Thank you. Thank you,' she said.

'Remind me not to take the piss out of your tea-making skills anymore,' said Paterson. She smiled at him.

'Yeah, and remind me not to sexually harass you anymore,' said Clocks.

'You can do, guv. I don't mind,' she said. 'Every little helps.'

'Okay,' said Paterson. 'Moving swiftly on . . . a quick hello to DC Carrie Gedmine who will be joining us for the foreseeable future. It would seem that Tetley doesn't have the stomach for police work after all and called in sick today.' A few people snorted their contempt. Clocks scowled at them. He didn't like the man personally and felt the same, but he wasn't going to even allow the chance of a few snide comments.

'DI Clocks and I have a few things to update you on. First up, we went to the morgue yesterday. Preliminary findings on these children indicate that they were alive before they were skinned.' He paused to let that one sink in.

'The pathologist is of the opinion, and bear in mind that at the moment it is just an opinion, that these children were asphyxiated somehow for a period of time. Why? Glad you asked. We have no idea at the moment. I want someone to check all national databases to see if we have any recorded cases of this type of behaviour being reported. Volunteers?'

Jackie Hartnett put her hand up.

'Thank you, Jackie.'

Johnny Clocks scribbled in the actions book to show that she'd been allocated that particular task.

'Also, a man phoned in late last night and asked to speak to me. I wasn't about, so the uniform in the control room spoke to him — said the guy was pleasant enough, spoke politely but was insistent that he spoke to me. Said he had info about the case. Told again that I wasn't available, he left a message. He said, over and over, "let her go".' A few people frowned. 'The uniform told him it wasn't possible and he very kindly threatened to slice my face off.' Everybody frowned.

'Can only be an improvement if you ask me,' said Clocks. The frowns turned into smiles — all except for Carrie; her frown deepened.

‘Yeah, thanks for that.’ Paterson turned to Clocks. ‘The tape is being analysed for background noise, accent, et cetera. That right?’

Clocks nodded. ‘Yep. Any clue will do.’

Jackie Hartnett spoke. ‘So, do we have any idea what the connection is between the two?’

‘Nope. Not yet. I want that dug into today. We need to find out as much as we can about Elizabeth. What her story is, where she comes from, relationships, anything. Monkey said yesterday that she has a brother, so it may be him but we don’t know. DI Clocks and I are going out to him later today to see what we can find out.’

DC Ronnie Doneghan — Dusty to the squad — yawned. He’d finished at 1 a.m. and didn’t get to his bed until three, and was up again at five, in the office at six. For that, Clocks cut him some slack and didn’t bollock him for the yawn.

‘All right. Dusty, you’ve got an update for us re the house itself. The floor is yours.’

‘Thanks, guv,’ said Dusty. He remained seated as he tapped his fingers on his tablet.

‘As you all know, the house revealed some pretty unpleasant things and Monkey gave you all a very brief update yesterday as to what was found. I’ll go back over yesterday’s list and I’ve now got a fuller inventory of everything they found. Don’t bother writing this lot down, it’s not necessary and chances are you’ll run out of ink. Here we go.’ He looked down at the tablet and read off the bullet-pointed list.

‘One pair of child’s hands in a paper bag in a kitchen drawer, one teenager’s head in the kitchen freezer — female, frosted. Several skulls in the kitchen cupboard — missing the jaws. One in the sink that had cereal in it. One on a coffee table that had dead flowers in it. One penis being used as a curtain drawstring. Definitely not the guv’nor’s. It was way too big.’

Clocks gave him the finger.

‘One hollowed-out torso that was being used to store a number of human bones. Five faces. Children’s. These all had elastic bands threaded through the skin so they could be worn as masks. A pair of crudely stitched trousers made out of human skin — child size. A jacket made out of the skin of a human child. The legs of a young girl, possibly ten or eleven years old. The human teeth hanging on strings like a door curtain. Two bags of entrails. They were vacuum sealed, can you believe? There were three small ears, each of which had a cigarette stub standing upright a bit like a ciggy holder, I guess. Four place mats made of human skin. A face stretched out to make a small cushion cover. Six eyeballs and two pairs of lips. Three sets of ears hanging on a string like a necklace. A cornflakes packet containing toenails and a packet of Rice Krispies with three human fingers inside.'

'Bloody 'ell', said Clocks. 'Times 'ave changed. When I was a kid all you got in a packet of cereal was a plastic toy.'

One or two of the team chortled. Paterson shook his head.

'Two feet belonging to a young girl, side by side and wearing white socks and red shoes. The right arm of a teen-age girl with pink nail polish, something that we're not sure of yet but it looks like it came out of some poor little sod's insides. Three scalps complete with hair. We're saying they came from females at this stage because of the length. Colours are brown, blonde and rusty ginger. One of those scalps was placed on the severed head of a small child — like it was being used as a wig holder, y'know? And, get this . . . in a corner of a room was a leg — hollowed out, if you can believe it, and it had an umbrella standing in it. A fucking umbrella!'

'Probably didn't wanna get the floor wet,' said Clocks.

'In the downstairs bathroom in the bath itself were traces of human hair, more teeth and blood. And of course, there were the bodies themselves. The boys are doing a proper search on the upstairs and the basement today and I think they're going to start digging up the garden, too.'

Everybody in the room was an experienced detective and everybody looked rattled. All of them had seen their fair share of dead bodies over the years but none had ever heard of anything like this.

'Was Tetley over at the house all day yesterday?' said Toni Bell.

'Yeah,' said Paterson.

'No wonder he's gone sick, then. Don't fucking blame him.' There was a collective nodding of heads.

'Who did door-to-door?'

'I did,' said Dusty. 'Only needed one of us in the Lynton Road house and I volunteered Tetley. I had a word with the immediate neighbours. They weren't much help. All they could say was that, as far they knew, the woman lived alone. Bit of a recluse. Didn't talk to anyone and didn't have any visitors apart from a tall woman who turned up roughly once a month. Always had a kid in a wheelchair with her.'

The room went silent.

'Could be how they're getting kids into the house,' said Jackie. 'Maybe drugs them up, plonks them in the wheelchair and off she goes.'

Paterson nodded. 'Do we know who she is?' He looked at Dusty.

Dusty shook his head. 'One of the neighbours thought she might be a sister but wouldn't swear to it.'

'Descriptions?' said Paterson.

Dusty checked his notebook. 'Not much. Tall, thin, always wore dark clothing. Never hung about.'

'What time did she arrive?' said Paterson.

'Usually after dark.'

'She stay over?'

'Not as far as I know, but no one ever saw her leave in the morning or during the day, so I'm guessing she left in the small hours.'

'Any car? Van? If the kids are in wheelchairs, I'd expect to see something like that, unless of course she lived local.'

A few people scribbled in their notepads.

'What about the kid in the chair?'

'Again, not much,' said Dusty. 'It was dark.'

'So, we don't know if it was the same child going in each time?'

That question pricked up a few ears.

Dusty shook his head. 'No. We don't.'

'Did anyone ever see a male going into the premises?'

'Nope. Nothing said about a man going in.'

'Okay,' said Paterson. 'Two priorities now . . . this mystery caller and the possible sister with the kiddie in a wheelchair. I want something by the end of the day.' The detectives started to leave their seats when Paterson spoke again. 'Listen up. When this story breaks, the media storm will be massive and intense. No one says a word. Neither confirm nor deny. Refer anyone to the press office.'

CHAPTER SEVENTEEN

There was a knock on the door. Clocks got up and opened it. Jackie Hartnett stood there.

'Profiler's here, guv.'

Clocks shook his head. 'Show him in, Jack.'

She stood aside and allowed a man of about forty years old step past her and into the office. The first thing Paterson noticed was his hair. It looked like it had dodged a wash and a comb for a good few weeks. He wore a checked shirt with the sleeves rolled up and a pair of brown corduroy trousers. A battered old leather school satchel was hanging off of his left shoulder and he topped off the look with a pair of Jesus Creeper sandals. With socks.

Clocks looked him up and down, a sneer on his face. The man, Thomas Case, nodded politely. Paterson was suddenly conscious of his own dress, which was in stark contrast to Case: a two-grand Gucci watch fitted snugly on his wrist; his navy blue tailor-made Armani suit fitted him like a glove; and his Louboutin shoes probably cost more than this man's car.

'Mr Paterson?' He took his hand. 'Nice to meet you. My name is—'

'Thomas Case. I know. Nice to meet you. Please, take a seat.'

'Thank you. I appreciate the opportunity to work with you on this case.'

Johnny Clocks frowned. 'What'd you mean "work with us"? You're not working with us, mate. Oh, no. We're gonna tell you as little as possible, you're gonna jot a few things down on a bit of paper, type it up, then you leave and we toss it in the bin when you've gone. Thanks for comin'. It was a pleasure.'

Thomas Case looked at Johnny Clocks, mortified. 'Er, I'm sorry? I don't understand. I'm here to help you draw up a profile of the man who called Mr Paterson threatening to cause him bodily harm.'

'Bodily 'arm? That's a quaint way of puttin' it. Bodily 'arm. Threatened to peel 'is bleedin' face off.'

Case nodded.

'An' how'd you know it's a man?'

'What?' said Case.

'A man. You said it was a man. How'd you know it's a man who made the call?'

'Er . . . well . . .'

'That's a leap, ain't it? You don't know anythin' about this case yet and you've already decided it's a bloke. That's called cognitive bias, mate. You come in 'ere with your preconceived notions and you're blinded by your own mind. Could be a woman. Could be a kid. Could be a pensioner. Nobody knows and you're off to a bad start straight away.'

Thomas Case looked both confused and startled. 'But . . . but . . . it's the information I've been given. A male.'

Paterson could see the man flush and he bet that right now he was wishing the ground would open up and take him straight back to the halls of academia.

'Well then, it's your lucky day then, mate,' said Clocks. 'It *was* a man who made the call so, write down a few details for us and let us get on with the job. Ta-ta.' He waved him away. 'Go on. Off you fuck. Men at work.'

'Enough, John.' Paterson scowled at him. 'No need to be rude.'

'Wasn't being rude, guv. Was being honest. If he gets his pants bunched up his arse over this, wait 'til he sees the photos.'

'Mr Case . . .' said Paterson. 'Thomas . . . I apologise for DI Clocks. He's not a big fan of the old psychology and I have to admit, neither am I. But I know you have a job to do and I'll make sure you're treated courteously and professionally. Just ignore DI Clocks. He was just playing with you. His idea of banter. I'm afraid he's what we call "stuck in the past". Round about the seventies I'd guess.'

'I see,' said Case. He gave Clocks a weak grin.

Clocks glared at him. He was going to have his fun one way or the other.

'I take it then that you already know some facts, yes?' said Paterson.

'Er, yes. Some.'

'Good. I'll make sure you're brought fully up to speed. We'll get you started with the crime scene photos, what we know about the woman so far and the conversation the uniformed officer had with the man who called in leaving threatening messages.'

Case looked interested at that point. 'Yes, I had a very brief glance at the notes on the way over. Interesting.'

'Is it? Why's that?'

'Well, it's unusual for serial killers to work in pairs. Highly unusual in fact. It is so rare—'

'Who said they were working in a pair? There you go again. All we've got is one in custody for two murders and a bunch of kiddies insulating the walls.' Paterson winced at Clocks's insensitivity. 'Then someone phones up and tells us to let her go. Don't mean he's working with her, does it? It might be her son sitting at the table wonderin' where his bloody dinner is. Might be a nutter who's just on a wind-up. Knows she got nicked and thought he'd try it on. Take us off in the wrong direction. It happens.'

'No, no, I just meant—'

'Yeah, I know what you meant. You fired up some sort of cockamamie theory in yer 'ead on yer way over an' now you want to prove it to yerself.'

Paterson wrinkled his nose. 'Cockamamie? What does that mean?'

'It means 'load of ol' bollocks'.'

Paterson was satisfied with that. 'Mr Case, we'll get to see just how interesting this man is when we catch him,' he said.

A sharp tap on the door pulled them all out of their thoughts. Jackie Hartnett poked her head around the door looking anxious. 'Guv. Pick up the phone. Now. I think he's back on for you.'

Paterson reached for the phone and hit the speaker button. He waved Jackie into the room. She closed the door behind her. Thomas Case quickly pulled out a micro digital recorder and pressed the red button.

'Superintendent Paterson speaking. What can I do for you?'

Silence.

'Hello. Can I help you?'

'You're looking for me.'

'Am I? Who are you, then?'

'I'm the man you're looking for?'

'Which one? I'm looking for about half a dozen at the moment.'

'Lynton Road.'

'Okay. What can I do for you?'

'Let her go.'

'Who?'

'The woman.'

'What woman?'

'Mr Paterson, I'm in no mood to play stupid games with you. Let her go.'

'Nope.'

'Let her go.'

'Who's she to you, then? Is she your wife or sister or something?'

'She's no one.'

'Well, she must be someone, mate, or you wouldn't be phoning me up telling me to let her go, would you? Is it your mum, maybe?'

'Let her go.'

'You know what she did yesterday? Killed two men and injured another. Badly. Two policemen.'

'Unlucky for you. Let her go.'

'Doesn't seem the sort of thing I'd just do. No. I'm not a fan of letting murderers go.'

'You will let her go.'

'And if I don't?'

'I will wear you.'

'Come again? You'll "*wear* me?" What'd you mean?'

'I will take your face.'

Paterson clenched his fist. 'That a fact, is it?'

'Yes. I will peel your face off your skull. Slowly. Painfully.'

'You can try your luck, but I don't fancy your chances too much.'

'Your face will be my face.'

The blood pounded in Paterson's temples and he took in a deep breath before he spoke. 'Most likely that will be a big improvement for you. You're a tough nut threatening me on the end of a phone, fellah. Why don't you set up a meet and we can chat about it in person. You can bring your knife, wave it around, and I'll kick your black heart out the back of your chest. Fancy your chances?'

'Last time. Let her go.'

'Go fuck yourself, arse-wipe.' Paterson slammed the phone down. He looked across at Thomas Case who had a look of total bewilderment on his face. 'Turn that off, right now,' he said, indicating the recorder.

Case clicked it off immediately. The two men looked at each other.

'So gimme your assessment,' said Paterson.

Thomas Case was clearly upset at the way things had gone. Whatever he was expecting when he took on the case, it would not have involved the senior investigating officer in charge of the investigation to behave the way Paterson had just done and he certainly wouldn't have expected him to antagonize the only lead they had. His ethics were about to cause him a problem. Should he shut up or report him. He chose the latter.

'My assessment? Of whom? You or him?'

Paterson's was enraged. 'What did you say to me?'

Case looked uneasy but stood his ground. 'In all my years, I have never witnessed a police officer talk to a suspect in that way. Do you realise what you've done? You've made him angry and who knows what he'll do now. He may kill again because of you.'

Paterson came around the table fast.

'Ray! Don't,' said Clocks as he moved to block him.

Paterson stopped.

'I'm sorry, sir, but I'm going to have to report your behaviour and the fact you may have jeopardised your own investigation.' He turned to leave and came face to face with Jackie standing in front of the door. He looked back at Clocks, standing in front of Paterson. Paterson tore his glance away from Case and turned it to Clocks. They nodded to each other. Clocks turned around.

'I'll show you out, mate. It's all right.' He crossed the room and took him lightly by the arm. Jackie stood aside to let them out.

* * *

As they walked through the office and out to the stairs, Clocks stopped Case. 'Look. I know you're upset. We all are. Mr Paterson don't normally behave that way but we're all under a lot of pressure, mate. You understand, don't ya?'

Emboldened by his having taken a stance, Case wasn't going to let it go. 'I'm sure he is. I'm sure you all are. But don't you understand what he may have done back there?'

'Yeah. You said. But don't underestimate him. He went off at him for a reason.'

‘What reason?’

‘Dunno yet. You went all goody two shoes on ’im. Never got the chance to ask before you shot yer crack off.’

‘What? He shouldn’t threaten suspects.’

‘To be clear, ’e didn’t threaten ’im. He goaded ’im. Different thing all together.’

‘Why do that?’

‘Because it unsettles them. If the bloke’s unsettled, challenged, it might cause ’im to make a mistake, maybe draw ’im out into the open. May bring ’im out to come after Mr Paterson. Who knows?’

Case waved Clocks away. ‘Whatever. That’s not how you do it.’

‘I’m sorry. Who the fuck are you to tell us how to do it? You’re a book reader not a fuckin’ copper. You could write what you know about policin’ on the back of a stamp with a crayon.’

Case backed up a step. ‘Well, I’m sorry. I’m still going to report him.’ He held up the recorder. ‘And this tape will be the eviden—’

Clocks snatched it off of him and threw it out of an open window. ‘Oops!’

The recorder made a shattering sound as it hit the ground four floors below and was followed immediately by someone shouting, ‘Oi!’

Clocks poked his head casually through the window. ‘Sorry,’ he said. ‘Didn’t see you.’

A uniformed officer stood looking up at him, his face red with anger. ‘You fucking idiot!’ the copper shouted up.

‘Fair point,’ said Clocks. He pulled his head back in and turned his attention back to a stunned Thomas Case.

He put his hands in his pockets. ‘Anyway . . . lovely to meet you, Mr Case. Thanks for coming an’ for all your ’elp.’

‘You . . . what the fuck is wrong with you two?’

Clocks shook his head and shrugged. ‘Dunno. Maybe you can draw up a profile of us now you’ve got yer mornin’ back to yerself.’

‘That was my personal property.’

‘What was?’

‘That was. My recorder.’

‘What recorder?’

‘Are you joking, Clocks?’

‘DI Clocks to you, son.’

‘That will go in my report too.’

‘What will?’

‘That you threw my recorder out of the window.’

Clocks shrugged again. ‘Dunno what you’re talkin’ about, mate.’

‘You nearly killed someone. He’ll be a witness.’

‘I doubt that very much. Anyway, you’ve wasted way too much of my time, so go. Off you fuck, and be careful now. Mind you don’t fall down the stairs on yer way out. That would be tragic.’

CHAPTER EIGHTEEN

'Superintendent Paterson . . . Good to meet you. DI Clocks . . . Good to meet you too.' Detective Chief Inspector Carolyn Henson was a striking woman in her early forties. Painfully thin, she looked like she'd had or was still struggling with some sort of eating disorder. Her demeanour was that of someone used to being in charge and not one to let things slip by her. With five years in the Met's Child Abuse Investigation Unit, she was well versed in the figures and reasons why children went missing in the UK.

'This is Debbie Lane. She's part of the Global Missing Children's Network.' Debbie Lane, also in her forties, nodded to Paterson and Clocks.

'Thank you both for coming in. I take it you're up to speed with what happened yesterday?' said Paterson.

'We read the reports, yes. How is it that we can help you?' said DCI Henson.

'To be honest, I'm not actually sure you can with this one, but I was wondering if you could perhaps put some meat on the bones of it for me.'

'Go on,' she said.

'I was hoping you might be able to tell me a little bit about the woman living in the house, a Miss Elizabeth May?

We've found out a few things already . . . that she has a brother, Marcus, living in the sticks and a sister that went missing years ago. When I say *missing* I mean she left the family home due to alleged sexual abuse by the father. We're going off to see the brother after we've finished here today. I just wondered if she was in any of your databases.'

'Name doesn't ring a bell.' DCI Henson turned to her colleague. 'Debs?'

Debbie Lane shook her head.

'What's the possibility of Elizabeth or Marcus being part of a paedophile ring operating around these parts?'

'Could be. But we would have to dig deeper. A lot deeper. I'm happy to do that but, tell me, were any of these dead children sexually assaulted either before or after death?'

Paterson frowned. 'Not that I'm aware of. I'm still waiting for full reports from the pathologist and labs.'

'I would be surprised if they have been. Don't get me wrong. We all know that some paedophiles kill and they sometimes do that horrifically, but not like this. Not like the pictures we've seen anyway.'

'How can you be sure?' said Clocks.

'Experience. Think about it. If there was a gang, that could be as few as say, four, but it could go up to about fifteen, twenty. Believe me, this would have leaked out before now. Someone always talks. Has to show off, show pictures. Post them on the Internet — the dark web. And remember . . . although there are plenty of paedos on the dark web, it's not typical for them to engage in this sort of behaviour. I know it sounds odd, but there's a good percentage who would be horrified by this and would have sent in anonymous links to the police.'

Clocks shrugged. 'Why's that then? Worried they'll get a bad name?'

DCI Henson gave him a wry smile. 'Strangely enough, something like that, yes. They might be sick, but there's levels of sick and these deaths, well they're a whole new level. Trust me, this isn't your bog-standard paedophile. Someone would have talked.'

'The kids we found behind the walls . . .' said Paterson. 'Some of them had been dead for some time judging by the state of decomposition. We're obviously in the process of trying to identify them and track down their families to give them the bad news but I understand that sometimes not all missing children are reported. Is that right?'

DCI Henson nodded. 'Oh, yeah. Happens more often than you would think.'

'Well, why the hell aren't they reported, for Christ's sake? Surely the parents would be going out of their minds with worry?'

'All different reasons. Sometimes the kids just up and run away for whatever reason. Often the parents are just glad to see the back of them and couldn't give a shit. Glad to have them out of the house. To be fair, ninety-nine percent of them are devastated but that one percent . . . well, that one percent may have far darker reasons.'

'Such as?' Clocks folded his arm across his chest.

DCI Henson turned to look at him. 'Let me ask you a couple of questions. Do you come from a good home, Inspector? Loving parents who fed and watered you? Put a roof over your head, gave you a warm bed? Helped you with schoolwork, bought you a bike, that sort of thing? If they did, lucky you.'

Clocks said nothing.

'No drink problems? No drug problems? No sexual abuse?'

Clocks remained silent.

'In that space is where the one percent live. Some of these parents, if we can call them that, will willingly sell their child for their next drink, their next fix. Prostitute them out for a tenner a time to paedos. Doesn't matter to them. The next fix is all that matters. Some have been known to even sell them to sex traffickers for a grand. A thousand pounds. Can you imagine what they can do with that sort of money? They can drug themselves into oblivion. Hell, they might even overdose if we're lucky. So, they're not going to report their child missing, are they?'

'Fuck me blind! Sellin' their own kids . . . What's wrong with these people?'

'I just told you. The three D's . . . drink, drugs and desperation. A shitload of desperation. And, there's worse . . .'

'There fuckin' better not be,' said Clocks, his anger palpable.

'Of the one percent there is another one percent that actually have children purely so they themselves can sexually abuse them.'

Paterson shook his head while Clocks looked genuinely appalled.

'Fuuuuuck off!' he said.

'It's true, I'm afraid. We've had cases where paedophiles abuse their own children, often as babies, and then when they get older, pass them around.'

'All right,' said Paterson. 'That's enough.'

DCI Henson was on a roll. 'And then of course, there's the traffickers. These are the bastards who snatch kids off the street, shopping centres, beaches, swimming pools, parks and then spirit them off out of the country to be sold into the sex trade. They do get reported, of course. Then there are those who act as a middleman between rich couples with a shit-ton of money and no fucking scruples at all. Those ones, though, often end up living a decent life.'

'All right, we get it,' said Paterson. 'So how big a problem is it?'

Debbie Lane cleared her throat and handed both Paterson and Clocks a sheet of A4 paper with a pie chart and columns of figures. 'In the UK, in any one year, there are roughly — *roughly* — one hundred thousand children reported missing.'

'What? An 'undred thousand?' said Clocks.

'Give or take.'

'Give or take what?'

'Ten or twenty thousand. It fluctuates.'

'Ten or twenny thousand! That's not a fluctuation. That's a bloody battalion. How the fuck do an 'undred and twenny thousand kids go missing? That's lunacy.'

'The good news, though, is that most of them are found quite quickly. Usually within twenty-four hours. Kids run away. Kids wander off. So much easier now that Mum and Dad are always glued to their fucking mobile phone screens and not taking any notice of where their kids are.'

Paterson rubbed away a small tear that was threatening to spill over. 'Back to this . . . At this stage, we're still going to assume that all of these poor little sods were reported missing and that somewhere out there, there are some parents who will at least get some form of closure. Carolyn, can you liaise with my team and help them navigate their way through the identification process and hopefully do a match-up of your databases?'

'Of course. Anything else I can do?'

'Not unless you can find a way to make sure that parents, grandparents and carers all keep a closer eye on their kids.'

Detective Chief Inspector Henson nodded. 'We should be so lucky.'

CHAPTER NINETEEN

The curtains of No. 68 Alfriston Road gave a little twitch as Paterson and Clocks pulled up on the gravel driveway and stepped out of the Mercedes. Clocks stretched out his back and looked at the house. Big, white and with fields at the back.

'He's doin' all right for himself by the look of it. Nice little drum 'e lives in.'

Paterson nodded. 'Yeah, not too shabby, is it?'

'What's he do for a livin', again?'

'Architect,' Toni said. 'They're never hard up, are they?'

Clocks shook his head. 'Wouldn't 'ave thought so. 'Ere, when you're talkin' to him, 'ave a word and see if he can design you an extension for your wallet. You could always use a bigger one, couldn't ya?'

Paterson closed the car door. 'Nah, you're all right. I'm happy with this one, John. It's slim but it holds five of my black credit cards. That's enough for me.'

'What about cash?'

'What about it? Who carries cash anymore? Thing of the past, mate. No one wants the bloody stuff.'

'I fuckin' do! I'll 'ave it if no one else does. I ain't proud, mate.'

'Well, that we know,' Paterson gave Clocks a grin. 'John, before we go in, do me a favour.'

'What?'

'You know what.'

'Do I?'

'Yes.'

Clocks nodded. 'Oh. You want me to be a good boy an' behave meself. Don't wind 'im up, right?'

'Yep. That's exactly right. If he's the bloke who phoned me up threatening to slice my face off, I don't want to do anything to give him the impression we suspect him of it.'

'Why?'

'Well, for starters, we don't know what's in that house, we don't know what he's capable of, we don't know if anyone else is in that house with him. And if he manages to do a runner we may not be able to find him for a while. Maybe never. So let's play it by ear and see how it goes.'

Clocks shrugged. 'Whatever.' He rang the bell and his face showed disdain as the doorbell played a tinny version of Clair de Lune.

The door opened and Marcus May stood in the entrance. 'Can I help you gentlemen?' His deep voice carried a hint of both menace and inquisitiveness.

Paterson turned to look at him. Memories flooded his brain. Most of them carried pain and embarrassment. Pictures flashed into his head of the beatings this man had handed to him in tournaments, and the sarcastic taunts afterwards had left marks on him that he had long buried.

'Marcus,' said Paterson. He pulled himself taller and walked toward the man, his hand extended. 'D'you recognise me?'

Marcus tilted his head to one side. Paterson was shaking his hand before Marcus realised who it was.

'Paterson? Ray Paterson?'

Paterson gave a slight nod.

A look of surprise and happiness spread across Marcus May's face. 'Paterson! It is you. My God, man, what the hell are you doing here? How long's it been? Don't tell me. Fifteen years? Must be.'

Johnny Clocks frowned. He wasn't a fan of people who made a fuss.

'Jesus, you look well. Really well.'

'Thank you, Marcus. See you've kept yourself in shape.' Paterson couldn't help but admire the man's physique. Muscles exactly where they should be and about eight percent body fat were covered by a tight white T-shirt. His hair had thinned quite a bit though, which pleased Paterson.

Marcus looked slightly embarrassed but that was probably only something he'd learned to do to help people feel less inferior around him. 'Yeah, you know. Looking pretty fit yourself. Who's this?' He lifted his head towards Clocks.

'I'm sorry. This is John. Johnny Clocks. We work together.'

Clocks flashed his palm up.

'Sorry it's so late,' Paterson said, 'but I needed to talk to you about something.'

'You're all right. It's not that late. Come on in, come in, both of you. Christ, it's good to see you after all this time.' Marcus stood aside and let the two men into his home.

'Wife's in the greenhouse doing a bit of late-night potting. Karen!' he called. 'Karen! Go in the living room, Ray.' He pointed to a room that had the door open.

'Take a seat, gents. You're a tea man if I remember, aintcha, Ray? I'll get you a cup of tea.' He looked at Clocks. 'Tea for you, too, mate, or you a coffee man?'

'Gin, vodka, whisky or beer man to be honest, fellah. But if coffee's all you've got . . .'

Marcus grinned over at Paterson. 'I like him.'

'That's because you don't know him.'

'Pick your poison then, gents.' Marcus headed over to a large drinks cabinet.

'Marcus?'

Paterson turned to see Karen May, Marcus's wife, in the doorway. She was short with blonde hair pulled into a ponytail. A pair of pink-framed glasses framed malachite green eyes set in an elfin face that could have seen her run for Miss World back in the day. The only flaw he could find was a small scar on her right cheek. On her hands were a pair of dirt-covered gardening gloves that fitted tightly. She began to tug at the fingers of one of them as she walked into the room.

'Karen,' said Marcus. 'Come and meet an old friend of mine.' Paterson and Clocks both stood. 'This is Ray. Ray Paterson. We used to fight together when we were kids. Haven't seen him in years.'

'Hello, Ray.' She held out a delicate hand to shake his.

'Hi,' Paterson said. 'Nice to meet you. This is John.' He jerked his head towards Clocks who was looking at her like he'd found his favourite meal on the menu.

'All right, love.' He tried not to stare.

She smiled at him as if used to men feeling awkward in her presence.

'Hello, John. I'm all right, thank you. Thanks for asking.'

'Ray and John were in the neighbourhood and . . .' Marcus stopped himself. 'Actually, why are you here? Sorry. Don't mean to be rude but I haven't seen you for ages and . . .' He shrugged. 'Not that it's not good to see you.'

Paterson smiled at him. 'Yeah, sorry. Never got to say, did I? I'm here on business. *We're* here on business.'

'Oh.' Marcus nodded. 'What sort of business? You want something designed? I can do that for you. Mates' rates, of course.' He winked at Paterson.

'I said that to him outside. Said you could design and build him a bigger wallet.' Clocks grinned over at Karen.

'That's right. I'd forgotten. You're worth a good few quid aren't you? Sod the mates' rates then.' He chuckled.

'Don't need anything built or designed, Marcus. Police business.'

Marcus's face dropped. 'Police? You're a copper?'

'Yep. Superintendent.'

'Wow. Good for you. Good for you. Always knew you'd do well for yourself.'

'Thanks,' said Paterson.

'So, why are you here, Ray? Not holding a grudge, are you? Haven't come to nick me for kicking the shit out of you all those years ago, eh?'

And there it was. Paterson had wondered how long that would take. Clocks grinned.

'All in the past, mate. And it was just a competition. Means nothing.'

'So . . .' Marcus gave Paterson an expectant look.

'I'll get to it. Sorry, can I just ask? You had a sister, didn't you? Whatever happened to her?'

'Bev? Dunno. She left home when she was young. Haven't heard a word from her in years. Could be anywhere. Why'd you ask?'

'You seen the news lately?'

'No. Don't watch it that often. Why? What's happened?'

'Do you know the address 1365 Lynton Road?'

Marcus shook his head. 'Should I?'

Paterson ignored the question and pulled out his mobile phone. He swiped through some photos before holding it toward Marcus. 'Do you recognise this woman?'

Marcus peered at it for a second then turned to Karen. 'No. No, I don't. Should I?'

'I think you probably do. Her name's Elizabeth.'

Marcus peered at the photo again. A mug shot taken at the hospital complete with blood and bruising. He shrugged. 'No. I don't but, Jesus. What happened to her?'

'She fell down the stairs a few times,' Clocks chimed in.

'She murdered a police officer and seriously wounded another,' said Paterson, his tone colder.

'Oh God!' Karen swayed slightly and pressed her hand to her mouth.

'So, you do know her?'

Marcus took on the look of a helpless child as he turned between both officers. 'I'm sorry. I'm so sorry. She didn't . . . she wouldn't . . .'

'Yeah, well, she did and she did, mate.'

'I haven't seen her . . .'

'We know,' said Clocks. 'For years. You said.'

'So is this your missing sister, Beverley? Is she using another name now? Is she called Elizabeth now?' Clocks's tone was more insistent.

'Thing is, Marcus,' Paterson said, 'the social services have you down as next of kin and first point of contact. They've been writing to you about her for some time about her mental issues, so you might want to rethink your stance on not having seen her for years.' He kept his eye on Marcus as he weighed him up.

Marcus nodded. 'Yes, yes, you're right. I'm sorry. Please, sit down again. I'll tell you what happened.' He walked back over to the drinks cabinet and filled three glasses with vodka. Karen declined.

Marcus sat down opposite Paterson, his hand shaking as he chugged the entire glass of vodka. Clocks raised his eyebrows and nodded.

'Look. Here's the truth of it. I've actually got two sisters.'

'Two?' Paterson feigned surprise. 'I only remember you ever mentioning one.'

'Bev's the one I haven't seen for years. She took off when she was young. Elizabeth? She's a different story altogether. She had a lot of issues as a child. A lot. She was diagnosed with severe mental problems from an early age and, to tell the truth, Mum and Dad couldn't cope with her. She was violent, quick-tempered. Awful. Healthcare services did help a bit but nowhere near enough. We just couldn't get her the right help that she needed and they wouldn't hospitalise her even for her own safety.

'Things came to a head when she was about twelve. She attacked Dad — stabbed him three or four times.' He shook his head at the memory.

'Why'd she do that?' said Paterson.

Marcus shook his head. 'Said that he had raped her. Been raping her for years.'

'Had he?'

Marcus looked both annoyed and exasperated at Paterson's question. 'I dunno. Probably. But you have to understand . . . she made all sorts of allegations all the time.'

'Like what?' said Clocks.

Marcus sighed. 'Sex assaults against everyone . . . me . . . Dad . . . Mum . . . Beverley . . . the postman . . . the ninety-five-year-old woman three doors down and the paper boy. That was a complete mystery, that one. We never even had the papers delivered, Ray. She was off her nut. Mum ran off. Couldn't cope with it anymore. Bev legged it first chance she got. Dad was desperate. Didn't know what to do with Elizabeth so he locked her away and told me not to say anything about her to anyone. We moved away and that was that.'

'That was that?' said Paterson. 'He locked her away? Jesus. That's fucked up.'

'Yeah, well. He was desperate and, truth be told, ashamed of her. Stigma of mental health and all that.'

Paterson shook his head. 'And you said nothing to no one?'

'Nope. I was a kid. I was frightened. I'd lost my mum and my sister. Dad was in a right state. I didn't know what to do . . . I just did as I was told.'

'So, 'ow come she's living in Bermondsey on her own?' Clocks was looking distinctly agitated as Marcus's story unfolded.

'Dad died. I think it was the strain. Anyway, I couldn't look after her, could I? So, I called the social in. They freaked out and took her into care. Ironic, really. Only wanted to know once I'd lost my entire family. Bastards. If they'd have helped out sooner . . .

'Anyway, she went away for a while. Ended up in a mental hospital somewhere in Camberwell. After a couple of years, they moved her out into Lynton Road so she could live on her own, be independent and all that but . . . well, she wasn't up to it.'

'Did she get any help when she lived alone?'

'Some. But, not enough as far as I'm concerned.'

'I take it you didn't help?'

Marcus sighed. 'When you say it like that, it sounds bad, I know. But I don't know what to do, how to handle her. I'm not trained to deal with her and, to be honest, I don't want her making any bloody allegations against me anymore. I'm married. I've got a child. I've got my own firm. People depend on me for their livelihood and the last thing I needed was your mob carting me off to the nick because my mad sister got a fit in her head and decided to say I was boinking her. You can understand that, surely?'

Paterson rubbed his chin, feeling the stubble on it. Marcus was making sense. 'Did you say you have a child?'

Marcus sat up. 'Yeah. Little girl. Alice.'

Paterson smiled. 'Good for you, fellah. How old?'

'She's eight,' said Karen.

'Eight? Wow. Bet she's a handful?'

'No,' said Marcus. 'She's a real angel, mate. Doesn't give us any problems at all. You got any kids, Ray?'

'Me? No. No time for that, I'm afraid.'

'He's got a really big car though,' said Clocks, a mischievous grin on his face.

'Where is your daughter? Be nice to meet her,' said Paterson.

'She's staying with a friend for a few days. As you can see, we're a bit cut off here so it's difficult for her to play with kids. Not like they can just pop round after school. We normally swap about. Couple of days she has a friend here, then a couple of days she stays with a friend. It's not ideal, but it works.'

Paterson nodded. 'Yeah. Can't be easy for you.'

'It's all right,' said Marcus. 'We're used to it now. It's just the way it is.'

'Talking of kids,' said Paterson, 'Have you ever heard her make mention of someone called the Childmaker?'

Marcus gave him a curious look. 'Childmaker? No idea. What does that mean?'

'Your sister kept saying that the Childmaker was coming and that he was going to hurt us.'

'That's a new one. I never heard her say that before.'

'The thing is,' said Clocks. 'When we turned the 'ouse over, we found a few other things that, quite frankly, disturbed us.'

Marcus turned his attention to Clocks. 'Like what?'

'Shitload of dead kids bricked up behind the wall in the basement. Various bits missing from them. Found all sorts of stuff in the house. Skulls, bits of bodies. Looked like a serial killer's pick 'n' mix counter.' Paterson winced at Clocks's insensitivity.

Marcus looked horrified. Karen started to cry, shaking her head violently.

'So, we're thinking that she didn't do that all by herself, y'know? Must 'ave had some help from somewhere.'

Marcus stared at Clocks. 'What? Me? You think I had something to do with it?'

'Dunno. Maybe. You did lie to us, didn't you?'

'That's . . . I told you. We locked her away. When she was released, we had no contact.'

'But, you did, didn't you?' said Paterson. 'The social said you did. Letters prove you knew of her and had some involvement with her.'

Marcus stood up sharply and got right into Paterson's face. Paterson didn't flinch but crossed his hands in front of his genitals, just in case.

'Listen. Don't come in here after all these years and accuse me of murder. I don't know anything about it. Nothing. Y'hear me?'

'Didn't say you were involved, Marcus. Said you were lying and that's never a good thing when you talk to two 'tecs from the murder squad.'

'Nothing to do with me. End of.'

'Good to know. Now, do us both a favour and get out of my face, Marcus. Make's me a bit edgy.' Marcus didn't budge.

'Marcus!' Karen barked. 'Stop it. They have to ask.'

Paterson, his face two inches from Marcus's, smiled. 'We do.'

'Right,' said Clocks. 'Can you two ol' pals not get all punchy again? C'mon. Pack it in.'

Marcus backed off, his eyes fixed on Paterson. 'Sorry, Ray. I was out of order.'

'No worries. Difficult thing to talk about. I get it.'

'D'you 'ave an idea, *any* idea, why there would be dead kids in the basement?' said Clocks.

Marcus turned away from Paterson. 'No. But she did lose a baby.'

'What?' said Clocks.

'Got herself a boyfriend and ended up pregnant. Lost it. Maybe it's something to do with that.'

Paterson frowned. Interesting. 'Where's the boyfriend now?'

'Six foot under. She lost the baby and apparently, he stepped in front of a lorry. Depressed. Mental problems himself.'

'Fuckin' 'ell.' Clocks shook his head. 'She don't 'ave much luck, does she?'

'No. She doesn't. Her life's been shit.' Marcus dropped his head and fixed his gaze on the carpet. 'All of our lives have been shit and it sounds like they're going to shit yet again.'

'Well, as her brother, we're going to need you to come to the nick and give us a full statement,' said Paterson.

'About what?' Marcus's eyes were still fixed downward.

'Basically, what you've just told us. We need to get an overarching picture of her and the part you and the rest of your family played in her life. You may be able to tell us something important. Anyway, I'll send a car over to pick you up tomorrow or the day after.'

Marcus nodded. 'Fine. I'll be here. If you're done, I'll show you out.'

Paterson and Clocks said their goodbyes to Karen and followed Marcus out into the hall. Paterson stole a glance out through the patio doors and into the fields behind.

'You really are isolated out here, aren't you, Marcus?' he said.

'Suits us. No one to bother us. No neighbours popping round when you don't want them.'

'Is that your nearest neighbour?' said Paterson. He nodded toward the field out back.

'Yeah. Why?'

Paterson shrugged. 'No reason. Just asking.'

'That's old Lee Angel. Must be in his eighties now. Lives there with his wife. Heard he was supposed to be a right villain in his day. Armed robber. Shotguns. Sad story really. Had it all once. Got old. Kids fucked off on his money and lived the life of Riley. Never sees them now. Wife is a nice old lady. Not fond of the Old Bill, as you would expect. They've been together for a dog's age. Better part of sixty years now.'

'Sixty years! Blood 'ell,' said Clocks. 'That's a right old Mills 'n' Boon story that one.'

'Mills and Boon?' said Paterson as he stood in the doorway.

Clocks rolled his eyes. 'Yeah. You must of 'eard of them? Published a shit-ton of romance novels for the last, I dunno, billion years. That's how people used to get their jollies before Internet wanking took off in a big way.'

Paterson shook his head, baffled by some of the things that rolled around inside Clocks's brain and by the fact that he wasn't capable of stopping them from spilling out of his mouth.

The two men said their goodbyes and Paterson reminded him that a car would be sent for him.

Marcus May watched the two men climb into the car and closed his door.

'What'd ya reckon, Ray?' said Clocks as he pulled the seat belt across his chest.

'Nothing to tie him to anything but he's lying like a lunatic.'

Clocks nodded. 'I take it you noticed, then?'

'What? That there's not a single picture of his daughter anywhere and no toys lying around? Yeah, I noticed.'

'Thought you had. Still, they may be telling the truth. Perhaps she is with a friend. It happens.'

Paterson started the car and pulled away. 'Yep. It does. But I'm thinking if he's lied about not having a second sister for so long plus he lied about his dad dying, I'm pretty sure we can't trust a fucking word that comes out of his mouth.'

'D'you think he'll do a runner?'

'Honestly? I doubt it. Look around you. Big house, his own company. No. Too much to keep him here at the moment. Besides, if we played it right, and I think we did, he's got no real reason to think we think he's involved with the murders themselves.'

'He got a bit showy-offy in there, though. Bit defensive.'

'That's just his way. Aggressive bully. No, he was always an arrogant prick, so my money's on him staying put for the time being.'

'We puttin' him under watch?'

'I'd like to, but it's not going be too easy, is it? Flat fields and no trees for — what — half a mile? The only place suitable is the old boy's house and, from what Marcus said, he's not exactly pro-police.'

'I'll get some checks done on the old boy when we get back. Time might have mellowed him.'

Paterson's phone rang. He nodded a few times then hung up.

'Problem?' said Clocks.

'Information.'

'Where we goin' now, then?'

Paterson glanced at the clock on the dashboard. 'Back to Lynton Road.'

CHAPTER TWENTY

Paterson and Clocks drew up outside the Lynton Road address and, after signing in and pulling on shoe covers, walked back into the house. Senior Forensic officer Tony Kent, greeted them with a surly look. Neither of them had left him with a good impression after their attendance at the scene of the murder of a Muslim man whose head was the only thing showing on the shore of the Thames. Taking bets on whether the man's head was attached or detached and then deciding on whether or not the best way to find out was to kick it or hit it with a golf club had not been his idea of professionalism. He had a point.

'Mister . . . ? I'm sorry,' said Kent, 'I've forgotten your name.'

'Detective Superintendent Paterson.' He didn't bother offering to shake hands with Kent.

'Yes. Paterson. Thank you for coming so soon.' CSI Kent ignored Johnny Clocks completely, a fact that didn't seem lost on him.

'What are you still doing here? I thought you guys all went home at five.'

Kent grinned. 'We do normally, but with one prisoner in custody and this house being what it is, we've been ordered to work until midnight to secure as much evidence as possible.'

'So, why d'you call us back here?'

'I thought you might want to see this.' Kent held up a sealed plastic bag. Inside was a letter from Barclays Bank dated earlier in the year.

Paterson and Clocks both peered at it. It was addressed to a Mrs B May with an address in Hertfordshire. Paterson took out his mobile phone and took a photo of it. Clocks did the same.

'The missing sister?' Paterson said to Clocks.

'Looks like it could be,' Clocks replied.

'Where did you find this?' Paterson said to Kent.

'It was down behind the cooker. I don't know, but I'm assuming it slipped down there at some point and she either wasn't aware or just forgot about it.'

Clocks ripped open the envelope.

'What the fuck?' said Kent. 'What d'you think you're doing?'

'Openin' the letter,' said Clocks. 'How else will I know what's in it?'

'You moron. That's evidence. We have ways of opening letters.'

'Do ya?'

'Yes.'

'Are they anything like mine?'

'No they're not. It's a delicate process.'

'Would you 'ave 'ad to take it back to the lab?'

'Yes, of course.'

'Thought so. Ain't got time for all that fannyin' about. Me prints are on file so do an elimination set and we're good to go.'

CSI Kent shook his head, his face pained. He looked at Paterson for some help. He didn't get it.

'Clocks has a point. If this is who we think it is, there's a good chance it's the person who's killed all of these children.'

'And that's all the more reason to preserve the bloody evidence!' snarled Kent. 'What he's just done could give a defence team an open shot at goal!'

'Well don't tell 'em,' said Clocks. 'Tell 'em it was open when you found it.'

Kent looked mortified. 'What? What? You want me to lie?'

'It would 'elp immensely.'

'No. I'm not lying to cover your dumb arse, Clocks. No.'

'Didn't think you would. Worth a try, though.' Clocks turned to Paterson. 'The letter's nothin' important, guv. Notification of change in interest rates.'

Paterson grinned. 'Fancy giving it back to her?'

Clocks's face lit up. 'Oh, yeah.'

Paterson looked back at Kent. 'Y'know what . . . I might have been wrong about you. You are in fact a useful tool.'

Kent frowned.

'What? I don't understand.'

Paterson and Clocks headed for the door.

'He said you were a useless tool.' Paterson pointed to Clocks who was already at the street door.

Kent gave Paterson the finger and a dry smile. But Paterson had already gone.

Paterson slid into the driver's seat and fired up the engine. He slammed the accelerator to the floor and screeched away from the kerb at the same time as Clocks put the blue light and siren on.

'What you thinkin', Ray?'

'We know that a woman was seen going to Lynton Road with a kid. Might be the same one, might not be. We know Elizabeth has a sister who is apparently on the missing list and has been for years *but* . . . what if she's not missing after all? What if she's been going to Elizabeth with her victims? Maybe she's the killer, maybe she's involved. Whatever, we've got to talk to her.

'Give the office a ring for me. Tell Dusty to call up a friendly magistrate and get a full search warrant for the address. Get the troops together and ready to travel. When you've done that, call that knob, Anderson. Tell him we've got a good suspect and to bell the Chief Constable of Hertfordshire. Get him to tell them we're coming over today mob-handed as soon as we've got the warrant from the magistrate. Tell him we're happy to have a couple of his carrot crunchers come with us but to stay in the background. I also want to know everything about this property and its occupant before we get there. He can call it over.'

Clocks tapped the screen of his phone a few times and pressed the phone to his ear. 'We tooling up for this, guv?'

Paterson thought about it. 'Yep. With this nut job, best we take a few guns with us. Get authority for everyone on the squad who's firearms trained. We need it done now.'

'You're gonna need to get authority for the guns if we're going over to another force's ground,' said Clocks.

'You reckon we'll get authority from Anderson?'

'Fuck, no! No way will he want us stamping about in the sticks waving guns around.'

Paterson shrugged. 'That's what I thought. So, I won't ask him. Better to do it and apologise to the discipline board he'll inevitably put me on than not do it and some other crazy bitch tries cutting us all up.'

'Point of interest . . . you do know that Hertfordshire have their own gun crews, don't you?'

'Course I do, but they're probably still carrying the same sort of gun that Billy the Kid had. We'll stick to our own.'

A voice answered Johnny Clocks and he asked to be put through to Commissioner Anderson urgently.

An hour later they were back in the briefing room cracking open a bottle of vodka. Jackie Hartnett wasn't impressed.

'A solid lead, guv?' she said.

'Looks like it but we can't hang around on this one. We're going over to carrot land. Hertfordshire.'

Jackie frowned. 'They won't like that. Especially if we're going over gunned up.'

Paterson slugged back his vodka. 'Tough. I don't have time to play nice and ask them to go and pick her up for us.

If that fucker's there, *we're* bringing her in. Anderson's on the case for us.'

'Good.' She raised her mug of tea. 'Be nice to wrap this one up nice and early.'

'You 'eard from Dusty?' said Clocks.

'No, guv, not yet. He said he'll ring as soon as he's got the W.'

'Well, he better fuckin' hurry up. I'm getting antsy.'

'You were born antsy.' Jackie walked back to her desk.

'Finish that,' said Paterson 'and then we'll go and book out our firearms. Jack! Downstairs in five! Book out a weapon, meet us in the yard and I'll brief everyone there!'

Clocks necked the glass and followed Paterson downstairs where Superintendent Chris Hammer, the officer authorising the use of firearms, was waiting for them.

'Off for some fun then, Mr Paterson?'

'Hopefully. Got a lead on the Lynton Road killer. Better to be safe than sorry.'

'Fair enough. But if you want to be safe, why is Timex getting a gun?' He nodded toward Clocks with a wry grin. Hammer and Clocks had been friends for a long while. They went through basic training together, passed their driving courses at the same time and, for a while, were a formidable team on the streets of Bermondsey, but Hammer was the smart one who studied for promotion. He was also the one who gave Johnny Clocks the nickname that had stuck with him throughout his service. It was only people of a certain rank and length of service who still used that name. Most people had another name for him these days but it was a swear word that related to the female sexual organs.

'Cheeky sod. I'm the only one who can shoot straight. They need me.'

Superintendent Hammer eyed him carefully. 'Not what your reports say. According to your stats it seems highly likely you wouldn't hit the floor if you fell over.'

'Don't you be worrying about me, Chris. I'll be fine. You go an' sit in yer nice warm office and set up a few pointless meetings. Me an' Ray'll go catch the bad boys.'

'No time for meetings today, Timex. I've just taken delivery of a new fifty-two-inch TV for the office. I've plugged it into the PVR recorder and I'm catching up with a recording of *Antiques Roadshow*. Be careful out there.'

Paterson topped and tailed the paperwork and he and Clocks went out into the yard to wait for his team to arrive. He leaned back on the car and looked up to the heavens. There was a lot to think about, a lot to sort out before they got to the address. It was all very well having guns but he knew he needed a properly trained and properly kitted out rapid entry firearms team to get inside and secure the property.

His phone rang. 'Paterson,' he said. 'You had better be fucking kidding me.' Paterson glanced across at Clocks. 'We're all ready to go, sir. Warrant on its way.'

Andersons voice filled his ear. 'That's the way it is, Paterson. The Chief Constable said that his people are more than capable of storming the house and bringing her in if she's there.'

'I don't give a toss what he said or what they're capable of. These murders are on our ground, we've housed her and we're entitled to go nick her. Tell the CC his job is to back us up and that's it. Tell him!' Paterson's body trembled with the rage built up inside him.

Johnny Clocks dropped his head and shook it from side to side. By now, a few other members of the squad had joined them and had stood back while Paterson argued with Anderson.

'I have told him. But it's his constabulary, his area. He has authority there, not me.'

'Oh, for fuck's sake. Grow a pair and tell him we're the bloody Met and it's our body and we're coming for her. Don't let him push you around.'

'Who the hell do you think you're talking to, Paterson? I'm the bloody Commissioner of Police. Don't you dare tell me what to do and don't be so damned impertinent.'

Paterson shook his head. 'Then don't be so weak. I was under the impression that you were on our side.'

'Sides have nothing to do with it. Jurisdiction does.'

'I knew we shouldn't have fucking contacted them. What's the point? Fucking politics and jurisdiction bullshit.'

'You were right to run it past me first. You had to. You don't tramp onto another force's ground smashing doors in without telling them. Bad show.'

'Bad show? Look, you should know we don't have to tell them if we're coming to arrest someone. But I wanted to do it the right way and show professional courtesy.'

'You do if you're taking guns. You should know *that*, Paterson.'

'Guns? Who said we're taking guns? I never said that.'

'You're going over without them, then?'

'That was the plan. Mob-handed should do it.'

'I smell a lie, Paterson.'

'Can't think why.'

'Doesn't matter anyway. It's irrelevant.'

'So that's it, then? His boys go nick her and we act like a cab firm and just go pick her up?'

'That's about it. Now, stand down, Paterson and wait until you hear from them. Do not go out there under any circumstances. Do not.' The phone went dead. Paterson stared at the phone's screen, silently mouthing curses at it.

'So. Bad news I take it, guv?' said Clocks.

Paterson stared at him.

'I'll go an' put the kettle on, then.'

'None for me, Clocksy.'

'What? You love a cuppa tea.'

'I know do, but it'll be cold by the time I get to Hertfordshire.'

CHAPTER TWENTY-ONE

Two uniformed police officers from Hertfordshire Constabulary sat in their patrol car and watched with mild interest as a line of four cars raced past them with blue lights flashing and sirens blaring, unaware that they were watching officers from the Met who were acting in direct defiance of a lawful order from the Commissioner of Police. They never called it in or questioned where the convoy had come from. None of their business.

'How much further?' said Paterson.

Clocks peered at the GPS on the dashboard. 'According to this, about two miles. Looks like most of it is country road.'

'Kill the music.'

Clocks switched off the sirens but kept the blue lights on. The cars behind did the same.

'Anywhere we can park up close to the address?'

'A couple of streets nearby. I'll tell you where to go when we're closer.'

Paterson nodded, keeping an eye on the twisty road ahead of him.

'You thought about what we're gonna say to Anderson when we get back?' Neither had mentioned it on the drive over. Clocks had been busy talking on the phone with the office manager, trying to get as much info on the address as they could without flagging anything up on the system. They were already concerned that Hertfordshire Police would be mobilising and didn't want to alert them that they were coming.

'Yeah. I'm thinking that if the carrot crunchers are already there, we can just say we nipped over early to make sure we wasted no time in the handover.'

'What? Mob-'anded and with SCO19 with us?'

'Yeah, why not? We can say we had no idea what they might've found inside so we made sure we were prepared.'

'No one's gonna buy that shit. You know that, right?'

'Why won't they?'

Clocks shook his head and looked out as the countryside flashed past him. A city boy to the core, too much greenery always made him uncomfortable. There were too many things like horses, sheep and cows for his liking. And birds. Strange-looking ones with coloured plumage, nothing like the drab grey pigeons and brown sparrows you got in Bermondsey. He knew where he was with them.

'Because it's a load of ol' fanny.'

'I know, but this is down to me. I'll just say I never relayed Anderson's message to you lot so you just did as I instructed.'

'And if the carrots are already there?'

'Then we take over.'

'And if they're not already there?'

Paterson smiled. 'Then I'll say we pulled up a couple streets away to do a walk past and wait for the locals. Turns out that on the walk past I saw a woman at the window and, believing it was our girl, called everyone on the hurry up. Couldn't take the chance she was going to do a runner.'

Clocks wrinkled his nose while he thought about it. 'It's definitely thin but it might work. Anderson'll want your dangle berries on his desk one way or the other.'

'He can have them. I haven't used them for a while so, no loss.'

Clocks chuckled. 'Speaking of not gettin' any, what's the score with you an' Carrie then?'

Paterson gently swerved to avoid a pheasant that wandered into the road.

'The fuck is that thing?' said Clocks.

'You're joking?'

'I'm fuckin' not. You see the size of it? Looked like a little gay turkey.'

'It's a pheasant. Dumbest bird on the planet.'

Clocks looked at him. 'I've heard of them. What all you money people go shootin' at the weekend, innit?'

'Not all of us, mate. Some of us like to round up vagrants and chase them through the fields.'

Clocks shrugged. 'Fair enough. No one likes a tramp, do they?'

Paterson sighed. It was still difficult to know whether Clocks was serious or not sometimes.

'So come on then . . . spill. You back shaggin' her?'

'Not even funny, John. When this is over, she's off the squad and back to her old job.'

'She won't like that. Not now she's with 'er Raymey Waymey.'

'And who's fucking fault is that?'

Clocks grinned at him. 'You're welcome.' He looked at the GPS. 'Take the second left. It's a one-way dogleg. Pull up as soon as y'can.'

Paterson did as he was told and brought the convoy to halt doing his best to make sure all of the cars were hidden by a line of bushes. The last car in the line swung itself across the road blocking any cars that might try to enter. Once all the cars had stopped, Paterson drove forward to see if any Hertfordshire police were present in the target road. They weren't. He spun the vehicle around and drove back to the little convoy. The cars emptied out and their occupants formed a huddle in the middle of the road.

'Okay,' said Paterson. 'Here's the deal. I've decided DI Clocks here is going to do a walk past the address to see what he can see. I need two people at the back of the house in case she does a runner. If she does, be very, very wary. Remember what this woman may be capable of. I'd prefer to nick her but you need to protect yourselves. Understood?'

Everyone nodded.

Clocks was long gone. As soon as Paterson had mentioned 'walk past' he'd set off. Five minutes later he was back.

'Right, listen up. Good news is we're definitely ahead of the local yokels. We're looking at a detached house, pretty big, four, five bedrooms maybe. Place looks dark though. Not big windows. There's nothing on the drive so she may not have a car or she may be out.'

'Can she see us approaching?' said Paterson.

'If she's upstairs then, yeah. Stevie Wonder could see us from up there. If she's downstairs, not so easy. If she's not there, then not at all.'

'Neighbours?' said Lyndsey, ignoring the little quip.

'House either side. I'd guess maybe thirty feet between them.'

'Door?'

'One at the front. Looks like it'll go if we 'it 'ard enough.'

Paterson swept his eyes across the team. 'Okay, folks. Here's the score. Inspector Kitchener and two of her team will force rapid entry on my authority. Me and John — sorry . . . DI Clocks, will be right behind them. Everybody else is to wait until told the property is safe. When the shit hits — and it no doubt will — as far as you're all concerned, you knew nothing and just did as I instructed. We clear?'

Again, everyone nodded.

'Then let's go.'

The crowd of officers dispersed, Dusty and Jackie ran off to get to the back of the house while the others formed a queue, backs to the bushes. Lyndsey led the way as they made their way along the street, Sergeant Kevin Eaton behind. His job was to put the door in and he carried the 'enforcer', a small handled battering ram designed to take out door locks.

Lyndsey, Eaton and a third officer, PC Feeney, kept their eyes firmly on the entrance to the door as they made their way along the garden path, weapons drawn. Paterson and Clocks watched for any sign of movement from the upstairs.

Lyndsey and PC Feeney flattened themselves against the wall either side of the door as Sergeant Eaton holstered his weapon and swung the enforcer. No one was hanging around. With a loud crack, the door flew inward and banged itself against the wall. Eaton stepped back as Lyndsey and Feeney rushed in. Eaton dropped the enforcer, unholstered his Glock and rushed in behind them.

'Police! Police!' Lyndsey shouted. 'Armed police!'

Paterson and Clocks entered the house seconds later. Lyndsey moved through the house with Eaton, kicking doors open as they went.

'Clear,' Lyndsey shouted before moving on to the next. PC Feeney moved into the hallway to allow Paterson and Clocks to climb the stairs. Paterson was first, gun drawn and held two-handed in front of him. At the top of the stairs he could see a bedroom to his right, a smaller room dead ahead and, by peeking around the corner, a third room at the end of the hall. There was another corner to be turned once this floor was clear. He could hear Lyndsey downstairs kicking at a door, followed a few seconds later by the shout of 'Clear!'. He felt his stomach sink as he realised there was no one downstairs. That meant someone was waiting for them in one of these rooms or the bloody house was empty. He was hoping someone would jump out. They didn't. A grandfather clock chimed from somewhere around the corner.

Paterson and Clocks cleared all four bedrooms and the landing room toilet. The place was immaculately neat and tidy as if no one had been living there for a long time. Paterson looked out of the upstairs window, just in case Miss B. May had done a runner and was on her toes across a field. What he saw, he didn't like.

'Well, this sucks,' said Clocks. 'Looks like a B an' B. What are the chances of gettin' out of 'ere and fuckin' off back to Bermondsey without anyone knowing? Make out it 'ad nothing to do with us?'

'By the look of it, pretty slim. Look . . .' He pulled back the net curtain to let Clocks see the convoy of police vehicles hammering along the same road they'd taken. Sirens were blaring and lights were flashing.

Paterson shook his head.

'Oh, shit in a hat an' punch it! That's a bitch.'

They trudged downstairs to join up with Lyndsey and the rest of the team.

'Nothing?' Paterson said to Lyndsey.

She shook her head. 'Nah. Nothing. All the windows are closed and locked. The patio doors are closed but unlocked, but I wouldn't think that's overly unusual in this area. Seems pretty decent.'

'Still,' said Paterson, 'she could've done a runner.' He looked out into the street as he heard the first of the police cars screech to a halt and doors slam. He heard shouts of 'Police! Stand still!' He walked outside to see four cars skewed at odd angles across the road and at least half a dozen uniformed officers out of their cars and running toward them. In front of them and more troubling to him, were two firearms officers, fully tooled up, machine guns held high.

'You!' one of them shouted to Dusty. 'Down on the ground.' Dusty ignored him, choosing instead to meet his stare.

All of Paterson's team refused to comply but offered no overt resistance as the uniforms shouted panicked instructions to them. As far as they were concerned the Met officers could have been anyone. Paterson pulled out his warrant card and walked out into the garden. Clocks did the same. They held their cards up high so that everyone could see them clearly.

'It's okay, boys. We're police, too. From London. I'm Superintendent Paterson. We need to talk.'

'Down on the ground,' the other officer shouted. Paterson frowned.

'Here's my ID, mate. I've told you who I am. Take it and verify it.'

'I said to get down. Now do it. Both of you.'

Johnny Clocks sneered. He wasn't getting on his knees for anyone. Last time that happened he was tied up and had petrol poured over him.

'Calm down, fellah,' Paterson said, 'we're Met. We're here for the same reason as you. House is empty though.'

'Last time!' the man shouted. 'Get down on the ground!'

The firearms officer's eyes widened as his peripheral vision picked up Lyndsey and her team of five as they all emerged from the house fully kitted and heavily armed. The man's attention shifted away from Paterson and Clocks and honed in on the hardware they carried.

'Hello, gentlemen,' said Lyndsey. 'Seems to be an over-reaction going on here. Weapons down please, gents, and we can talk.'

The two Hertfordshire firearms officers didn't take too long before deciding to do as she requested.

'What the fuck's going on here?' said the elder of the two. 'Who are you and why are you here?'

The back of one of the car doors opened and a uniformed superintendent stepped out. Clocks grinned.

'As we said, we're here for the same reason as you. We came for the occupant of this house.' Paterson said to the firearms officer.

'Who's in charge here?' roared the uniformed superintendent.

'That'll be me, sir. Detective Superintendent Paterson. We're with the Homicide and—'

'I don't give a shit who you are. You have no jurisdiction to be here. Why wasn't I informed?'

'You were,' said Paterson. 'Our commissioner had a conversation with your CC.'

'I was told you were coming to pick up a prisoner, if we got one. Not that you were coming over here playing fucking John Wayne and waving guns around — and, by the looks of it, forcing your way into a property without a warrant.'

'Got one of those.' Paterson nodded toward Dusty who pulled out a sheet of A4 paper. He handed it to a constable.

'Seems we arrived before you boys and so we waited. Thing is, I saw the curtains twitch upstairs and believed the suspect was about to do a runner. Couldn't take the chance on her getting away or tooling herself up so we went in. Sorry if we breached protocol, but we couldn't take a chance on anyone getting hurt. You understand.'

The superintendent, a stocky man with a red face and a temper to match, wasn't buying it. 'Bollocks!' he spat.

Clocks had had enough. 'That's not nice, is it?'

The superintendent wheeled around. 'And who the fuck are you?'

'DI Clocks. But you can call me Timex or Clocksy. I'm good with either. You can also call me Thrush if you want.'

'What? Thrush?'

'Yeah.'

'Why would I call you that?'

'Seems I can be an irritating cunt from time to time.'

The superintendent glared at him. 'Well, Detective Inspector, you're in a world of shit now.'

'Thought I could smell something.' Clocks sniffed the air.

'What?'

'Shit. Thought I could smell something. Wasn't sure if it was the cows around 'ere or a uniformed superintendent 'aving to leave his office and do a bit of police work.'

'You think this is funny, Inspector?'

'Little bit.' Clocks held his thumb and index finger close together to emphasise his point.

The superintendent's face went redder and a little vein popped out on his forehead. 'I'll have your bloody jobs for this.' He pointed his finger at Clocks. Clocks smiled.

The superintendent stepped forward and jabbed it towards Clocks's face. 'Did you hear me, son?'

Clocks stood stock still, his face impassive.

Paterson closed his eyes for a second. 'Sir . . . please . . . don't do—'

'Shut up!' The superintendent hadn't turned from Clocks. 'I'm talking to the junior here.'

Clocks raised an eyebrow. 'Get your finger out of my face.'

'What? Who the hell do you think you're talking to?'

'Last chance.'

The superintendent looked bewildered. The Hertfordshire force obviously weren't in the habit of talking back, let alone uttering what appeared to be a threat. Like an old-school bully type, he opted to double down. 'I don't know who you think you are, son, but you're in a world of trouble.'

Clocks grinned, lop-sided. 'Oh, no. Is the world of trouble anything like the world of shit we're in? Anything but that.'

'You have no idea, son. No idea.'

'Do yerself a favour, mate. Get yer finger out of my face and don't call me *son*.'

The superintendent left his finger just a second too long. Clocks grabbed it, pulled it up and forced the hand down at the same time. The uniformed officer dropped straight down onto his knees. Clocks stared at him impassively as he roared in pain and anger. Several of his officers moved forward to help but were met with severe looks from Paterson's team. They decided to stay where they were.

'John . . .' said Paterson. 'That's enough, mate. Let him up.'

Clocks never took his eyes from the man. 'When he apologises.'

'John. Come on.'

'When he says sorry. I can't stand a fuckin' bully. You know that.'

'Yeah, I do know that. But this isn't gonna help the situation, John.'

The superintendent's face filled with fury. 'Let me go! Fuck you?'

'You heard what I said. I will when you say sorry. You're a bully, aintcha? Except, you don't get to bully me. I don't give a fuck who you are or what your rank is. You don't treat people like that. Now, say sorry or we do this until you do. Makes no odds to me. I'm already in the worlds of shit and trouble, remember?'

The superintendent's eyes blazed up at him. He was already humiliated but now Clocks was rubbing it in.

'John!' Lyndsey shouted. 'Stop playing about with him. Let him up!'

Clocks looked across at Lyndsey, then back at the officer on the ground. 'Your lucky day. The missus has spoken.' He released his grip and the superintendent grabbed his injured finger, pulling it into his chest. He stood up and squared up to Clocks. Paterson stepped between them.

'Don't,' was all he said. And the superintendent didn't.

'Good,' said Paterson. 'Now, we can all go back to your nick and have a proper debrief, or you can sulk for a while and bang in a report about us being here and your little run-in with my DI. What'd you say?'

The superintendent eyed him up and down. 'I'm taking the second option.'

Paterson nodded slowly. 'Okay. And when you do, we'll counter with the fact that you and yours were way, *way* too slow to mobilise. Fuck me, we drove all the way from the middle of London and still beat you tractor chuggers here. Then we'll say that you got all rowdy and threatened my DI here. Now, I reckon if we do that and the complaints boys start digging into your background, I'm betting that this won't be the first accusation of threatening and intimidating behaviour toward junior officers.'

The superintendent's face fell. The last part was obviously true.

‘So, given that I have twice as many witnesses as you, would you like to rethink your position here? S’up to you.’

The superintendent stayed silent for a moment. ‘Debrief it is.’

‘Good man,’ said Clocks. ‘You know it makes sense.’

CHAPTER TWENTY-TWO

As they rode up in the lift to the fifth floor of New Scotland Yard, Clocks tapped his toe against the metal wall and looked up at the digital floor indicator.

'This is gonna be a riot,' Paterson said.

Clocks shook his head. 'Don't think so, Ray. I think we might have pushed him a bit too far this time. You heard him on the phone. I thought he was gonna burst a bollock.'

'Shame he didn't.' Paterson couldn't help but grin at the thought of the Commissioner of Police for the Metropolis actually bursting one of his testicles.

'I'm pissed at that superintendent though. Didn't think he'd grass us up like that.'

'He had to, John. The story would have got out one way or the other. Better it comes straight from the horse's mouth, I suppose. Just hope he hasn't mentioned you assaulting him and making him look like an idiot in front of his troops.'

'I bet he's skipped over that bit,' said Clocks.

'I'll bet. Right, listen to me . . . For the last time. This is on me. You tell him I misled you about the trip to Hertfordshire. Far as you're concerned, we had authority.'

'I did have authority. From you.'

Paterson nodded. 'That's it. Stick with what I've told you. At least he might leave you on the case.'

'Fuck him. If he boots you, he boots me. Simple as. If he don't, I'll throw a sickie with a bit of the ol' stress and he can sort the shit 'imself, can't 'e?'

The lift chimed and the doors slid open onto the fifth floor. They walked along a corridor lined with photographs of previous commissioners until they came to the reception desk.

'All right, love?' said Clocks. 'Paterson and Clocks here to see the commissioner for our weekly bollocking.' He took a quick look around the reception area. 'Where's Sue? On 'oliday?'

The lady behind the counter, whose lapel badge revealed her to be Donna Leem, was on a temporary contract from an agency, replacing the full-time receptionist, Susan Adams.

'No. I'm afraid she's gone sick for a while. I'm standing in.'

'Sick? Whassamatter with her? Nothing bad, is it?'

'I think she's sick of him.' She jerked her head towards Anderson's office. 'Likes to shout a lot, doesn't he?'

Clocks nodded. 'Yeah, he does. Don't take no notice of him, love. He's a dick.'

Donna smiled.

'Can we go straight in?' asked Paterson.

'Afraid not. He told me to tell you to wait outside and to let him know when you've arrived.'

'Oops,' Clocks said. 'Naughty schoolboy time for us. No worries, love. We'll be good boys.' They sauntered off toward the waiting area. Clocks turned back to Donna. 'Listen, love. We could be waiting here a while so, no pressure or anything, but Sue always used to bring us a cup of tea and a sticky bun while we wait. You gonna be a sweetheart too?' He gave her a wide smile and a thumbs up.

Fifteen minutes later, Clocks, with his feet resting on the edge of a magazine-laden table, finished off the last of his bun and downed the rest of his tea just as Commissioner Anderson jerked open his door and issued a terse command.

'Inside, the both of you.'

Clocks removed his feet lazily from the table and stood up. Keeping his voice low he said to Paterson, 'He better not start 'ollerin' and 'ooting when we get in there.'

'You're shitting me, right? That's what we're here for.'

'I'm just sayin'.'

Both men walked into Anderson's office to find him already seated back behind his desk. He fixed his eyes on Clocks as they made their way toward him. Neither said a word.

'Sit down. Both of you.'

'Sir, before—'

'Shut up, Paterson. This is not the time that you talk. Understood?'

Paterson raised a single eyebrow in reply.

'What the fuck were you two thinking? I gave you clear instructions that you were only supposed to pick up any prisoner that Hertfordshire took from that property, didn't I?'

Paterson nodded.

'But you ignored me and stormed the place like a couple of fucking wild west cowboys, didn't you? And you dragged in firearms officers from SCO19.'

'Wasn't quite like that, guv,' said Clocks.

Anderson turned his gaze to Clocks. 'Why don't you fucking tell me how it was then, Clocks.'

Clocks frowned. 'Guv—'

'Don't call me *guv*, Clocks. When you address me, you bloody well address me as *sir*. Clear?'

'Yes, guv. Crystal. Can I just ask . . . are you angry about something?'

'What?' Anderson looked dumbstruck.

'Are you angry about something? I ask because you don't normally swear. It's unusual for you.'

'No, Clocks, you fucking idiot! I'm beyond angry. I'm fuming!'

'Okay, fair enough. But can I just pull you up on your swearing then? There's no need for that, is there? That's not very professional. Now, I don't mind a bollocking or whatever it is you're going to do to us but, let's keep it civilized.'

Paterson rolled his eyes.

Anderson's face flushed and he bunched his fists as he looked at Clocks's impassive face. 'You think this is joke, Clocks? Do you?' The anger in his voice was barely contained.

'No. Just sayin' . . . bollock me professionally, please.'

Anderson spun towards Paterson. 'What the fuck is wrong with this man?'

Paterson shrugged. 'Hard to tell, sir. There's a lot of theories being bandied about, but . . .' he shrugged again.

'You have both wilfully disobeyed a direct order from the Commissioner of Police and brought this force into disrepute, and by the looks of it neither of you give a toss.'

'That's not true, sir,' said Paterson. 'I'm the one that disobeyed you. Not Clocks. I kept him in the dark and everybody else too.'

'Nah. He's talkin' bollocks, guv,' said Clocks. 'I 'eard you shouting down the phone at him and decided I was going anyway so, yeah, I disobeyed you too. Wilfully.'

'So, we can add lying to the commissioner too, can we, Paterson?' Anderson sat back in his chair.

'Cheers, John,' said Paterson.

'Welcome,' said Clocks.

'You know I can suspend you both right here, right now, yes?'

Both men nodded.

'Give me one good reason why I shouldn't?'

Clocks looked around the room. 'Beats me.' He shrugged.

'I can, sir,' said Paterson.

Anderson waited.

'Because, whatever you think of us, and I know it isn't much, you know that we're your very best bet for finding out who did this and bringing them down quickly. I know you don't want to admit it, but inside, you know it's true. So, yes, you can suspend us, but once this breaks properly in the press, they'll wanna know why we're not on it and you'll have to issue a statement to the effect that we were until we went to execute a warrant on a suspect's address that turned out to be a negative and *then* you decided to suspend us.'

'My God, man, you think a lot of yourselves, don't you?'

'It's right though, isn't it?'

'No, it fucking well isn't?'

'Guv'nor,' said Clocks, 'language.'

Anderson ignored him. 'I'll simply tell the press you disobeyed a direct order.'

Paterson smiled. 'You think they'll care about that? Far as they're concerned, we went to do our job.'

'You forget, Paterson, that we will feed the press what we want.'

'And we'll feed them something to the contrary.'

Anderson leaned forward. 'So, now, leaking to the press, too? And a form of blackmail?'

'In for a penny, sir.'

'All right. All right. I'll admit you two get results but know this . . . you will be under close scrutiny at all times through this case. You will report to me personally at the end of each day with updates. You will do exactly as you're told from this point forward and you will *not* go back to Hertfordshire for any reason without first contacting me or unless I give you explicit authority to do so. Do you understand?'

Paterson said nothing. He glanced across at Clocks, who was grinning.

'Same goes for you, Clocks. Do *you* understand?'

'You know me, guv. Wouldn't dream of it.'

'And a discipline panel will be convened in the near future for the both of you,' said Anderson. 'Understood?'

'Sir,' said Paterson, 'I expected no less.'

'Guv?' said Clocks.

Anderson was not amused. 'It's *sir*. Call me *sir*, for God's sake. What do you want now?'

'I was just gonna say, guv. Do we 'ave to keep doing these silly discipline panels? We always get found not guilty so, just seems a waste of everyone's time to be honest.'

Anderson shook his head slowly. 'Just get the fuck out of my office, the pair of you. Now!' Anderson waved his hand.

Paterson and Clocks stood up and headed for the door.

'Oh!' Anderson called. 'You will both be interviewed tomorrow in relation to the attack on CI Lambert.'

Paterson and Clocks turned.

'Excuse me?' said Paterson. 'Interviewed? What do you mean *interviewed*?'

'Routine, Paterson. That's all. Background stuff. Don't worry. If I could pin it on you both, I absolutely would. One way of getting rid of the pair of you. Now get out!'

'Hold up,' said Clocks. He planted his feet, ready for a row. 'Are you for real? Did you just say you'd fit us up with Lambert's shootin' or did my ears go a bit dodgy on me?'

'I never said I'd fit you up. I said I'd pin it on you if I could. What I meant was—'

'What you meant was what you said. An' there you are, the bloody Commissioner of Police, always bangin' on about us being dodgy an' bent sayin' you'd fit up two innocent men just 'cause you don't like us.'

Anderson flushed. 'That's not what I meant at all, Clocks, and you know it.'

'Do I? I only know what I 'eard an' what you said an' luckily . . .' Clocks pulled his mobile phone out of his jacket pocket and held it up. 'Luckily I set it up to record before we came in 'ere so who's fucked now then? I'll give you a clue. That's right, sir. It's you. See you at the discipline meeting except, if I'm not wrong, yours will be with an outside force. No coverin' up for you, guv.'

The redness in Anderson's face drained away rapidly.

Clocks spun around on his heels and headed for the door. Paterson at the doorway, a grin on his face, stepped away as Clocks stormed out leaving the office door wide open.

'Door!' Anderson hollered.

Clocks ignored him. Ten seconds later the door banged shut behind him.

Donna grinned at them both.

'Thanks for the tea and cakes, sweet'eart,' said Clocks. 'They were lovely. Listen . . . Sorry, but I think we've pissed him off again. Might take it out on you for a bit.'

'Don't worry about it,' Donna said. 'My old man shouts louder than him.'

She signed them both out and waited for Anderson to start showing off.

Paterson jabbed his finger on the lift button.

'I probably don't need to ask this but, did you really record him, John?'

'Nah. Did I fuck. But he don't know that, does he? He'll be sweatin' blood 'n' bullets from arse'ole to breakfast time now, won't he? Now he'll know what it's like to 'ave shit 'anging over yer 'ead for weeks on end. Might not be too quick to keep threatenin' discipline panels all the time if he thinks he's the recipient of one.'

Paterson grinned and jabbed the lift button several times.

'You all right, Ray?'

'Nope. Not really.'

'S'matter?'

'Two things . . . First, I told you that it was on me, my fault, and you overrode me.'

'Yeah, because it's not. I'm a big boy an' I made my own decision an' you're not taking the fall for it. Fuck him.'

Paterson shook his head.

'And the second? Lambert?'

'Yeah, Lambert. Anderson's clearly fucking trying to put this on us. He made that perfectly clear, didn't he?'

'Yeah, of course. Desperate, ain't 'e? Again, fuck him.'

'I intend to. One way or the other.'

'Ooh. That sounds ominous, Ray.'

The lift door pinged open.

DAY 3

CHAPTER TWENTY-THREE

9:30 a.m.

The interview room on the third floor of Lambeth House was a large, modern affair with plenty of natural light and comfortable chairs. Gone were the days when officers were interviewed in cramped little offices with hard wooden seats. Back then, it was a psychological attempt to intimidate, but the police, enlightened as they now were, had been persuaded that airy-fairy was the way forward.

On one side of the desk was Detective Chief Superintendent Ronnie Box. He was a thirty-two-year man, coming up for retirement, and had spent the majority of his career behind a desk, most of it investigating corrupt police officers. Next to him was DI Kim Parsons. She looked to be about the same age as Paterson. She wore slightly tinted designer glasses and an expensive suit. She was on the way up, Paterson thought to himself. This was just a stopover job for her CV. Always helped on an interview board if you could show you'd helped to bang up the odd bent copper. She had a file in front of her and would be the one operating the evidence TV, a screen that allowed all parties present to see exactly what evidence was being shown so there could be no disparity.

Sitting next to Paterson was Superintendent Peter Lacy. He'd been a Federation representative for the last ten years and was known to be a tricky bastard, not afraid to challenge any officer if he thought the line of questioning was outside the parameters of the interview's purpose. He played with a straight bat and expected others to do the same.

Fixed to the ceiling in a corner of the room, a single camera hung down, its little red light blinking to show that the interview was being recorded. Paterson knew he was probably being watched on monitors in another room and God knew how many other experts were taking a keen interest.

At the opposite end of the large office, Johnny Clocks was in exactly the same position. Two officers to interview him, although his were of lower rank, and two observers with professional qualifications in the psychology of men.

The interviews had been scheduled to take place at the same time in order to ensure that one wouldn't have the opportunity to tell the other what sort of questions they'd been asked. Although the interview had been sold to them as being just a part of the investigation into Lambert's shooting, both Paterson and Clocks went in knowing they were suspects and this was just a bullshit fishing exercise. They would play the game, but they'd play it their way. Control was key.

Superintendent Box ran through the preliminaries, informed Paterson why he was being interviewed, that he wasn't under arrest and that he was free to leave any time he wished. With that out of the way, the interview began with a few benign questions designed to help build rapport and nothing of any significance. Ten minutes in, Superintendent Box started to steer things in a different direction.

'Mr Paterson, thank you for coming today. I've explained why you're here, it's just to help us get some background information on DCI Lambert and the interactions you had with him. If I can just clarify . . . DCI Lambert reached out to you for help with regards to the case he was working on. I understand that it was not too dissimilar to a case that you had a couple of years ago in which a man was murdering women and carving a single word into their chests. Is that correct?'

'Sir,' Paterson kept his answer curt.

'I understand that you refused to help. Is that correct?'

'No, sir. Not correct, at all. I didn't refuse to help. Lambert came to ask for any insight we might have as he believed the cases were very much the same. I could see *some* similarities, but not enough to shed any light on his investigation. Lambert suggested a copycat killer. I disagreed with him.'

A picture flashed up on the screen above their heads. The torsos of two young girls, each with a word carved into them.

'The one on the left is from your case and the one on the right is from Lambert's. They look similar to me.'

'As I said, some similarities but, as I said to him, there were other factors that led me to believe it wasn't a copycat in the true sense of the word.'

'And they would be?'

'Method of death for one. My boy incapacitated his victims by throttling them. This one hit them with a hammer in the throat or something.'

'That's hardly conclusive.'

'Fair point, but if we're talking a copycat — correct me if I'm wrong — they generally tend to copy the original's kills in as much detail as possible. Am I right?'

Box ignored his question.

'So, what else do you want me to say? I genuinely didn't think there was anything I could help him with and I'll stick by that. If I thought I could have helped him, I would have. Of course I would.'

Superintendent Box kept his eyes on Paterson, clearly looking for any little signs that might tell him that he was lying. Any little twitch, his eyes darting away for a second, change in breathing, a bead of sweat. Paterson wasn't fazed in the slightest. Box nodded slowly and looked at his pre-briefing notes.

Paterson had a fair idea of what was in them. He was tagged as psychologically damaged due to the death of his wife, Lisa, and his friend and mentor, DS Dave Jordan. His expected upward trajectory in the Met had come to a grinding halt when he put a bullet between the eyes of the man who had killed them both, Detective Constable Adam Walker. The note, from Paterson's Met-imposed psychiatrist, would no doubt label him as suffering from some sort of personality disorder, a politically correct term for a sociopath. Box was no doubt treating this hearing as an opportunity to find out if he was turning to the dark side.

'Okay,' said Box, 'moving on . . .'

* * *

Johnny Clocks listened carefully as Chief Inspector Richard Bradbury informed him that he wasn't under arrest and was free to leave but, as they were investigating the shooting of DCI Lambert, they would appreciate any help he could give. Clocks nodded when asked if he understood.

'Thank you, John. May I call you John?'

'Please yerself,' said Clocks. 'Can I call you Dick?'

'I'd prefer to be called Richard, if you don't mind?'

'Fair enough.'

'Thank you. Now, I understand that DCI Lambert came to see you to discuss a case he was working on. A couple of girls had been murdered in much the same way as a case you and Mr Paterson worked on. Is that correct?'

'Nearly.'

CI Bradbury frowned. 'Nearly?'

'We went to see him. He called. We went.'

Bradbury looked down at his notes. Clocks figured he was either trying it on or he hadn't done his homework properly. He settled on both.

'Indeed. Yes. Sorry. And I understand that you didn't help him. Can I ask why?'

Clocks shifted in his seat. 'Wasn't a question of not 'elping him. He asked if we thought it was a copycat at work. We said no. We gave our reasons and that was it.'

The same side-by-side images that had been shown to Paterson now flashed onto his screen. 'You don't think this is the work of a copycat?'

Clocks shook his head. 'Nope. I'll grant you there are similarities but from what we were told and what he showed us, no we didn't think it was a copycat as such.'

'Interesting.'

'What's interestin' about it, then?'

'Well, from where I'm sitting, it does look like a copycat killer was emulating the murders in the Walker case. I'm just surprised that you couldn't, and apparently *still* can't see it.'

'And yer point is?'

'Nothing. I'm just trying to get the background to your relationship with DCI Lambert.'

'We didn't 'ave a relationship. We met a coupla time re his case an' that was it.'

CI Bradbury cast an eye over Clocks. 'All I'm saying is, my understanding is that the pair of you were not particularly friendly toward him at this—'

'Oh, turn it in. What are you talking about, *not friendly to him*? Since when does not agreeing with someone's evaluation of a case mean we 'ave to be all cuddly with 'em when we tell 'em somethin' they don't wanna hear. Jesus.'

'Let me phrase it differently. You were both uncooperative.'

'Matter of opinion, Dick.'

'Richard.'

'Potato — potahto, mate.'

Clocks sat back in his chair and straightened out his legs.

'Let me stop you there, Mr Clocks. You need to understand that while this a fact-finding investigation I'm not, and never will be, your mate, so please ensure you address me by my rank from this point on and show some respect.'

Clocks grinned. Here we go. His Federation rep shifted uncomfortably in his seat. He'd represented Clocks a few times in the past and knew the score. When Clocks had asked him to tag along, he'd been reluctant at first. Then eventually he'd sighed and said that he might get some entertainment out of it at least.

'Sorry, Chief Inspector,' Clocks said. 'Do carry on.'

'Thank you,' said Bradbury. 'Going back to the photos, can you tell me why you thought there were dissimilarities?'

'The way they were killed was different. Ours strangled his victims, Lambert's hit 'em in the throat with somethin'. Dunno what.'

'Could it have been a fist, perhaps?' DS Sharpe said.

CI Bradbury shot him a look.

'I'm sorry. Who are you?' said Clocks.

'Sergeant Sharpe.'

'*Sergeant*, Sharpe?'

Sharpe nodded.

'What you doin' talkin' to me?'

'Excuse me? I'm asking you a question. Simple enough. Would you like it asked another way?'

Clocks leaned forward. This idiot had bit and he was going to reel him in. 'Yeah. I'd like it asked by someone who knows what they're doing.'

DS Sharpe coloured up.

'I have the right to be questioned by an officer of at least one rank above me. You ain't that, so be a good lad an' go an' make us all a cuppa tea while the grownups talk about big boys' stuff. Two sugars in mine and, if you've got any, a couple of digestives would be nice. Away you go.'

DS Sharpe now burned with anger and embarrassment. He scowled and looked about to say something when CI Bradbury chimed in.

'Can I just say, if this was a formal interview then, yes, you would have that right but, as I've already stressed, this is not formal. This is fact-finding. That's all.'

'Bugger,' said Clocks. 'Seems you are on the ball. Well spotted, that man. Could still do with a cuppa though, seeing as 'ow we're all gettin' on so well.' He beamed a smile at DS Sharpe. 'When you're ready, son.'

* * *

'Can you tell me, did DCI Lambert have any enemies that you know of?'

Paterson eyed Superintendent Box warily. He knew that they were getting to the good part. The only thing that surprised him was how fast he was going.

'I have no idea. Why would I?'

'When you met, did he ever mention having enemies? Any difficulties with anyone in particular?'

'No.'

'Did he mention that he'd upset anyone recently?'

'No. To be honest, I don't know why you're asking me this. You need to ask the people he worked with. I hardly knew him.'

'We've done that. He'd upset a few people in his time, of course, but no one springs to mind as a suspect.'

'Can't help you then. Sorry.'

Box nodded. 'I understand that during the case, he felt the need to place you and DI Clocks on his list of suspects. Is that right?'

'So I've heard.'

'Why do you think he did that?'

'No idea.'

'Are you sure?'

Paterson eyed the man carefully. Now it was taking the turn he was expecting. 'Can only think he was pissed that I couldn't help him.'

'Seems a bit extreme to put you on the list of suspects just because he was pissed off at you.'

'I think we're veering off the path here, gentlemen,' said Superintendent Lacy. 'This sounds to me like you're heading toward questioning Mr Paterson as a possible suspect in Lambert's assault. Would I be right?'

Box glared at Lacy but gave a curt nod. 'Forgive me. But this is a relevant part of the questioning.'

Lacy returned to his notepad. 'We'll see.'

Box turned his attention back to Paterson. 'And you found out you were a suspect, yes?'

'Yes.'

'How did you find out?'

'He sent the wrong man to follow us. Who sends an undercover into a pub full of local coppers? Strange face sticks out a mile.'

'How did that make you feel, knowing you were suspects in a murder case?'

Paterson leaned forward and looked Box in the eye. 'If I'm honest, a bit like I feel now. Pissed off at the cavernous stupidity of the notion. Now, before we go any further, as my Fed rep just said, this looks to me like we're no longer having a *friendly chat*, as you put it. Looks to me like you're definitely weighing up whether Clocks and I are responsible for his shooting. Let me tell you now, so we're clear . . . it had nothing to do with us. *Nothing*. Understood?'

'I didn't say it did.'

'Yeah, but you're going to. So, I've answered your little fishing questions upfront and unless you're ready to arrest me, we're done. I've got work to do.' Paterson stood up.

'I still have a few quest—'

'I'm sure you do. Then, as I said, you best nick me. Because I've told you what I know and that's it.' He shoved open the glass door and stormed out into the office causing a few heads to turn his way.

* * *

'We'll have tea in a minute, Mr Clocks. We've only just started,' said CI Bradbury.

Clocks shrugged. 'Fair enough. I'm not stayin' long anyway. I just wanted the lad to have something useful to do with 'is time.'

'Sorry? You're not staying long, did you say?'

Clocks nodded. ''Sright.'

'I think I'll be the judge of that, Mr Clocks. Don't you?'

Clocks fixed Bradbury with a cold stare. 'No. I don't. As far as I know, I'm not under arrest. And if I'm not under arrest then I'm free to go. Correct?'

'Correct.'

'Then, as I said, I won't be stayin' long if you intend to drag out this silly little game just to piss me off.'

'Okay,' CI Bradbury said. 'If we can just move on, then perhaps we can all get on with our day. Can I ask, do you know much about DCI Lambert?'

'Nope. Only that he got shot. Why would I know much about him?'

'No particular reason. Just asking. Would you happen to know if he had any enemies?'

Here we go then, Clocks thought. *Cut to the chase*. 'I would 'ave thought so. Why you askin' me? I didn't know 'im.'

'I know, but sometimes people open up to people they don't know particularly well. Strange really, but there it is. Did he mention upsetting anyone recently?'

'No he didn't. But I'll save you the trouble of this silly little game we're playin', shall I? Then we can all get back to work.'

CI Bradbury looked confused.

'We all know that he'd put me an' Paterson in the frame for the dead girls. So, we were fucked off with 'im, for sure. But being fucked off and being responsible for 'im getting shot is a big ol' leap even for you boys. So before you even go there . . . nothing to do with us, okay?'

'I never suggested it was. Why did you say that?'

'Because I ain't the fuckin' idiot you think I am. Lambert was all right to talk to, but shit at bein' a copper from what

I saw. Seems to me he couldn't find his arse with both 'ands tied behind his back an' because he couldn't, me an' Ray were his stopping point. You need to go and find out if he'd upset any bloody criminals and stop soddin' about trying to fit us up for it.'

'Excuse me? No one's trying to *fit you up* as you put it. We're just trying to find out if you knew of anyone who'd upset him recently.'

'Yeah. We 'ad. An' I told yer. He'd upset us, too. Don't s'pose we're the only ones either.'

'He'd upset a few people, of course,' said Bradbury. 'Inevitable in our line of work I suppose.'

Clocks snorted. '*Our* line of work? What would you know about our line of work? You sit behind a computer day after day typing up silly little reports an' chasing coppers. Easy targets. Don't s'pose you've seen the streets since you finished yer probation.'

That seemed to hit home. Bradbury twitched and then sniffed. 'There are other ways to serve,' he said, sharply.

'No there's not. In my book, you're either a copper or you're not.'

'Is this what you do, John?'

'Do what?'

'Go on the defensive. Attack people as a way of deflecting.'

'I ain't deflectin' anythin' and I'm on the defensive because you and Anderson are tryin' to stitch us both up like a coupla kippers an' I ain't 'aving it.'

'Anderson? You mean Commissioner Anderson?'

'Yep. That's the fellah. Pulled me 'n' Paterson in his office yesterday an' said if he could, he'd pin it on us. Sounds like a stitch-up to me.'

'Doesn't sound like the sort of thing Mr Anderson would say.' CI Bradbury made a few scribbled notes.

'You'd like to think not, wouldn't you. But he did an' I 'ave proof.'

'Proof?'

'I recorded him.'

'Can I hear it?'

'Nope. Not yet. When I'm ready.'

'When you're ready?'

'When I'm ready.'

'And when will that be?'

'Dunno. When I'm ready.'

CI Bradbury shook his head.

'You gonna open an investigation into him, then?'

'I don't have any evidence. Only an allegation.'

'You don't 'ave any evidence against me 'n' Paterson but it ain't stopped you investigating us, 'as it? I can smell a cover-up comin' on.'

'Be careful, Inspector Clocks. I don't like the insinuation.'

'Never mind. You'll get used to it. I am.' Clocks turned his head up to the video. 'Let the record show that I have today accused Police Commissioner Anderson of attempting to pervert the course of justice and that Chief Inspector Bradbury seems unwilling to investigate that allegation in what I can only consider to be a cover-up at the highest level.' He smiled at Bradbury.

'Well, thank you for that, Inspector. Just for the record, I haven't refused to investigate your allegation, it's just that you haven't presented any concrete evidence. I will, however, begin an initial enquiry but can I remind you that it is a criminal offence to waste police time and a disciplinary offence to make false accusations and withhold evidence. I would expect to hear your recording as part of my enquiry. Please ensure you keep it safe.'

'Will do,' said Clocks.

'Okay. Well, let's clear something up once and for all. No one is trying to put you in the frame for anything. But I have to say that your demeanour would suggest that you may know more than you're letting on.' Box leaned back in his seat.

'Is that right? Well, best you put on yer big boy pants an' nick me then. 'Cos if you don't, we're done, all right?' Clocks gave Bradbury the hard stare, willing him to arrest him.

'Mr Clocks,' said DS Sharpe. 'Perhaps we could calm things down a second and—'

'Who rattled your cage, tea boy? You sit there nice an' quiet while yer boss works out what to do next. I'm thinking that, right about now, he's wonderin' if he should arrest me — chances are he's forgotten the words of the caution an' don't wanna embarrass 'imself — or whether to boot me out an' keep us in play a bit longer to see if we 'ang ourselves. But then he knows that's not gonna 'appen either so he's in a bit of fix now, ain't he?'

The room fell silent for a few seconds.

'I've no intention of arresting you, Mr Clocks. But our investigation will continue until such time as we find out who did shoot DCI Lambert. Or perhaps ordered it.' The little dig didn't go unnoticed.

'Well, best of luck to ya. I really do 'ope you catch 'im.'

'Who said it was a him? I didn't?'

Clocks looked a little stunned for a second. 'That's right, you didn't, did ya. No doubt you an' yer mates watchin' this will be 'aving yerselves a right ol' wank when you play the tapes back, thinkin' I've slipped up.' He shook his head. 'Good luck with that.'

'You really are a cocky one, aren't you, Clocks?' said DS Sharpe.

'So it's been said, tea boy. Now, it's obvious I'm not gonna get me tea an' biscuits out of you, so I'm done with this silly little game. I'm off. Places to go, people to see, things to do. You know 'ow it is?' He looked back and forth at his interviewers then pushed his chair back and stood up. 'Well, p'rhaps you don't. Ta-ta.'

Clocks nodded to his union rep and wrenched open the heavy glass door. As he stepped out into the main office, he saw Paterson come storming out of his interview from the other end. They locked eyes across the office and headed toward the lift.

CHAPTER TWENTY-FOUR

As they rode the lift to the ground floor, neither man said a word to each other. Their faces showed that each was locked in their own private thoughts, seething with anger and about ready to blow. The doors pinged open and they stormed out, pushing past the throng of irritated people desperate to force their way in and chain themselves to their desks.

They attracted the eyes of the security guards as they made their way across the foyer. They were obviously men with an anger inside. The guards must have decided that, as they were leaving the building, it wasn't worth challenging them.

Once out in the street, Paterson stopped and turned to his friend. 'What'd they say to you?'

'I'd imagine it was the same as they said to you by the look on yer face when you came out. Stitch up?'

'Yeah. Bastards really want to put it on us.'

'Course they do. We know that. Why wouldn't they?'

'What? Why *would* they?'

Clocks looked exasperated. 'Jesus, Ray. Come on. They've been after us for ages. You know that. Lambert put us in the frame for the dead girls on 'is manor and the commissioner 'ates us. He's desperate for it to be true. We both know we've probably been under twenty-four-hour surveillance for Christ knows 'ow long and they've come up short. We catch out their surveillance guy and they're seriously pissed at that. Don't tell me you thought they were gonna let it go, surely.'

Paterson shook his head. 'No, not really. Hoped they would.'

'So they've got two cops who sail a bit too close to the wind, a few dead girls that died in a similar manner to one of our cases, we more or less blanked Lambert when we met up with 'im an' they know we know Lambert put us in the frame for the dead girls. We're known to be a little bit loose with the law an' when Lambert gets shot, who better than us to bung in the frame? Fuckin' 'ell, I would.'

'I see that. But when Lambert was busy getting himself shot, we were tucked up kicking the fuck out of their undercover boy in a pub full of coppers.'

'An' that's why they ain't nicked us. If it was us investigating us we'd be thinking that the two dodgy bastards arranged to have him whacked while we're sittin' in a pub packed out with witnesses — an' not just any ol' witnesses . . . Ol' Bill witnesses. Don't get better than that, does it?'

Paterson sighed. 'No. No it doesn't. So, what now?'

Clocks looked across the road at a little café they'd used before. 'Well, first things first. I'd say it's time for a full nosh up an' we put this down while we concentrate on catching the crazy fucker we're after. We'll deal with this afterwards.'

'Where are we going? One of your greasy spoons?'

'Yep. Maria's. Next street over. Best grub in . . . well, that street.'

'Sounds wonderful.'

'It is. An' while we're in there, I'll tell you all about 'ow I wrong-footed them an' now they 'ave to investigate Anderson.'

'You didn't?'

Clocks grinned. 'Oh, I did, mate. Told 'em I caught him out on me phone an' I'll give it to 'em when the time's right.

Framed ol' Anderson up like a Rembrandt. That should keep 'em all a bit busy for a while.'

Clocks pushed open the door to the café. 'Maria! 'Ow you doin', sweetie?'

An Italian woman in her sixties beamed him a smile that lit up the dreary little café. 'Johnny boy. Is good to see you. Come. Give old Maria a hug.'

Paterson chuckled. 'Clocksy, I don't tell you this enough. I bloody love you, mate.'

'Fuck off bender, I'm about to cop off with Maria here.'

CHAPTER TWENTY-FIVE

Two hours later, Paterson and Clocks were back in the main office. Clocks caught up with Monkey Harris who told him that information was still trickling through but nothing that would advance the case any further than adding another sheet of paper to the file and he now busied himself making notes of the meeting he'd just had. Paterson, still fuming, sat behind his desk staring at his mobile phone. On the screen was the name of his lawyer, Anthony Lune. Lune was as good as they came and at three grand a day he was worth every penny. The only question was whether Paterson called him up now and gave him the heads up on today's meeting or ride it out a bit longer to see where things went. The sudden ringing jerked him out of his reverie.

'Paterson,' he said.

'Ray. It's me. Marcus.'

'Hi, Marcus. What can I do for you?'

'Got some info for you regarding Beverley?'

'What is it?'

'Don't want to say over the phone. But I've been digging around and found some papers.'

'And?'

'And it gives a possible address for our missing sister. Don't know if it's still current but it's a start.'

'Is it in Latent Avenue, over in Hertfordshire? If it is, we visited it. Nothing there.'

'It's Hertfordshire but not the road you said.'

Paterson nodded. 'Okay. Lemme grab my pen?'

'Think it would be better if you came and got it, Ray. I've found some interesting stuff about her.'

'Like what?'

'Like, she got married a few years back.'

Paterson's mind lit up. If the sister was delivering children to Elizabeth at Lynton Road, maybe it was her husband who was the Childmaker.

'Hold on. If you haven't seen her for years, what are you doing with paperwork with her address on it and knew that she had a husband. Why didn't you mention it yesterday?'

'Ah, well. To be honest, when I started making good, she wrote to me a few times to tell me what a shit life she was having. She was on the earhole for money. Gave me some old sob story about her husband beating her, threatening her and their kid, all that old toffee. After about the third letter, I shoved them and the rest that came in a drawer. Never bothered opening them. They stopped years ago and, to be honest, I completely forgot about them.'

Paterson rubbed his face. 'Marcus, I'm up to my eyeballs. I don't have time to come all the way out there for some papers that may or may not be of any use. Tell you what. Take photos of it all and send them to me as attachments. I'll give you my email address.'

'What? Email? Sorry, mate. I don't know about all that attachments shit. I have secretaries for that sort of thing. Can just about understand how to send and receive texts.'

'Can't your wife do it?'

'Yeah, she could but she's not here. Gone out for the day. Look, I can put them in the post signed for, but I doubt they'll get to you by tomorrow. Plus, they could still get lost.

You know what the post is like at the best of times. Rather you got them yourself. Up to you, mate.'

Paterson sighed. 'I'm on my way.' He hung up and wandered out into the main office.

'Clocksy,' he said.

Clocks looked up, glad of the break from his two-finger typing. 'Yes, guv. S'up?'

'I've just had a call from Marcus May. Wants me to go out and pick up some paperwork he found on the missing sister. Got a possible address for her.'

Clocks frowned at him. 'Why don't he just take some pics and send 'em in?'

'Reckons he don't know how to.'

'Wanker.'

'Yeah, he always was.'

'So, we goin' now?'

'Nope. You're not. You've got work to do here. I'll go.'

'Er, no. That doesn't sound good to me.'

'It's the way it is, John. Anderson gave us explicit instructions not to go, didn't he?'

'Yep. He did. So why you goin'? You lookin' for trouble?'

'Yeah. Fuck him. I'm a dead man walking anyway. Just a matter of time, really.

'Why don't you just give 'im a bell. I'm sure he'll let you go over there for that.'

'Yeah, he probably would but I'd hate him to think he'd bullied me into doing what he says.'

'You've turned into a right little tinker, aintcha?' Clocks chuckled.

'You can hold the fort until I get back can't you?'

'I should think so. I've been watching you and I've gotta be honest an' say your job looks like a piece of piss. From what I've seen of it, all you do is just strut up an' down all day pointin' at things an' tellin' people what to do. Don't seem to be that 'ard. I reckon I can handle it.'

Paterson grinned. 'I'm sure you'll handle it. Just don't abuse it.'

'Wouldn't dream of it. Might as well get started. Dusty!'

'Guv'nor,' Dusty Doneghan said, startled.

'That breakfast I 'ad this mornin' didn't touch the sides. Be a love an' go an' get me a cuppa tea an' a fried egg sandwich from the canteen. I'm starvin' again. Oh, and don't be givin' me any lip about it either. The guv'nor's goin' out so I'm in charge now.'

Paterson raised an eyebrow. Dusty raised his middle finger.

'Look at that, guv! Fuckin' cheek. No bloody respect for the rank anymore, is there? This job's gonna be a lot tougher than I first thought, Ray. You'll 'ave to give me some tips on orderin' people about when you get back. Sure you don't want me to come with you?'

'No. No point. I'll pick someone up. Must be someone out there.'

'Toni!' Clocks shouted across the office. 'We got anyone out on the street can go for a quick trip with the guv?'

Toni tapped her computer. 'Looks like the only one who's not tucked up to their eyeballs is Carrie.' She grinned across at Paterson.

He rolled his eyes. 'Find out where she is and tell her I'll come pick her up.'

Paterson wasn't keen but he knew he needed to be professional and thought it might be a good opportunity to try and find some common ground and work their shit out.

* * *

Fifteen minutes after Paterson left the office, Dusty, on the phone, looked over at the group and frantically waved his hand at them. He caught Monkey Harris's eye.

'Guv,' Monkey said to Clocks. 'Dusty's got something.'

As they both moved toward Dusty's desk, he thanked whoever he was talking to, hung up and finished scribbling on his pad. He looked up and smiled.

'Whatcha got?' said Clocks.

'That was the psych hospital. Mad Elizabeth is apparently lucid and wants to talk.'

Clocks bolted for the door.

'Want me to call Paterson back to the office?'

'Nope,' said Clocks. 'No point.'

'Ask for the doctor . . . Lena Stanton!' Dusty called as Clocks disappeared through the door.

Clocks came running out into the yard heading toward his BMW just as Jackie Hartnett was parking up.

'Whassamatter?' she said, a look of alarm on her face.

'Jump in!' Clocks shouted. 'I need a Doris with me.'

She did as she was told and slid into the seat next to him. Clocks hit the siren and blue lights and screeched out into the street.

'Where we going?' said Jackie.

'We're off to the nut 'ouse. Our lady of Lynton Road is no longer off 'er bonce apparently. So we're gonna go an' chat with 'er before she gets the chance to go mad again.'

'That's why you needed me? Because she's female?'

Clocks craned his neck to look at her. She was struggling with her seat belt and he copped a good look down her shirt, open by one button too many.

'Nope. I need you to make the tea. Dusty flat out refused. I was gonna bring Toni but she was too busy making fairy cakes an' ironing a coupla shirts for me.' He spun himself back around, a grin on his face.

CHAPTER TWENTY-SIX

On their arrival at the hospital, Jackie and Clocks met Dr Stanton at the reception desk.

'Thank you for coming.' Dr Stanton was a tall, slim woman in her fifties. The most striking thing about her was the colour of her eyes. One brown, one blue. Clocks couldn't stop staring at them. 'I know you'll want to go straight through but, before we do, I need to tell you about her condition as it stands.'

'Go on then. Hurry up.'

'She is lucid, but dozy. Her system is full of anti-psychotic drugs so her memory of events will not necessarily be perfect.'

'No one's is, love,' said Clocks. 'I'll take that into account.

'Doctor Stanton, if you don't mind, Inspector. I'm not fond of the term *love*.'

Clocks looked deep into her eyes. 'Jesus. Sorry. Everyone's so sensitive these days.'

Dr Stanton ignored that remark. 'What you have to remember is that whatever she says in there may not be admissible as evidence in any criminal prosecution you bring against her. I'll come in with you to act as an independent witness and, if needed, can attest to her state of mind at the time. There's a little room next door with two-way glass and a colleague of mine, Dr Lenny Wing, will be observing and taking notes of his own.'

That was fine by Clocks. All he wanted to do was to clarify her position in this whole sorry story and where and how she managed to capture the children. More than anything, he wanted to know why: why those children had been so brutally murdered and cut to pieces; why various body parts were strewn around the house and used as ornaments; perhaps most importantly, how she got so badly broken in the first place.

'Her return to some sort of normality is fragile at best and she could slip back into psychosis at any given moment. All I ask is that you tread lightly, be careful what you say and try not to upset her. If you do, she's likely to retreat back into her own world and this time it may be harder to reach her in the future.'

'No worries there, doc. I actually run the Met police nice 'n' cuddly courses. They go down a storm with the bunch of pansies we've got in the job these days.'

Jackie intervened. 'Guv, got a sec?'

'What?'

'Doctor, excuse us for a second, please.'

Clocks was perplexed as Jackie took him by the arm and led him away.

'Whassamatter, Jack? Something wrong?'

'Guv, don't take this the wrong way, but I think it's best if you go in the room with the other doctor and I talk to Elizabeth May with Doctor Stanton.'

Clocks looked at her. 'What? Why?'

'Well, despite all that bollocks you just gave her, you are not the sensitive caring soul you make out to be, are you?'

'No, not overly.'

'So, if you go in there and tick Elizabeth off which, let's face it, you're bound to do at some point, we'll get nothing. So . . .'

'Oh, I get it. You're sayin' you don't trust me to behave.'

'That's it. Don't trust you to behave in the slightest.'

'You may have a point.'

'I do have a point. A bloody good one.'

'I'll go and sit with Doctor . . . Benny or whatever his name is.'

'Lenny,' she corrected. 'And I appreciate that.'

'But hang on . . .I appreciate you're all girls together an' all that but I seem to remember you an' 'er having a right ol' roll around in the interview room, and if I recall correctly you punched 'er lights out, didn't you?' He pointed to her strapped-up hand.

Jackie nodded. 'Yes. I did. I'm hoping she won't remember me though.'

'It was only yesterday, Jack.'

'Yes, all right. I know, but she was mad yesterday.'

'So, you think that because today she's not too mad, she'll also have amnesia?'

'A girl can dream, can't she?'

Clocks shrugged. 'She can indeed. All righty then. Let's give it a run.'

They returned to Doctor Stanton.

'Sorry about that, love — sorry! Sorry. *Doctor* Stanton. My colleague here just wanted to remind me that the whole point of me bringing a girl with me was not in fact to just make the tea but to be able to talk to another girl in some sort of mysterious way that I can't. So, if it's all right with you, I'll go and sit with your mate Kenny.'

Dr Stanton shook her head. 'Follow me. And his name is Lenny.'

* * *

Jackie entered the room to find a fragile looking creature, scared and tearful, looking at the big wooden desk in front of her. She dropped her bag by the side of a chair and sat herself down opposite Elizabeth May. 'Miss May. Thank you for agreeing to talk to me today. I really appreciate you taking the time to do this. If, at any point, you feel unwell and want to stop, please just say so.' She decided not to make mention of their earlier meeting, hoping that she would have no memory of it. From the look of her, she didn't appear to.

She was quieter now, certainly quieter than when she attacked Jackie and headbutted her own solicitor.

Elizabeth May lifted her head. She looked drawn and pale, her lips thin and her hair a straggly mess. She hugged herself. Bony arms wrapped around her shoulders and twiglet fingers gently caressed the cold, pale flesh. She nodded.

'Okay. Thank you, Elizabeth.' Jackie tried to maintain a gentle demeanour. She had to tread carefully and not do anything to make Elizabeth withdraw back into her own world. What she really felt was disgust and anger, and she knew that when angered she was not a person to be around. She bit her lip in lieu of punching the woman opposite in the mouth. 'Can you remember what happened when the police came to your house?'

A nod.

'Did you know why they were there?'

A nod.

'Can you tell me please, in your own words, what happened?'

Elizabeth stared into space, her eyes darting from side to side as she replayed her version of events back in her mind. 'I killed them.'

'Who, Elizabeth? Who did you kill?'

'The man. And the policeman. Serves them right, coming into my house to steal my children.'

'What children, Elizabeth? Tell me about your children?'

'I love him so much?'

'What? Who? Your child?'

Elizabeth looked down at the floor and stayed quiet.

'Elizabeth?' said Jackie, gently. 'Who is it you love? Please tell me.'

Elizabeth lifted her head and sat up straight.

'My husband.'

'Excuse me?'

Elizabeth smiled.

'Elizabeth, you said *husband*. Is that right?'

'Yes.'

'I didn't know you were married.'

'It's a secret.'

'Why is it a secret?

'Because he said so. He said it had to be a secret.'

Jackie's heart skipped a beat. She knew too well what that phrase meant.

'Why did he tell you to keep it a secret, Elizabeth? What happened?'

'It's a secret.'

'Okay. I understand. What's his name?'

Elizabeth smiled. 'I won't tell you.'

Jackie took a deep breath. 'Why not?'

'It's a secret.'

Jackie nodded. A lot of secrets. 'I see. But I was thinking. If you tell me his name and where he lives, perhaps I can get him to come and see you. Would you like that? I can do that for you.'

Elizabeth's face took on a wistful look. 'Yes. Very much.' She folded into herself and put her head down. In a whisper, she said, 'We had a baby. A beautiful baby. She . . . died.'

'I'm sorry to hear that, Elizabeth. What was her name?'

'Alice.'

'Alice. That's a very pretty name. I'm so sorry that happened to you. That must have been very painful for you both. How old were you when this happened?'

'Thirteen.'

Jackie managed to look startled and confused at the same time. 'Thirteen? Are you sure, Elizabeth? That's very young. *Very* young.'

'I'm sure . . . yes, young.'

'When did this start, Elizabeth?'

'When did what start?'

'When you started sleeping together, having sex.'

'When I was . . . five, maybe six.'

Jackie tightened her jaw as she listened to Elizabeth recount her abuse as a simple fact, not a violation.

'Did you tell anyone?'

'No. We loved each other.'

'You do know that it's wrong to do that, don't you? On so many levels. You were a child yourself.'

Elizabeth's eyes flashed with a look that said she was tired of justifying their love to strangers. 'It isn't wrong. It isn't. Not if you love each other.'

'Okay,' said Jackie. 'I'm sorry. Didn't mean to upset you. We'll come back to that later. Can I ask what happened to Alice?'

'She died.' Elizabeth's eyes brimmed with tears.

'I know she did, I know. And I'm sorry to hurt you again but I would really like to know what happened to her. Please.'

Elizabeth looked around the small room, her head swivelling about slowly, as if she was looking for something. 'He killed her.'

Jackie stiffened. 'Who did?'

'My husband.'

'Why did he do that, Elizabeth?'

'He said she was ugly.'

Jackie winced. She turned to Dr Stanton to see whether she was still safe to push on with her questions. Dr Stanton nodded.

'I'm sure she wasn't, Elizabeth.'

Elizabeth looked at Jackie, her eyes full of pain.

'She wasn't, lady. She was beautiful.'

'What happened to little Alice? After your husband killed her?'

The tears rolled down her cheek as Elizabeth's mind searched the past.

'He cut her up into little pieces . . .'

'Dear God . . .' The words slipped out of Dr Stanton's lips before she could stop herself.

'And then what happened?' said Jackie.

'He cooked them.'

Dr Stanton stood up abruptly. ' I . . . I . . . I don't think . . . I'm sorry. Sorry. I don't think I can listen to any more of this. Not this.'

Jackie could see that the colour had drained from the doctor's face and had been replaced with a slight greenish tinge. Dr Stanton bolted from the room leaving Jackie and Elizabeth alone.

Elizabeth was grinning. 'Where is she going?'

Jackie took a deep breath. 'Some people get a bit upset when they hear about bad things that happen to children, Elizabeth. She'll be all right.'

'I don't care anyway.'

Jackie stared at Elizabeth. 'I need to ask you about your house, now. Do you mind?'

Elizabeth shrugged. 'If you want.'

'When we searched it, we found a number of children hidden behind a wall in the cellar. What can you tell me about them?'

'My children . . .'

'Your children. Okay, yes. Can you talk to me about them, please?'

A cruel grin played on Elizabeth's lips for a second or two, then passed.

'What about them? They're mine.'

'I know.' Agreeing with a suspect was a tactic for getting them to feel safe and not judged, but it was all Jackie could do to stop herself from backhanding her across the face. Her rage was building. She took another deep breath and pushed on.

'Elizabeth, I have so many questions. Please don't take offence at anything I say. I'm just trying to understand, okay?'

Elizabeth looked at her and said nothing.

'Who put them there?'

'Me and my husband.'

'Why?'

'Because they were not good enough.'

Jackie frowned. 'For . . . ?'

'For me.'

'Why weren't they good enough? Was something wrong with them?'

'We tried,' Elizabeth said.

'Tried what?'

'To get it right?'

'Get what right? I don't understand.'

Elizabeth shook her head as if in admonishment to the idiot woman sitting opposite her, judging her.

'To make a child. *Make* a child. Of our own.'

Now Jackie stayed quiet. But not for long. Just long enough to collect her thoughts.

'So . . . let me get this right . . . You're saying to me that you and your husband were killing other children and . . .' She shook her head at the thought of what she was about to say. 'And cut them up to use as parts to physically make yourself a child? To replace the one you lost?'

'Yes. They were different sizes. Boys and girls. You can't make a perfect child out of a boy and a girl. I told him that. He knew that, but we tried. It was fun.'

'Fun?'

'Fun. Yes.'

Jackie felt her grip on the interview start to slip. The room started to spin. She fought it off.

'So . . . just so I'm sure . . . you took parts from living children and tried to make a child out of them. Is that what you're saying to me?'

'Yeah.'

'Jesus . . .'

Elizabeth laughed.

'You knew your husband was doing this?'

'Yeah. I sent him out to get them.'

Jackie stayed quiet.

'We cut them all up but it was my child to make. Not his. You know what men are. Useless. But I did it. I made a beautiful little girl out of all the children he brought me.' She shrugged slightly, giggled and gave Jackie a sideways grin, like a naughty little girl telling a secret to her mum.

Jackie fought down the bile that she could taste in the back of her throat and forced herself to speak. 'Where is she, Elizabeth? Where is your daughter now?'

Elizabeth May put a finger to her lips then whispered. 'With him. Her daddy. It's his time with her. She has so much energy.' Elizabeth's face brightened and she sat herself up, energised at the thought of her daughter. 'She runs, always running around. Always playing, singing, clapping. She loves to clap. She loves to sing . . . play. I need to rest.'

'Can you tell me where they are?' said Jackie.

Elizabeth's face changed. No longer happy, nor animated. Her eyes narrowed. 'Why? Why d'you want to know?'

Jackie took another deep breath. She had to phrase this right. 'Because I'd love to see her. I bet she is such a beautiful little girl and I've never seen a girl that's been made before, not in such a special way.'

Elizabeth's forehead crinkled slightly.

'Please, Elizabeth. Please let me see her. I don't have any children so I would like to buy her a pretty little dress if you'd let me.'

Elizabeth gave Jackie a big smile. The idea of her little girl in a pretty dress obviously appealed to her. 'She's at home with him.'

'Home? Where's home? Where does he live?'

Elizabeth nodded. 'In their special place.'

'Special place? Where's that?'

'Behind the wall.'

Jackie frowned. '*Behind* the wall? I don't understand. What wall? What are you talking about?'

Elizabeth giggled again. 'The wall in the house.'

Jackie was close to losing her rag. 'Whose house, Elizabeth?'

'My husband. Marcus's, silly.'

Jackie sat bolt upright.

As soon as she heard the cup shatter on the hard, tiled floor, Jackie knew that Clocks was up and running out of the room. 'Elizabeth,' she said. 'I have to go now.' She pushed back her chair and stood.

Elizabeth gave her a supercilious look which flipped Jackie just a bit too far. 'Very quickly. I just wanna say . . . I hope to God you suffer a painful death and rot in hell, you fucked-up crazy bitch.'

* * *

In the little room with the two-way glass, Lenny wrinkled his nose as the detective ran out after her inspector.

CHAPTER TWENTY-SEVEN

Marcus stood in the centre of the bedroom and watched Paterson's approach through the net curtains. As he stepped out of the car, he saw that he had a woman with him. They chatted to each other as he opened the garden gate. It was time to withdraw. He moved to the safety of his daughter's playroom — *his* playroom, hidden behind a swing-out bookcase.

He put a finger to his lips. '*Shhh* . . . we have guests, Alice. They want to take you away from me.'

'Why, Daddy? Why do they want to take me away?'

Marcus turned to the child he called his daughter: Alice Two. So beautiful and so precious to him he could scarcely breathe. She wore a pink ribbon in the thin strands of dead hair that clung wispily to the blackened head of a child called Jess. Jess was seven years old when Marcus took her from the park just a year before. In life, she had been like any child of that age: happy, curious, adventurous and full of life. And then Marcus and his sister took her from under the nose of a mother who was too busy with her Facebook and Instagram accounts to pay more than a scant amount of attention to the child she professed to adore.

The milky eyes of the ragdoll corpse of young Jess stared into nothingness, sat lifeless in a small chair. Covering her stitched-together body she wore a pink summer dress, white ankle socks and a pair of black ill-fitting patent shoes. Stitches covered her joints where she had been sewn together from the parts of other children they had stolen and dismembered: a leg from six-year-old Shania; another leg from seven-year-old Emma; both arms from an eight-year-old called Olivia; the hands of a young girl named Amelia — her fingernails were what attracted them. Here and there, small bits of catgut stuck out where Alice had been stitched together but the nylon had not been cut neatly enough.

'What's that?' said Marcus. 'No. These are bad people. Now, no more questions. You must keep quiet, angel. Please. Daddy will send them away.'

Marcus closed the door with a slight click then swung back a small wooden block to reveal a single peephole. A surge of adrenaline bolted through his system. His heart was beating so fast, threatening to hammer its way out of his chest. This was being alive.

In his head, he heard her voice, sweet and gentle. 'Are you going to let them take me, Daddy?'

'No, no sweetie. Daddy will never let them take you from me and Mummy. Never.'

'Will you hurt the bad people, Daddy?'

Marcus pulled his lips tight against his teeth. 'I don't want to, sweetie. Now . . . please be quiet.'

'Daddy?'

'Yes, sweetie. What is it?'

'Kill them for me, Daddy. Kill them both.'

Marcus smiled. 'Anything for you, my angel.'

* * *

The ride over to Marcus May's house had been mostly in silence. Neither Paterson nor Carrie knew what to say to each other, so the journey was made up of long pauses and work-related small talk. As they pulled up outside the house,

Paterson breathed a sigh of relief. He vowed to talk to her properly on the way back.

Paterson rang the bell and waited. He rang again after a few seconds. Nothing. He stepped back out onto the driveway and looked up at the upstairs windows. Nothing out of place that he could see. He looked across at Carrie. She shrugged.

'You said he called you, yeah?' she said.

'Yeah.'

'So, where is he?'

'How am I supposed to know? He said to come straight over.'

'Perhaps he ran out of milk or biscuits or something.'

'Doubt it. His car is over there.' He nodded toward a silver Range Rover parked next to the boundary fence. 'Try the door,' he said.

Carrie twisted the handle and the door swung open. 'If he has gone out, seems he forgot to lock the door.'

Paterson walked toward her. 'This is the sticks, Carrie. Doubt they worry about that kind of thing too much here.' He stepped inside. The place was filled with silence. 'Marcus! It's me, Ray. Ray Paterson.' His voice made a faint echoing sound. 'Marcus! You here?'

The two police officers looked at each other and shrugged.

'I'll have a wander upstairs,' Carrie said. 'Big house. Maybe he can't hear us.'

Paterson nodded and headed toward the patio doors in the living room. 'He might be out in the garden. I'll have a quick look. Wait for me.'

'What?'

'Wait for me. I won't be a second.'

'I'm a big girl, Ray. I'll be fine.'

* * *

Clocks swerved the car across the road into the path of oncoming traffic. He waved one arm frantically to get the panicking drivers coming toward them out of the way. One car, driven by a woman who looked the wrong side of ninety, didn't see him and pootled on steadily. He braked hard and swung the steering wheel violently. The back of the car slid before he got it under control again. As he straightened the car up, he took a few seconds to hurl a volley of expletives at the old woman.

'The fuck is an ol' bird like that doin' drivin'? Nearly fuckin' killed us.'

Jackie said nothing as she felt her breakfast heading toward a rapid exit.

'Give Hertfordshire a bell, Jack. Tell 'em to get someone over there a bit lively. Urgent assistance needed an' all that.'

He pressed the accelerator and the front of the car lifted. Jackie gripped the grab handle with her left hand and the centre console with her right. Her legs were ramrod straight.

'Fuck's sake, Clocksy. Slow down!'

He glanced at the speedo. 'Seventy's not fast.'

'It's fucking suicidal in Tooley Street.'

'Nah, you're all right. Close yer eyes if you're worried.'

She did.

Clocks's right foot danced between the accelerator and brake as he weaved in and out of the traffic. 'Stop being a tart, Jack, and get on the phone. They could be in trouble. Come on.'

Jackie opened her eyes but kept her head down. If something was going to hit them, she didn't want to see it coming.

'Get out of the fuckin' road, you arse-wipe!' Clocks screamed at a young man, a suited and booted office worker with a big set of red earphones stuck on his head who'd stepped into the road without looking at anything other than his phone. The young man went white with shock as Clocks shot past him missing him by less than a foot.

Clocks glanced in his mirror as the young man stood stock still, the sudden adrenaline dump rooting him to the spot. 'Yeah. That woke you up, didn't it, you numpty?' He watched the young man recede into the distance. He turned his attention back to the road. Jackie ended her call.

'What'd they say?'

'They're on their way. They're not happy he's gone back there and not told them he was going.'

Clocks shrugged. 'Eh, who cares. Fuck 'em. Now call Ray or Carrie. Tell 'em not to go in that bastard 'ouse, if they haven't already.'

Clocks stood on the brakes, bringing the car to a violent halt.

'Jesus!' Jackie shrieked, 'what the fu—'

Clocks's head was already out of the window. Twenty feet away from him, a startled Lyndsey Kitchener looked shocked as he beamed a big smile at her. ''Ello love. Get in! Get in! Move, move, move!'

Lyndsey recognised the tone. Whatever it was he wanted, it was urgent. She wrenched open the back door and slid across the back seat, her hand slamming the door behind her as Clocks stamped on the accelerator again.

She shoved her head between the seats. 'What's goin' on?'

'Ray's in the shit,' said Clocks. 'An' Carrie. It's all gone tits up on us. You got yer shooter with yer?'

'What? My gun? No. Why would I have my gun?'

'Dunno. But you normally sleep with it under yer pillow. Don't think I don't know. I sometimes think you love that Glock more than me.'

'I love getting a bikini wax more than you, you knob. What the fuck is happening?'

Jackie quickly explained what had happened.

'Christ . . .' Lyndsey sat back in her seat and clipped on her seatbelt. She checked the inside pocket of her jacket and pulled out a set of plasticuffs. 'Got these, though.'

'Oh, yeah. They might come in 'andy.' Clocks slung the car into a hard right, narrowly missing a lorry, before straightening up again. 'P'rhaps we can sling them at 'im when he's killing Ray. What you doin' here anyway?'

'I'm off duty. I was shopping.'

'What for?'

‘Mind your own business.’

Clocks slammed his hand onto the car horn as he hit the brakes and swerved around an ashen faced pedestrian. ‘That’s ’urtful. I was only askin’.

‘You got any weapons then?’ she asked.

‘Only me devastatingly boyish charm and razor-sharp wit.’

‘Jesus. We’re proper fucked then.’

‘Ah well,’ said Clocks. ‘Fisticuffs it is then.’

* * *

Paterson looked through the glass of the patio doors and out into the garden. There was no sign of Marcus or his wife. He tried the handle of the door. Locked. As far as he could tell, unless you walked around the front of the house to get into the back garden, this was the only other exit leading there. He raised his head slightly and pulled himself up straight. Something was off. He could feel it.

A muffled thump from upstairs brought him back into the room.

‘Carrie!’ he called. ‘You okay?’

Silence. He walked out into the hallway and shouted up the stairs. ‘Carrie. Everything all right?’ He listened. Nothing. ‘Carrie!’

He started up the stairs.

CHAPTER TWENTY-EIGHT

Paterson had a gnawing feeling in the pit of his stomach that something was wrong. Very wrong. He made his way carefully up the stairs, conscious of every little creak each step made, although he knew logically it made no difference. If someone was in here with them, he already knew about them. His focus of attention was firmly on the landing ahead. He could see that at least one door was partly open and every step upward gave him a wider view of the layout. At least two other rooms, each door closed.

The open door was nearest to him. 'Carrie?' he said, quietly. No answer. 'Carrie? You okay?'

He pushed the door open gently. It creaked as it swung back to reveal Carrie lying face down in a pool of blood.

'Jesus! Carrie!'

Instinct took the place of caution and Paterson rushed into the room.

As he knelt down to her he sensed something moving in fast behind him. Before he could turn, a thick polythene bag was yanked down over his head and the full weight of Marcus May ran into him, knocking him onto his stomach. Paterson's face banged against the bare floorboards, stunning him for a second or two. It was all the time Marcus needed.

He jammed his knee between Paterson's shoulder blades and pulled the bag tight, lifting Paterson's head up and back. Paterson panicked and grabbed at the polythene, tearing frantically at it, desperate to get it off of him, to breathe. The taste and smell of plastic fuelled his muscles and he squirmed around violently, trying unsuccessfully to throw Marcus off.

Paterson's own panic was now his biggest enemy. His vision blurred as the bag began to fill with condensation from his own breath. He roared with rage, twisting, fighting, desperate to throw Marcus off of his back. He couldn't. Marcus was too well trained, too strong and too determined. Paterson couldn't claw at the bag and fight him off at the same time. His vision blurred as his eyes filled with tears.

Gradually, Paterson's muscles weakened. His hand dropped from the bag and slapped onto the floor. He tried to push himself up. Too weak. His hand went back to the bag but dropped again. The bag was pulled tighter.

With just a few twitching kicks and jerky arm movements Paterson finally stopped fighting. Marcus kept the pressure on.

Through the misty bag, Paterson could just make out the blurred, wet shape of Carrie lying still and lifeless and the last thought he had before the darkness engulfed him was that she was dead. And it was his fault.

CHAPTER TWENTY-NINE

'Try giving 'em a bell, again, Jack. One of 'em's gotta have their bloody phone on.' Jackie looked at her phone log. Nine calls to Paterson, seven to Carrie. She was as worried as Johnny Clocks but kept it under control better than he did. Clocks reckoned he was still a good twenty minutes from May's house even though the traffic was light. This time, he hoped the locals would get there first but he wasn't banking on it.

Someone answered.

'Ray? Ray? It's me, Jackie. Are you okay?'

Clocks glanced across at her. Lyndsey pounced forward, head between the front seats again. Clocks mouthed 'put it on speaker.' Jackie nodded and tapped the screen. Silence.

'Ray!' Clocks shouted, keeping one eye on the road. Where are you, mate? Listen, don't go in that fuckin' 'ouse, you 'ear me? Turns out Marcus is as nutty as 'is nutty sister. He'll likely be hiding in there somewhere. Wait till we get there.'

A small chuckle from the speaker turned Clocks's blood cold. They were too late. 'The nutty fucker's not hiding anywhere.' His voice was quiet. Calm. In control.

Clocks grimaced. 'Ah. You heard that, then, did you, Marcus?'

'I did.'

'No offence, mate.'

'None taken.'

'Where's Paterson? And the girl?'

'That's not important.'

'It is to me.'

'But not to me.'

'Okay. Okay. Listen up, Marcus my ol' son, an' listen fuckin' carefully. You'd better not 'ave hurt either of them.'

'And if I have?'

'Then your fuckin' life won't be worth tuppence ha'penny, fellah. I promise you that.'

'Do you?'

'Yeah, I do. Now put Paterson on the phone, right now.'

'He can't come to the phone.'

Clocks took a deep breath. 'Why's that? Where is he?'

'He's sitting in a chair waiting for you but I'm afraid you're too late. Far too late.'

Clocks gripped the steering wheel so hard that his knuckles turned a deathly shade of pale. 'Too late for what?'

'To stop me.'

'I'm fuckin' tellin' you, mate. If you've 'armed either one of 'em, me an' you are gonna go a few rounds.'

Marcus burst out laughing then there was silence for a second or two. 'I really do hope so, officer. I truly do.'

Marcus hung up.

'Fuuuuuuccccckkkk!' Clocks screamed. He pushed the accelerator to the floor and swung the car into a dangerous bend on the blind side of the road. A car coming the other way left the road and slid into a line of bushes as Clocks hurtled past at eighty. Jackie had turned a whiter shade of pale and was clinging on for dear life.

Lyndsey had been thrown back into her seat. 'Jesus, John!'

Clocks tapped on the brakes and accelerator as he weaved the car around the country roads. Fifteen minutes top whack if he could keep this speed up. He couldn't. As he rounded a bend a tractor was coming the other way. Clocks had nowhere to go. He slammed on the brakes and slid to a halt two feet from the front of it. Window down, Clocks screamed at the driver to pull over. The tractor driver, a burly man in his early thirties, scowled at Clocks.

'D'you fuckin' hear me, son? Pull it over. Emergency. Move yerself.'

Clocks watched the driver pull up the handbrake and cross his arms. Clocks lost it and bailed out of the car. He ran to the driver's side. The tractor driver looked down at Clocks's face, red with fury.

'Oi, Tractor Jack! Get this lump of shit out the way or I'll kick you from arse'ole to breakfast time, I swear. Do it!'

The driver leaned out of the window. 'Fuck off, plod. You back up. This is my right of way.'

'What? Right of way? 'Ave a look at the blue light, mate? We're on the 'urry up. Wassamatter with yer?'

Tractor Jack shrugged.

'If you don't move it, mate, I swear to God I'll fuckin' drag you down out of there and move it meself.'

Jackie and Lyndsey both got out of the car and trotted over. Jackie looked up at the driver. 'Sir. Please. We're in a desperate hurry. We're trying to stop a murder.'

Tractor man looked unconvinced. Perhaps nobody ever got murdered around this neck of the woods. 'He can't talk to me like that.'

'Don't take it personal. He talks to everyone like that. Now, *please*. Back it up.'

'You back it up. Only five hundred yards. There's a space to pull in.'

Lyndsey had taken up a defensive position, watching this unfurl. She could see by Clocks's agitation that he was about to lose it big time.

Clocks grabbed at the door handle and yanked it open. Tractor Jack, alarmed, backed away. Clocks grabbed his leg and pulled on it, dragging the man half out. Instinctively, Tractor Jack grabbed onto the steering wheel and held on tight. It was off now. Jackie joined in, pulling at his other leg until he lost his grip and crashed down onto the ground with a sickening thump. As quick as he hit the ground, he was up again, a nasty graze on his cheek and blood in his mouth. He glared at Johnny Clocks and swung at him. Clocks ducked, came up, kicked him straight in the balls and smacked him on the jaw as he doubled over.

Tractor Jack went down on one knee, turned his head toward Clocks and caught another right-hander. This one knocked him spark out.

'Oh, shit,' said Jackie. 'Well done. More trouble. Thanks for that.'

Clocks dragged tractor man on the side of the road and dumped him on his face in a clump of stinging nettles. 'Sod 'im. Come on. We're wasting bloody time fannyin' about with him. Lynds! Back the car up a bit while I move this tractor out of it,' he said. He climbed into the driver's seat as Lyndsey jumped into the car and backed it up.

She sat there for a few seconds waiting for him to pull forward.

Clocks fiddled around with a few levers and crunched the gears before poking his head out of the window. 'Right. Anyone know 'ow to drive one of these fuckin' things?'

CHAPTER THIRTY

A dull throb in his head welcomed Paterson back into the land of the living. He opened his eyes very slowly and raised his head. His vision was blurry and it took him a few seconds to realise where he was and measure his situation. It wasn't good.

The first thing he saw was Carrie sitting opposite him. Her arms and legs were bound tightly to the chair with duct tape. A piece of tape covered her mouth. Her eyes were wide with fear. As he focused on her and struggled to pull himself together, he quickly realised two things: he was also bound to a chair with tape across his mouth and Carrie's look of horror was because someone was standing behind him. A sudden memory of the thick polythene bag over his head sent a huge surge of adrenaline through his system and he began to struggle.

'That's not going to help you.'

Paterson twisted his head to see Marcus stood behind him. In his hand was a surgical scalpel. Paterson looked back at Carrie. Apart from the cut on her head, she seemed otherwise unharmed. So far.

Paterson struggled again.

'Please, Ray. Calm down. You can't escape.'

He struggled for another few seconds before accepting that he was bound too tightly and was helpless. He closed his eyes.

Marcus, his hands behind his back, walked slowly around to stand in front of him. He grinned. Paterson eyed his kidnapper: six-three and solid muscle. No wonder he couldn't shake him off easily. His eyes were cold. Dead. Always was a vicious bastard.

'Now, Ray,' he said. 'I don't have too much time. I have been talking to your friend, John Clocks. He seems to be very fond of you.'

Paterson stayed still, watching Marcus closely.

'He is on his way to rescue you. He will be too late.'

Paterson's stomach knotted and he struggled again, balling his fists as he strained against the duct tape that held him firm and growling with fury.

'Please calm down. This will go so much easier if you don't struggle.'

Marcus brought his hands out in front of him.

Paterson stopped. His eyes widened as he saw the scalpel.

'This is what I'm going to do. You're a handsome man, Ray. Your face will be pleasing to look at on a wall.'

Now Carrie started struggling. Her voice was muffled but there was no doubting the anger in her tone.

Marcus ignored her.

'I'm not going to lie to you. This *will* hurt but not as much as you think. Right now, your fear and adrenaline are busily sending messages to your brain and between them they'll block most of the pain of the initial cut. Once I begin, you'll feel nothing more than a stinging sensation. The real pain will commence when I pull the skin from your face.'

He walked behind Paterson and put one hand on his shoulder. In his peripheral vision, Paterson caught sight of the blade. A cold rush of fear shuddered through his body.

'I am going to make an incision under the jawline starting here.' He touched Paterson's chin. 'I will then cut along the jawline until I reach here.' He tapped the left side of

Paterson's face just under the ear. I will then go back to the chin and repeat the procedure and I will end up here.' He touched under the ear on the other side. 'Once this is done, it is a matter of pulling up the skin slowly so as not to tear it as I separate it from your skull. However, it may prove necessary for me to have to cut about inside from time to time. Let's hope not, eh?'

Paterson's head shot forward, breaking Marcus's grip. He raged at the man behind him, his muscles straining to break the tape. Carrie was doing the same, desperate to break her bonds, her screaming muffled by the tape across her mouth, and bouncing around in her chair.

Marcus grabbed Paterson's hair and wrenched his head back. 'Let me give you some advice, Ray. Keep still. If you don't, the cut is likely to be jagged and deeper. I may hit the bone and that will be even more painful for you. Plus, if you don't keep still, I'll slice *her* open.'

Paterson stopped. It was useless. They were both dead. He knew it.

Marcus pulled Paterson's head back and exposed his throat, like a barber about to shave a customer. He held onto Paterson's head with a tight grip and pulled it onto his chest to steady him.

Paterson swallowed hard and trembled from head to toe. Sweat ran down his forehead and into his eyes and he moaned quietly between deep, heavy breaths. Carrie sobbed and dropped her head. She couldn't watch.

Marcus dug the scalpel into Paterson's chin. He winced. He felt the warm tickle of blood make its way down onto his throat. He steeled himself for what was to come next. Marcus carefully and slowly pulled the blade along the jawline.

Paterson screwed his eyes tight shut as he felt a coldness where the blade gently separated his skin and exposed his jawbone to the air.

Carrie looked up and wailed through her tape. Her high-pitched whine caused Marcus to look up for a second. He frowned and went back to work.

Through tear-filled eyes, Paterson saw the room spin as his vision closed down. Just as he felt Marcus start to open up the other side of the jawline, he mercifully passed out.

* * *

Clocks, Lyndsey and Jackie had given up on the tractor and were now running through a field the best they could. A combination of mud, long wet grass and cow pats everywhere slowed them down considerably. That and the fact that none of them had much recent experience of using their legs other than for walking made for slow progress.

Clocks's determination to help his friend saw him ahead of Jackie but behind Lyndsey, who was much fitter than him. His lungs burned like a boy who'd just chugged his first ever glass of whisky. He wouldn't get too much further. On wobbly legs that were ready to give up on him he staggered forward a few more yards before he fell over, his hand landing squarely in a cow pat.

'Fuck me . . .' He panted heavily, sucking in as much air as he could get hold of. Struggling to pull himself up, he looked toward Marcus's house, taunting him in the distance.

CHAPTER THIRTY-ONE

Commissioner Anderson was in a meeting with the head of Traffic Control when he was interrupted by an urgent call. He listened for a few seconds, nodded once or twice and lost the pleasant expression he had been wearing a short while before.

Conversation over, he banged the phone down into its cradle and stood up so fast his chair fell over. 'What the hell is wrong with that man?'

The traffic officer looked startled and said, 'Sir?'

Anderson looked down at him. 'I'm sorry. Something urgent has come up. I'm afraid our meeting is over. I'll reschedule.' He held his hand out. The two men shook hands and Anderson showed him the door.

He poked his head outside and spoke to his new, new PA, Karen. Donna had quit the night before. 'No calls for a while. I have things to do.' He spun around and stormed back into his office, banging the door behind him.

He dropped himself back into his chair, picked up his phone and punched in three numbers. He gave the recipient of the call five minutes to get into his office and to bring Paterson's file with her.

Four minutes later, Alex Forbes, the head of Human Resources, tapped on his door.

'Come.' He looked out of the large plate glass window overlooking the City of London, five stories below. He acknowledged Alex's presence before returning to his seat. 'I've just taken a call from the Chief Constable of Hertfordshire Police. He tells me that his control centre has just taken a call from a very agitated DI Clocks. It seems that Superintendent Paterson has gone across their borders again and into the house of Marcus May, the brother of the woman suspected of these child killings.'

'Has he gone to arrest him?' Alex asked.

Anderson shook his head. 'Not to my knowledge. It seems he went out there with a female colleague and that's it.'

'Is that a problem, sir?'

Anderson glared at her. 'Yes. It is a problem. Two problems to be exact. First, he received information yesterday regarding the possible whereabouts of a suspect in Hertfordshire. I spoke to the Chief Constable and he insisted that his officers would raid the house and that they go only to pick up any prisoner. I relayed that to Paterson and he wilfully disobeyed me. He and Clocks and a posse of armed police arrived before the Hertfordshire officers and stormed the house. It was empty but it caused all sorts of problems with the CC. I called Paterson and Clocks in and bollocked them and gave a firm instruction that they were not to go back unless I gave them authority to do so.'

'Second. If he is going out to make an arrest, Paterson should have contacted me in the first instance to get my permission and then I would have called Hertfordshire to inform them of his intentions and that an officer from the Met would be on their ground. Paterson knew this. Clocks knew this. And, *again*, they've disobeyed me. Considering it's just the two of them, they may need urgent backup and without knowledge of them even being in Hertfordshire, how would local officers know?'

'I see your point.'

'And if he isn't going to make an arrest, what the bloody hell is he up to now?'

Alex frowned. 'I'm sorry, sir. I don't know. Maybe he went to ask him some questions.'

Anderson put his hands behind his back and went back to staring out of the window. 'Maybe. But if either of those two scenarios were true, why didn't he take or at least inform DI Clocks? Those two are like bloody conjoined twins.' Anderson turned back to her, not expecting her to have an answer.

'The Chief Constable has sent officers to the address urgently as Clocks believes Paterson and the woman detective he's with could be in imminent danger. So, again, if he hasn't informed Clocks then he's up to something. Something bloody dodgy I would think.'

Alex gave a slight shrug. None of this sounded right to her.

'When this is over, I want Paterson suspended pending a full investigation. Am I on solid ground?'

'Do we know if he's been authorised by anyone at all? His commander perhaps?'

Anderson glared at her. 'I just said. I'm the only one who can authorise him and I absolutely did not.'

'Was he given a written instruction not to visit this man unless he had authorisation?'

'He knows what I told him.'

'Sir, with respect, that's not what I asked.'

Anderson fixed her with a stare. 'No. He was not given a written instruction.'

'Well, then, I have to say you may be on shaky ground without a written instruction. From what you've told me about both Paterson and Clocks, they will both likely deny you said that. Paterson could simply say that he received urgent information that necessitated him keeping a low profile. Murder investigation. Can't trust anyone. That sort of thing. I don't think failing to inform another constabulary of his being on their ground warrants his suspension.'

'Can't trust the Commissioner of Police? Are you serious?'

'Can't trust anyone these days, sir. That's what he'd say. That's what I would say if it were me. Can I just ask . . . does he need permission from Hertfordshire to arrest someone on their ground? Is he legally obliged to inform them of his presence?'

Anderson glared at her. 'No. Only if it necessitates the use of firearms. Then we have to inform them.'

'And has he taken a gun with him?'

'I have no idea. They did yesterday.'

'But we're talking about today.'

Anderson took a deep breath and pulled his shoulders back. 'Look . . . the man continues to break rules and regulations on an almost daily basis and it's about time he was brought to heel. I want him disciplined with a view to his dismissal. I need you to talk this over with Legal *today*. I need you to find out if there is anything, *anything* in that bastard file of his, that I can have him for. Find me something criminal in there that I can use to hand him his arse once and for all. Understood?'

'Sir?' she said.

'What is it?' As far as he was concerned, the meeting was over. She had her instructions.

She looked up at him. He didn't like what he saw there, a streak of stifled impertinence or insubordination perhaps. That was the heart of the problem: you allowed people like Paterson and Clocks to get away with insolence and indiscipline for long enough and the malaise soon infected others. 'Nothing, sir,' she said at last. 'Not important.'

'Come back to me this afternoon with something. Off you go.'

Alex stood herself up, looking flustered and irritated. Well she'd just have to learn to do her job and do what she was told.

CHAPTER THIRTY-TWO

It was the screaming that woke him up this time. It started as a small whining noise in his head and turned into a loud high-pitched squeal. He snapped his head up and saw Marcus standing behind Carrie. Her eyes burned with anger and she fought against her restraints, chair hopping in small movements around the room.

Marcus was smiling at Paterson as he raised the scalpel high. His eyes pleaded with Marcus not to do what he was about to do.

'It seems, Ray, that your friends are a lot closer than I expected.' Paterson could now hear several sirens in the distance. He knew they were coming for them. He knew they weren't going to make it in time. He shook his head. *Don't. Please don't.* He looked away.

'Paterson.' Marcus's voice changed. Deeper. Commanding.

Paterson looked at him.

Marcus smiled. 'Thank you. Now, pay attention.' He slowly pushed the scalpel into the side of Carrie's neck. Her eyes went wide and she looked straight at Paterson, unable to comprehend what had just happened.

Marcus twisted the knife then yanked it upwards and out. A jet of blood squirted out of her neck and sprayed around the room as she fought to release herself one last time. Marcus was careful to keep out of her way and he danced lightly from side to side until Carrie slowed down, her strength ebbing away with her life.

As life faded from Carrie Gedmine, Paterson hung his head as a deep despair took the place of anger. Acid-filled tears burned his eyes and dripped slowly onto the floor. His chest heaved as he began to sob. He could do nothing. Nothing.

In the distance, the sirens grew louder.

Marcus walked over to Paterson. He didn't move. If it was his time, he was ready. Not a bad thing really, he thought to himself.

Marcus looked down at Paterson then grabbed Paterson's hair and yanked his head back. They locked eyes.

Marcus raised the scalpel.

Paterson felt a sudden calmness wash over him. A peace he hadn't felt for a long, long time. An image of Lisa, his dead wife, flashed into his mind. Defiance in his heart, he was ready.

Marcus lowered the scalpel. 'I told you. It was this I would take.' He put his thumb on Paterson's cheek and pulled up the flap of skin. Paterson grimaced. 'But . . . it takes time and I'm afraid I don't have enough left. So, I will leave now but we *will* continue this, Ray. And I *will* pick up where I left off.' Marcus retreated quickly from the room.

Paterson closed his eyes and lowered his head. Three minutes later, he heard the sound of tyres screeching to a halt outside the house, shouting, panicked voices and the sound of running feet crunching on the gravel drive. The door was kicked in and the house filled with police officers, desperate to find them both.

The first officer that found them stopped in his tracks, clearly aghast at what he was looking at. Blood spattered the walls and ceiling. Carrie tied to a chair, head to one side, eyes staring, tape across her mouth, her clothing drenched in blood. Then he turned to Paterson and grimaced at what he saw.

The officer snapped out of it and shouted, a mixture of panic and fear in his voice. Feet scrambled up the stairs and more officers piled into the room to witness a sight that would probably stay with them their whole lives. There was no playbook for this scenario and they clearly didn't quite know what to do. One of them, an older PC, was the first to snap out of it and take charge. He grabbed at his radio.

'Control from Nine-Eight-Four. We need the paramedics here at the May house urgently. We have officers down. I repeat. We have officers down. I also need the duty officer and CID here. Now!' He looked to another officer standing by the door. 'Get a first aid kit from the car. Move yourself.'

The older PC pulled the tape gently from Paterson's mouth, talking softly to him as he did so. He panicked when Paterson's face started to move with the tape. He went even more gently and managed to remove one side without causing any more damage. The silver tape flapped back. Paterson instinctively licked his lips.

'It's okay, fellah. We got you now. An ambulance is coming. Don't worry.'

Paterson looked at him. The officer moved toward his arms and began to pull at the tape.

'Anyone got a knife?' he called to his colleagues. Paterson winced.

'It's okay. It's okay.'

* * *

Heaving, panting and sweating, Johnny Clocks pushed his way into the house behind Lyndsey. Jackie was still struggling to stand up and was a good five hundred yards behind.

'Where are they?' Lyndsey shouted to the first uniform she saw.

'Upstairs,' was the only reply she got.

'Ray! Ray! We're coming. We're coming.' Clocks struggled to get the words out his mouth and stumbled up the stairs. He was caught by one or two of the officers that lined the stairwell. They pulled him to his feet and helped him on his way.

As he reached the top of the stairs, he heard Lyndsey let out a small moan. He staggered into the room. The small semi-circle of uniforms turned as he held onto the doorframe for support. His breathing was the only sound in the room.

They stepped aside and Clocks saw him. Lyndsey was standing with her hand clamped over her mouth. She spun around, blocking out her view of the man she loved as a friend. Her eyes filled instantly with tears.

'Hi, Timex,' Paterson's voice shaky, barely audible. 'Where've you been? You're late again.'

'Oh, fuck. What the . . .'

Clocks fell to his knees in front of him. 'Jesus Christ, Ray.'

'It's all right, mate. Bad day at the office, that's all.' Paterson gave him the weakest of smiles.

One of the uniformed PCs, an older guy, had cut through the tape on Paterson's arms and legs and released him. The first thing Paterson did was gently touch his cheek. Clocks saw the extent of the wound now and closed his eyes.

'I'm Nick Damien, sir,' the older PC said. 'Paramedics are on their way. I've called for a first aid kit.'

Jackie stumbled her way into the room. She gasped when she saw Paterson.

'Oh, God! Ray!' She heaved the words out.

PC Damien tapped Clocks gently on the shoulder. 'Sir . . .'

Clocks looked up at him. The PC looked toward Carrie. Clocks followed.

'Oh, fuck. No. Carrie!' Clocks, still on his knees, slid across the room to her, totally unaware he was sliding through her blood.

'Oh, fuckin' hell. Carrie . . . Carrie . . .'

Lyndsey turned, her hand still over her mouth. She shook her head as she saw her friend and stifled a scream. Jackie's legs gave out and she collapsed into a sitting position.

The younger PC came running through the door carrying a first aid kit. He set it down by Paterson and opened it up.

PC Damien grabbed a handful of bandages and cotton pads, ripping the packets open with his teeth. 'Hold this under your chin, mate,' he said to Paterson and handed him one of the pads. It wasn't quite big enough to cover the cut but it would have to do. Paterson took the pad and PC Damien began to wrap a gauze bandage over his head and under his chin. He did the same for the other side. When he'd finished, Paterson tried to stand.

'Take it easy, sir. Don't move until the ambulance gets here. Please.' PC Damien showed genuine concern.

'I'll be okay, mate. It's just a nick,' Paterson quipped. 'Had worse than this shaving.' His voice was weak and shaky. The PC didn't seem to know whether to laugh or cry.

Damien and Clocks helped Paterson to his feet and held him for a second or two as he regained his balance. Paterson nodded. Clocks knew that the policeman in him was about to kick in.

'Everybody!' Paterson called.

Everyone turned.

'Outside, please. This is an active crime scene.'

The uniformed assembly just looked at him. A man with his face sliced open, covered in blood, bandages wrapped around his head and tied off into what resembled a set of bunny ears, his colleague dead and his other colleagues in a daze, and he was still taking control.

'I appreciate your help, I really do. But, you have to leave. Please assemble in the garden and wait for instructions. Come on. Out you go.' Paterson's voice was stronger now, firmer. He looked across at Carrie and took a deep breath.

The officers began to file out of the room until there was just Paterson, Clocks, Lyndsey and Jackie left.

'Where is he, Ray?' Clocks said. 'Where'd he go? You know, don't you?' Is he still in here? The mad sister said there was a room behind the walls. That right?'

Paterson shook his head. 'I think there possibly is a room. Maybe that's how he got the jump on us. But, no. He's gone. But he's not gone far. He left a few minutes before the locals arrived.'

'What? Why didn't you say?' Clocks looked out of the window, scanning the fields for movement. He saw him. 'There!' Clocks pointed into the distance. 'Fucker's runnin' for it. He's heading over to the old boy's house. The old villain.'

Paterson squinted into the distance. 'Gotta get to him in case he hurts them, too.'

Clocks noticed that Marcus's run looked ungainly. 'Is he carryin' somethin'?'

Paterson said nothing.

'He is. Looks like . . . fuck me! That's a kid, ain't it? He's carrying a kiddie, ain't 'e?'

Paterson spun around, nearly falling. Clocks grabbed his shoulder.

'Woah, there! Where d'you think you're goin'?'

Paterson shot him a *dumb question* look.

'Oh, no you're not, matey. Don't you even think about it. You wait 'ere for an ambulance. I'll go an' get 'im.'

Paterson shook his head. 'He's mine, John. Mine. You understand?'

Clocks had seen that look in his friend's eyes too many times to know argument was a waste of time. Something had clicked over in the back of Paterson's head and no one would stop him. Not now.

'Ray,' said Lyndsey. 'Please. Wait for the medics.'

He ignored her and made his way over to the door.

'You sure you're up to this?' said Clocks.

'Very sure.'

'We'll need a car.'

'Plenty downstairs.'

'Let's go and get one, then.' Paterson headed for the door.

'Ray . . . for God's sake!' Jackie said. 'Let the locals get him. You're in shock, for God's sake.'

'Nope. I'm a controlled rage. This is personal.' He looked across at Carrie for the last time. 'Personal.'

Jackie stood aside. She understood.

'Ray . . . Johnny . . .' Lyndsey said. 'Don't do anything stupid boys. Please.'

Both men half-ran, half-staggered down the stairs, adrenaline the only thing keeping them both going. Lyndsey and Jackie followed behind.

'I need a car,' said Paterson to the crowd of uniforms out in the garden. 'Whose is that four-by-four?'

'Sir,' said PC Damien. 'What are you doing?'

'Whose is it?' he said, ignoring the question.

'It's mine, actually,' said PC Damien.

'Keys,' said Paterson and he made a grabbing motion with one hand.

The PC hesitated for a second but caught the look in Paterson's eyes and threw him the keys.

'It'll be okay, mate,' he said to PC Damien. 'Just something I need to do quickly before I go to the hospital. Thank you for your help up there, fellah. I won't forget it.'

Paterson passed the keys to Clocks.

'You can drive today, John.'

As they stood by the doors, a shout went up and they heard the screeching of tyres on gravel. A black BMW slid to a halt and Marcus's wife jumped out of the car, a look of anxiety on her face.

'What's happened?' she screamed to a uniformed PC barring her way. 'What's going on?'

'Let her through,' Paterson called to him. 'It's okay.'

The PC stood aside and Karen ran toward the grim-faced group of police officers.

'Jesus Christ!' She looked at Paterson. 'What happened to you?'

'Courtesy of your husband. Turns out he's still the same vicious no-good bastard he always was. Except he's turned it up a notch or two.'

'I . . . I'm . . . so, so sorry.'

'Not as sorry as me, love,' said Paterson.

'Why did he do that?'

Clocks could tell by the look on her face where she was headed. He'd heard it all before. She was going to row herself out of any crimes, deny all knowledge, say she had no idea of the kind of man her husband was. That's what people did when the world was about to cave in on them.

'Oi!' said Clocks.

She turned to face him.

'You're fuckin' nicked.'

'What? Why?'

'Before you even start, love, there's no way you didn't know what he was up to.'

Karen looked genuinely perplexed. 'I didn't. Truly. What's happened? Tell me. Please!'

'So you don't know anything about him trying to be the next Geppetto?'

'What? I don't understa—'

'We know he's been cuttin' up kids and stitchin' them together to make a real child.'

Lyndsey caught Karen's arm as her legs seemed to fold up underneath her.

Clocks stared down at her. He felt no compassion. He'd seen it all before. 'Oh, get up, love. I'm not fallin' for that ol' bollocks.'

Lyndsey hauled her back up straight.

'I didn't know. I didn't. I swear to God.'

'Religious are ya?'

'Please! He's a good man. He didn't mean it. He didn't . . .'

Paterson snorted. 'Yeah. He's a good man. This and cutting a woman's throat was just an accident, wasn't it?'

'I'm so sorry. So sorry.'

Paterson shook his head.

'Where is he?' She was visibly shaking.

'He's busy doing a runner at the moment.' Paterson nodded his head toward the field behind him.

'You have to help him. Please. *Please.*'

'Help 'im?' said Clocks. 'Oh, yeah. That's just what we're gonna go do. Help him. I'm gonna help him depart this fuckin' world, love. That's the only help he's gettin' from me.'

Karen's eyes, full of tears, looked helplessly at him.

'Please. No. He's not well. He's sick. He has a condition . . . please. I'm begging you.'

'He's got a condition all right. It's called mad-as-a-bastard-itis. But don't worry, love. Doctor Clocks and Doctor Paterson have a cure lined up.'

Clocks called over to the group of uniformed locals. 'One of you 'ang on to her for me until I come back. She's under arrest.'

'Wait!' Karen said. 'I can help. I can help you.'

'To do what?' said Paterson.

'I can get him to give himself up. He'll listen to me. Please?'

'I don't particularly want him to give himself up. Kind of hoping he wouldn't.' Paterson unconsciously touched his jaw.

'Please — Ray, isn't it? You're friends. Old friends. He's not well. He needs help. You know that. Please. I don't want him hurting anyone else.'

Paterson looked at Clocks, then Lyndsey, then Jackie.

'Bring her,' he said.

Clocks shook his head. Bad idea.

Lyndsey pushed Karen into the back of the four-by-four, swept a pile of evidence bags and papers into the footwell and slid in next to her. Jackie got in the other side sandwiching the woman between them. Clocks spun the car in a 180-degree scanning the view as he went.

'There,' said Paterson. He pointed to a rickety wooden gate that led into the field where Marcus was running toward a house.

'Go straight through that gate, there.' Paterson said.

'It's locked,' said Clocks.

'Go straight *through* that gate,' Paterson repeated.

Clocks grinned. 'Yessir.'

He gunned the engine.

CHAPTER THIRTY-THREE

Johnny Clocks smashed through the gate sending bits of old wood flying in all directions. He bounced the car across the field until he caught sight of a little speck in the distance. Marcus was still heading for the house of old Lee Angel. From what Clocks could see, there was nothing beyond it for a mile or so.

'He's done for, Ray. He's gonna 'ave to make a stand in there.'

Paterson didn't answer. He stared ahead.

'What the fuck 'appened in there for Chrissake?'

'He was in the house. Hiding.' Paterson still stared ahead as he replayed the events back to himself.

'I was downstairs, Carrie went up. I heard a bumping sound, called her, got no answer, went upstairs and the fucker jumped me from behind and put a polythene bag over my head. He knew what he was doing. I couldn't get up. I blacked out and he had us both secured when I came to.'

'Jesus. Then what?'

The car bounced violently as it went over a large mound of earth.

'Then he started cutting my face off.'

Clocks stole a quick glance at Paterson. 'Did it hurt?'

‘Of course it fucking hurt. It hurt bad but not as bad as watching him kill Carrie.’

Karen let out a small sob. ‘I’m so sorry . . .’

‘Shut the fuck up, bitch,’ snarled Clocks. ‘You’re in the fucking shit too.’

He swung the wheel to swerve around a small herd of panicked cows who were already breaking into a trot.

Paterson looked to the house. ‘There. He’s gone in.’

‘What’s the plan, then?’

‘Simple. I go in after him.’

‘And me?’

‘You stay outside.’

‘Nope. He’s a big mental bastard who’s just cut yer fuckin’ face open an’ he ain’t goin’ down without a fight and we both know ’e can fight.’

‘Yep. He’s going to have to.’

‘Yeah, but I mean ’e can proper fight. He’s a right dirty bastard.’

‘Clocksy, you’ve never really seen me fight, have you?’

‘Couple of times an’ that’s what worries me. You fight like a little girl.’

‘Well, today is different. I’m going to kill this bastard with my bare hands. See if I don’t.’

‘I know you’ve got the ’ump but you’re forgettin’ we’ve got his missus in the back. Good chance she’ll grass you up.’

‘Is there? We’ll have see about that too then, won’t we?’

Clocks went silent.

They were about five hundred yards away from the house now. The door was closed.

Clocks shook his head slightly. ‘Can I at least come in an’ watch then?’

Paterson turned to him. ‘Nope. But listen, whatever happens do not interfere. You understand? Even if it looks like he’s got me, don’t butt in. I can handle him.’

Clocks glanced at him. ‘Really?’

Three hundred yards.

'Really. But, just in case he happens to kill me, run like fuck mate because he will be *severely* pissed off.'

Two hundred yards.

'Ha! I ain't runnin' nowhere. When you ever known me to run?'

'Just run, Clocksy. Lyndsey. Jackie. You too.'

'We can handle him between us, Ray. I'm sure,' said Lyndsey.

He half turned his head to speak to Lyndsey. 'Did you bring a gun?'

'No.'

'Then you can't handle him.'

One hundred yards.

Paterson looked back out the windscreen and began taking off the bandages on his head.

'What you doin'?' said Clocks.

'Making sure he can't strangle me or break my neck.'

'Christ. This isn't good. Your face is still bleedin'.'

'Badly?'

'Depends on your definition of badly I s'pose.'

Paterson could feel blood seeping out from his wounds. He figured bleeding was still a better option than Marcus strangling him with the bandages. 'Drop me out front, go around the back. If he runs, knock the prick down. Don't hesitate, John. We'll sort out the rest later.' Paterson opened his door and put one foot out.

'Mind yer face, Ray. If the fucker gets hold of that . . .'

Clocks jammed on the brakes and slid the car into a tight handbrake turn. As the tyres squealed and rubber burned the concrete driveway, Paterson stepped calmly out of the moving car and walked toward the front door. Clocks floored the accelerator again, straightened it up and disappeared around the back of the house.

Paterson walked up to the front door and booted it straight in. He stepped inside the hallway. Off to the right he could see a large open-plan living room with a couple of sofas, two comfy chairs, a coffee table and a sixty-seven-inch TV. The house was quiet, save for the ticking of a large grandfather clock. If he could pick a place for a fight, this would be it. Plenty of space. Leading off to the left at the back of the room he could see a large standing freezer. The kitchen. A more than adequate supply of weapons.

Paterson stopped in his tracks. On the stairs, he caught a glimpse of a small child sitting with its head pressed against the bannister spindles. Walking over, he felt his stomach turn as he realised what he was looking at. A patchwork child, blackened from rot, grotesque.

A groaning sound pulled his attention away. Cautiously, he made his way toward the kitchen making sure he was well away from the walls and out in the open space. As the kitchen came into view, he saw a pool of blood. Sitting in the middle of it was old Lee Angel cradling the body of his wife. Paterson could see blood seeping from a wound in his head but at least he was alive.

Lee looked up at Paterson, then back at his wife.

'Help her. Please.' Paterson knew he couldn't. She was way past that. He made a show of pressing his fingers to the carotid artery in her neck.

'I'm so sorry,' he said. 'She's gone.'

The old man let out a wail, the long drawn out moan of a man who had lost the woman he'd spent his entire life with. Gone in a second.

'Where'd he go, mate? I'll get him for you. I'll make him pay.'

The old man went back to cradling his wife.

'Listen to me. You can't help your wife now but you can help yourself. Hide somewhere in case he comes back. Will you do that for me? Please.'

Lee ignored him. Paterson could understand that. When his wife was murdered, all he wanted was to be with her. To hold her. To will the life back into her.

Paterson balled his fists. 'Marcus! Where you hiding? Come on out, you dirty motherfucker. Playtime.'

He listened carefully. All he could hear was the car outside. He looked through the living room window and saw Clocks sitting behind the wheel.

Paterson suddenly broke into a run, shouting, 'John! John! Move!'

CHAPTER THIRTY-FOUR

Clocks heard a loud bang as his window went in, showering him in glass. Jackie screamed. He ducked to his left instinctively but not far enough. Marcus, having punched through the glass, grabbed his hair and pulled him toward him. Clocks swung out blindly. Nothing connected.

Lyndsey, shocked, threw her door open and scrambled out of the car. Jackie did likewise. 'Stay there!' she screamed at Karen. 'Don't move.'

Marcus dragged Clocks out through the window. Clocks yelped in pain as his chest was dragged across the remnants of broken glass and the hard metal of the window frame. Marcus dropped him onto the ground at the same time as Paterson burst out through the back door.

Lyndsey rounded the car and lunged at Marcus. His vicious backhand stunned her and knocked her to the ground. He started to climb into the driver's seat. Jackie froze.

'John. Stop him!' Paterson called.

Clocks staggered to his feet and lunged at Marcus, grabbing onto his arm and pulling him backward. Paterson launched a flying kick at the car door and slammed it into Marcus's back. Clocks went with him as Marcus's momentum violently changed direction. He crashed down onto his back again. Marcus bounced off the bodywork of the car and fell.

Paterson ran around to Clocks. He could see he had blood coming from his cheeks and forehead. Bits of glass. His shirt was covered in blood. Christ. 'Stay there, John. Leave it!'

Clocks nodded. His priority was Lyndsey. 'I'm all right, Ray. Just fuckin' do 'im will ya.'

Paterson turned to see Marcus scrambling to his feet. He walked over to him. Marcus looked up. Paterson kicked his legs out from under him and sent him back down.

Marcus landed on his tailbone. 'Fuck!'

'Stay down,' said Paterson.

Marcus smiled and pulled himself to his feet. Paterson let him get up this time. Marcus staggered back onto the car for a second, his hand on his back. 'That fucking hurt, Ray.'

Paterson said nothing. His eyes cold. His heart colder still.

'You sure you want to fight me, Ray? You know what I'm capable of.'

Paterson turned sideways on to his opponent, dropped his left hand down to stomach height and held his right hand up. He wanted to fight.

'Okay. If it's what you want. Don't say I didn't warn you.'

Paterson knew that Marcus would go for his face. It was obvious. Whatever else happened, Paterson couldn't let him grab a lump of skin.

Marcus pushed himself off of the car and walked toward Paterson. He took up his fighting stance, similar to Paterson's but both hands up. He stepped toward Paterson and flicked his right hand out. Paterson stepped back, dodged the blow, stepped straight back in and punched Marcus square on the chin. The big man staggered back a couple of steps and shook his head.

He came forward again. Same move. Same result except Paterson hit him in the mouth, snapping the bigger man's head back.

Marcus scowled.

Over to Paterson's right, Johnny Clocks was helping Lyndsey to her feet and making sure that she was okay. Then he made his way hurriedly to the back of the car — Lyndsey had said something to him.

* * *

Marcus saw Clocks. 'Where are you going? Two against one, eh?'

'Nah. You two carry on playin' together. I'm lookin' for somethin'. Don't mind me.' Clocks put his head inside the back door, looking into the footwell. He ignored Karen.

'Please. Please don't hurt him. He's not well.'

'Too late for that sweet'eart. Fucker's ruined me suit. It's bloody covered in claret an' we both know 'e won't pay the cleanin' bill so, no. I'm fed up with people ruinin' me suits. Fuck 'im.' He picked up a large polythene evidence bag and slammed the door behind him.

* * *

Paterson never took his eyes off Marcus.

Marcus grinned. 'So this is it then, Ray. Right here, right now, I am going to finish what I started. I am going to take your face for my collection.'

Paterson simply waited.

Suddenly, Marcus charged at him. Paterson moved fast, swinging his back leg around, stepping to the side and avoiding the charge. As Marcus drew level with him, Paterson shoved him hard, taking him clean off his feet. Marcus crashed into the side of the car, his head denting the bonnet as his body jack-knifed sideways. He lay there for a second, stunned.

'Up,' said Paterson, his voice devoid of any form of emotion. He stood square on now. He wanted Marcus to charge him, and he did. Paterson took the full weight of the man and fell backward into a roll, his foot in the man's stomach. He pulled Marcus over the top of him and straightened his leg pushing Marcus high in the air and sending him crashing onto his back. Paterson was up and already turned waiting for Marcus as he landed.

Marcus groaned in pain. He lay there for a second or two, recovering his breath and composure. 'Shit. You been practicing, Ray? You were never this good as a kid. That was slick.' He hauled himself up and turned to face Paterson. 'Okay. I've got you now. Got your measure. We do this properly now.'

The two men turned sideways again and began to circle each other.

Clocks poked his head around the side of the car and saw the two of them circling. 'Fuckin' get on with it, will ya? Like a couple of ol' women, the pair of ya.' He leaned on the back of the car, folded his arms and watched. In his hand he held the large polythene property bag.

Marcus was the first to move. He swung a right. Paterson blocked it and kicked him in the lower shin. Marcus went down slightly.

Paterson backed up as the man got to his feet again.

'Not bad. Fast. Come on, Ray. Give me your face. Let me rip it from you.'

Paterson raised an eyebrow. Now was the time for trash talk. 'Come get it, babykiller.'

Marcus glared at him.

'You're a tough bastard killing and cutting up kids but when it comes to fighting man to man, you're a fucking waste of space. I thought you might be the challenge you once were, not the fucking joke you are now, you pathetic bastard.'

Marcus wiped away the blood drooling from his mouth and spat out the remainder. 'Is that so?'

'Seems to be. You're not doing too well at the moment, are you?'

'I've beaten you so many times before. You're nothing to me.'

'That's when we were kids. Tables have turned, eh? I remember when you used to be a right handful. I guess killing kiddies has made you weak. Kids don't hit back, do they? Oh, and by the way, before I kill you, just to let you know, Elizabeth's dead.' An outright lie designed to infuriate his opponent. 'And *I* killed her. Crazy bitch went for me. I ended up snapping her scrawny neck. Cracked it like a fucking twig. It was beautiful.'

Marcus's face contorted with rage. 'My sister?'

'Yep. Stone fucking dead and good riddance to the mad bitch. One fucking lunatic less to worry about.'

'You killed . . . my sister?'

'Why not? Someone had to. Gave me a bloody good feeling too.'

Marcus ran at Paterson, growling with pain.

Paterson stood his ground. He dropped low and punched Marcus in the stomach. It was like hitting a wall. Marcus grabbed Paterson's head and swung him into a headlock. With his free hand he went for Paterson's cheek and grabbed a flap of slippery skin. Paterson growled with pain as he felt Marcus grab his cheek and start pulling. Paterson saw Clocks move forward in his peripheral vision.

Paterson bent his knees and dropped lower. He elbowed Marcus in the balls three times in rapid succession. Marcus grunted with pain and released his grip enough for Paterson to drop lower. He reached back and grabbed the bottom of Marcus's trouser legs and pulled at them. Marcus fell backward, banging his head off the ground again. Paterson sprung up, turned and stamped on his face.

Clocks stopped abruptly. No doubt Paterson's words rang in his ears. '*Leave him. He's mine.*' Paterson hoped so.

Marcus's nose exploded under Paterson's shoe. He groaned and rolled his head to one side. Paterson kicked it back the other way.

Paterson could feel his cheek burn and he patted it with his hand. He hoped Marcus hadn't made the damage too much worse. 'Up you get, Childkiller. Long way to go yet.'

Marcus pulled himself into a sitting position before standing up. He held his hands up.

Paterson beckoned him on.

Marcus swung a left. Paterson blocked it easily but walked straight into a kick to the knee. A blinding flash of pain lit up in his head as his leg gave out from under him. He dropped low leaving his head exposed. Marcus kneed him in the face sending him sprawling. He stood over Paterson and reached down grabbing him by the shirt. He reached for Paterson's cheek again but the sudden weight of Johnny Clocks piling into him knocked him clean off his feet.

As soon as they hit the ground, Clocks rolled off and got to his feet.

'Come on then, you cowson! Let's 'ave it! Me 'n' you. Come on!'

Marcus pulled himself up yet again and his facial expression left no doubt that he was not in the mood to be fighting someone as inexperienced and hopeless as Clocks.

Clocks ran at him, head down. Marcus stepped aside and pushed downward with both hands, slamming Clocks face-first into the ground.

'Clocksy . . . no!' Paterson scrambled to his feet. 'Don't . . .'

Marcus swung a vicious kick into Clocks's stomach.

'Childkiller!' Paterson called. 'Come on! We're not fucking done yet!'

Marcus spun around and honed in on Paterson. He moved in fast.

Paterson knew he had only one real way to beat his man. Deception.

His face, smeared with blood from his nose, his arms dangling down by his side, he wobbled, looking like he could barely stand. Easy meat for Marcus. 'C'mon . . .' he slurred. 'C'mon.'

Marcus swung a punch and caught Paterson on the side of his head. Paterson dropped.

Lyndsey moved forward.

Paterson held up his hand. 'Leave him . . . mine.'

'Mine?' said Marcus. 'I don't think so. Up you get Paterson. My turn now.'

Paterson pulled himself up onto one knee and stopped. As Marcus moved in, Paterson stood up sharply and caught the backhand of Marcus's fist full in the mouth. He staggered back a few steps. Marcus backhanded him again, knocking him backward. Paterson dropped his hands by his side. His legs buckled. He spat out blood. 'C'mon . . .'

Marcus went in for a third backhander.

Paterson dropped his weight slightly and, with a speed that belied his demeanour, threw a tremendous punch that landed on the left side of Marcus's jaw. Marcus's legs gave way and he struggled to keep upright. Paterson dropped lower and punched him in the balls, doubling him over.

As Marcus fell to his knees, Paterson side-kicked his right arm between the shoulder and the elbow and did the same to the other side. Marcus had lost the use of his arms. Paterson kneed him full in the face, knocking his torso backward and his head hit the floor with a thud.

Seeing Marcus lying there, folded backward on his knees with his head on the ground, Paterson dropped his hands to his side. It was finished.

'Fuck me blind with a baseball bat,' said Clocks between rasping breaths. He was on all fours holding his stomach, trying to get up. 'Turns out you're not a big girly after all. Didn't know you could fight like that.'

Paterson turned his head toward him, Marcus still in his peripheral vision.

'How's your stomach?' he said.

'It's a bit upset,' said Clocks. 'And, you're welcome.'

CHAPTER THIRTY-FIVE

'Ray. Watch out.' Clocks warned as old Lee Angel came storming out of the back door of his house. Clocks noticed two things about him: he was walking with purpose, a man on a mission; he was pointing a double-barrelled shotgun in their direction.

Paterson had already seen him.

'Lee!' he called as the man advanced. 'Put the gun down.' He raised and lowered his hands couple of times. 'Please.'

The man ignored him and continued on.

'Ray . . .' said Clocks. 'Get out of the way.'

'Bastard killed my wife,' the old man raged. 'Stuck a kitchen knife in her throat. She didn't do anything to him. Why'd he do that? Why'd he have to hurt her? Why?'

Paterson saw the tears streaming down the man's face.

'I don't know. He's sick in the head. I'm so sorry, but please, don't do this. Let us deal with him.'

The old man stopped walking.

'Get the fuck out of my way, copper. I'll deal with him.'

'Can't let you do that, Lee. If you do, you'll be a murderer. You don't want to do that. You'll go away.'

'Big deal. I've done bird before. As it happens, for murder. I ain't fuckin' worried about going inside again.'

'Think of your family. They'll need you now more than ever.'

'They'll manage. Now get the fuck out of my way. Last time.'

'Lee . . .'

'Two rounds in here, copper. I only need one for him. You want the other?' He pointed the shotgun at Paterson's head. 'Do you? Do you?'

Marcus, unable to move his limbs, strained to raise his body into a kneeling position. He grinned and spat a thick gob of blood on the ground.

'Is he the scum that killed all those kids?' Lee jabbed the shotgun in Marcus's direction. 'Is he? He is, ain't he?'

Paterson nodded. 'Yeah, he is. He's going to prison for the rest of his life so your shooting him won't help. It just means he doesn't get to suffer. He needs to suffer.'

'He won't fuckin' suffer. He'll be put in a cell and given everything he wants. We both know how it works.' Lee walked forward again.

Marcus, much to Paterson's surprise, managed to pull himself back up into a sitting position and his head rocked forward. He shook his head before looking at Paterson. 'Don't let him shoot me, Ray. You're a copper.' Marcus's mouth and teeth were red with blood. He eyed Paterson, a slight grin on his face.

Paterson stepped forward. 'Lee . . . please . . .'

The old man raised the gun and pointed it at Paterson as he walked.

'Fuck off out of it, copper,' he said. 'Last time I warn you.'

Paterson had already worked it out. Lee Angel was close. Close enough for Paterson to disarm him. He was much the faster man and would have the element of surprise on his side. Paterson looked into the old man's eyes, rheumy from age and running with tears, he took a deep breath and stepped aside. For all the things he'd done, Marcus deserved to die and he wasn't going to take a bullet for him.

The old man stood in front of Marcus and pressed the shotgun to his forehead. 'We were married best part of fifty-one years, raised three kids, got five grandchildren. Same age as the kids you killed. We were good to you and your wife, you no-good dirty bastard, and you fuckin' do this to us.' Marcus closed his eyes a second before his head disappeared in a red mist of blood and bone.

'Oh, fuck!' Clocks shouted.

'Jesus!' Paterson's eyes widened.

The old man looked on as Marcus's headless body jerked back and collapsed into the dirt.

Lee turned to Paterson. 'I ain't going back to no prison, copper.' In one quick move, he swung the shotgun up and under his chin and pulled the trigger.

CHAPTER THIRTY-SIX

From the back seat of the police car, Karen May watched the scene unfold in front of her and gasped in horror as she watched her husband's head disappear and his body pitch backward onto the gravel path.

Tears filled her eyes as the man she had loved since childhood left her and she knew then that there was nothing left for her in this world. It was over now. She felt it then, the anger. The fury. She knew what she had to do. Take revenge.

She reached inside her blouse and pressed her hand against her left breast. The hardness of the flick knife she always carried pressed against her flesh. She bent down and snatched up a plastic bag, pushed her weight against the car door and stormed out of the vehicle, her focus on Paterson.

* * *

Clocks was the first to see her coming. 'Stay there, love.' He held up his hand.

She marched on.

Paterson and Lyndsey turned. Towards her. She had a look on her face that they had seen many times before. Not grief. Not despair. Pure hatred.

'You bastard!' she screamed at Paterson, still marching toward him. 'You fucking killed him. You could have stopped him. You killed my brother!'

In the second before she closed the gap on him, Paterson was confused.

'Brother?'

Karen lashed out and caught him on the cheek, lifting the flap of skin.

Paterson staggered backward, shocked, as Clocks and Lyndsey rushed toward her. 'Leave her!' Paterson shouted. 'Leave her!'

Karen took another swing but Paterson was ready. He blocked the punch and pushed her backwards.

In a moment, Paterson had it all figured out. 'You? You're Beverley? The missing sister.'

'Bastaaaaaarrrd!' she screamed.

'You're the Childmaker. Not him. Not Elizabeth.' He kicked her full in the chest sending her sprawling on the ground. 'How the fuck did I miss that? *You*.'

''You took my children away. You killed my husband. I'll fucking kill you too, you bastard.' She scrambled to her feet.

'That what the bag's for? You think you're gonna do to me what you did to the kids? Suffocate me? You fucking idiot.'

Paterson slapped her across the face hard, stopping her in her tracks. He snatched the bag off her and in one quick movement pulled the bag down over her head, then stepped forward and behind her pulling down and twisting the bag as he went, sealing off her air supply. Her back to him, Beverley could do nothing as Paterson pulled on the thick plastic bag.

'What's it like, bitch?' he said, teeth gritted and holding the bag tightly as Beverley thrashed about.

In the distance, a cacophony of sirens broke into the moment.

'Ray!' Lyndsey said.

Paterson ignored her and dropped to one knee bending Beverley in half.

'Ray! For Christ's sake! Don't do this! That's not the way. Don't!' She ran toward him. Clocks followed her. Beverley pulled out the flick knife. Clocks and Lyndsey stopped in their tracks at the sight of the blade.

'Knife!' Clocks shouted. Then he ran at the pair.

Karen couldn't get to Paterson so she was trying to get the bag off. She stabbed herself in the cheek once, twice, then stabbed a hole where her mouth was. Blood gushed out of the bag as the blade sliced her lips open. With air coming in, she dropped the knife and clawed at the bag, tearing it away from her face.

Paterson felt the tension loosen on the bag, quickly let go and instinctively rolled forward out of harm's way.

Beverley span around at the same time as Paterson. She coughed furiously as she sucked in as much air as her lungs would allow.

The sirens came closer.

Paterson darted forward and backhand-punched Beverley on the nose. She dropped like a sack of spanners and landed in a heap on the ground. Paterson stood over her. 'Someone secure and nick her,' he said.

Jackie rushed forward and fumbled around in her pockets. 'Shit! Anyone got cuffs?'

Lyndsey threw over her set of plasticuffs.

'Karen! Beverley, or whatever the fuck your name is, you're under arrest for multiple murders. You do not have to say anything . . .'

Jackie grabbed one of Beverley's hands and slipped the plasticuff on. She reached across and pulled up the other hand. There was a second of recognition and shock before Beverley May rammed the knife into her throat, burying it up to the hilt.

CHAPTER THIRTY-SEVEN

Fear gripped Jackie's heart as she staggered backwards, hands clutching at her throat. She made a gurgling noise as the blood began to seep out through her fingers and splashed onto the ground.

Paterson was the first to see what had happened. 'No!'

Clocks caught Paterson break into a run out the corner of his eye and turned to see what was wrong. Shock hit him like a hammer to the chest and paralysed him to the spot.

Beverley, laughing, was lifting herself up when Paterson's kick to the chin rocked her head backward and knocked her spark out. He turned to Jackie and caught her as her legs gave out on her.

'Oh, fuck. No!'

Jackie stared up at him as he lay her on the ground. 'Jack! It's okay, s'okay. I'm gonna get you help. It's coming. It's coming.'

The sirens drew closer.

Lyndsey dropped to her knees and held Jackie's hand. Tears filled her eyes as she looked at her friend.

Everything hit Clocks at once. Then he ran to her. Dropping to his knees beside her, he pushed Paterson out of the way, scooped her body up into his arms and held her. He saw the handle of the knife sticking out of her throat, saw the blood. 'Oh, fuck, Jack. Jesus! Jesus!' Her eyes darted from Paterson to him. She gurgled.

'S'okay. S'okay. It's gonna be okay. I've got ya. Help's coming.' Clocks's tone was as soothing and as reassuring as he could make it.

Jackie stared into his eyes. Her hands slipped away from her throat as life began to leave her. Her eyes flickered.

'No! No, Jack!' yelled Clocks. 'Stay with me! Don't close yer eyes. Please. Listen to me! Stay awake! Stay awake!'

Paterson took her other hand and held it tight as he watched her close her eyes.

'Shhh, shhh. S'okay. Help's comin', Jack. You stay with me, hun. I've gotcha, I've gotcha, You'll be all right.'

Paterson stood up at the sound of urgent shouts behind him.

'Police! Stand still!'

Two Range Rovers had skidded to a halt and the occupants were out of the cars and headed toward them. Two of them had guns pointing at Paterson.

Behind the Range Rovers, more cars were coming. One, a two-man paramedic vehicle.

Paterson looked at Jackie's body, but he couldn't process it. He shouted to them. 'Police! Get the medics here now! Officer down!'

'You! Get down on your knees. Do it!' An armed officer was pointing a handgun at him.

Paterson flushed up. Agitation was turning to blood-red anger and he wasn't getting down on his knees for anyone. 'D'you not hear me?' he growled. 'I said, *officer down*!' Get me the fucking medics, now!'

The firearms officers moved closer, separating from each other as they walked. One went towards Clocks and Lyndsey.

'You! On the ground. Show me your hands.'

Clocks ignored him and carried on holding Jackie and whispering to her.

'Fuck's sake, man!' Paterson shouted at him. 'Leave him alone! We're coppers! That's our friend. He's known her for years! Show a bit of compassion.'

The firearms officer ignored Paterson and circled Clocks until he could see clearly what was happening. And he didn't like what he saw. The white face of a woman, a knife sticking out of her throat and blood everywhere. 'You! Show me your hands! Do it now!'

Three more uniformed officers ran down to join their armed colleagues. All three pulled out their taser guns and pointed them toward the group.

Clocks was stroking Jackie's hair, matted with blood. He whispered, 'I'm sorry,' over and over again.

'Last chance. Show me your hands or else!'

Clocks stopped stroking Jackie's hair and lifted his head. Gently, he laid her down and let out a gut-wrenching scream that startled everyone. When he'd finished, Clocks hauled himself to his feet and wobbled as he struggled to keep himself upright.

Jackie's blood was everywhere. All over his face, his shirt, his trousers, his hands. He turned to face the firearms officer. Then he moved. Slowly. Deliberately. 'Fuck off!' he shouted.

'Hands. Last chance.'

Clocks started toward the armed man. 'Go on then, big boy. Fuckin' do it! Do it!'

Paterson shouted. 'John! No!' He ran toward him. 'What're you doing? Don't!'

Lyndsey was still on her knees, holding Jackie's hand and whispering to her, seemingly oblivious to Clocks's behaviour.

'Stand still!' the officer shouted to Paterson. Paterson ignored him and stood in front of his friend. 'John! Don't!'

Clocks tried to push him away.

'Come on, mate! Shoot me! Do me a fuckin' favour!' He tapped himself between the eyes. 'Put one there. See if you've got the bollocks!'

Paterson kept himself between Clocks and the firearms officer and pushed Clocks back. 'Don't shoot. Do not shoot!

He's unarmed. He's in shock. We're all in shock. Stand down! Stand down!'

Both firearms officers hesitated. Whatever had gone on here, if these were police officers as they claimed, they didn't want to have to shoot them. The officers with tasers began to circle the little group.

Clocks struggled to get past Paterson. 'Mate. Please. Just do it. I'm fuckin' sick of all this! Sick of it!'

His body went suddenly stiff as a board and he shook violently before falling to the floor like a plank of wood.

Paterson saw two wires hanging out Clocks's back and went for the officer holding the taser. 'You fuckin—'. Another officer tased Paterson in the back and he dropped to the floor next to Clocks.

The two men locked tear-filled eyes as they waited for their nightmare to get worse.

A gruff voice from somewhere above them said, 'Whole fucking thing's a mess. Jesus! Look at his face. Right, get 'em cuffed and off to hospital. Get forensics here. Both houses and everything in between is a crime scene. Somebody get onto the Met and inform them what's happened. And they better know what the fuck this is all about.'

'Pulse!' shouted a voice. 'We've got a pulse. Weak. Move!'

Paterson closed his eyes. Perhaps Jackie was tougher than he thought.

CHAPTER THIRTY-EIGHT

Sir Scott Anderson was not in the best of moods. He had been advised that it should be him who held a press conference to inform the public that the Childmaker and his sister were no longer a threat to society. That, he could handle. What stuck in his throat was that he was also forced to extol the virtues of detectives Paterson and Clocks and how Paterson had come within a hair's breadth of losing his face and his life.

The interview was being played back on every news channel. The sound on the TV was turned down but he was watching the part where he had to inform the public that Detective Constable Carrie Gedmine had been brutally murdered, Detective Constable Jackie Hartnett had been within a few minutes of dying and had suffered life-changing injuries, and that the last two victims of Marcus May were an innocent couple in their late seventies, in the wrong place at the right time.

He tore his eyes away from the screen and back to the assembled group of high-ranking police officers he had summoned.

'Fucking heroes, yet again,' he said, with bitter irony.

The room stayed quiet.

Anderson shook his head. 'I don't know how they get away with it time after time. Defies explanation.' It seemed he was talking to himself as opposed to the room.

'Sir?' Assistant Commissioner Sam Morne had been called in on his day off and wasn't in the mood to hear his boss whine on again about the two officers who had become his pet project. 'Why exactly are we here?'

The other two officers from the surveillance squad and the Chief Press Officer nodded their heads. It was a legitimate question.

Anderson returned from his musings and gave Morne the hard stare. 'We need to figure out how we handle this from here on in.'

'How do you mean? What is it we need to handle?'

The hard stare remained on him. AC Morne wasn't the sort to be intimidated, though. He'd worked with Anderson for long enough to have the measure of him. A vindictive bully whom he didn't much care for.

'Before this happened, my intention was to suspend them both for disobeying a direct order not to go to that house. He went. And, as a result, four people lost their lives. Four, for Christ's sake! And he beat the shit out of a woman. The problem here is how it looks, the optics, if I go through with that suspension.'

'Then don't,' said Morne. 'Yes, Paterson ignored your order but I'm sure he had sound reason to. Has he been spoken to yet?'

'No.'

'Then don't you think it best you find out the facts before you act?'

Anderson leaned back in his chair and stretched out his legs. His eyes never left AC Morne's face. 'Let's review the facts then, shall we? Fact . . . Paterson disobeys me. Fact . . . he gets a colleague killed. Fact . . . a second colleague is seriously injured. Fact . . . he gets his face sliced to ribbons. Fact . . . he gets an old woman killed. Fact . . . our killer gets his head blown clean off his shoulders. Fact . . . the man who executed him then blows his own bloody head off. Fact . . . if Paterson had obeyed me then DC Gedmine, May and the Angels would still be alive and DC Hartnett wouldn't be in intensive care. Those, Mr Morne, are the facts as they stand.'

'Yes, sir. I know those facts. But you've missed a few out. Fact . . . Paterson was carrying out his lawful duty as a police officer. Fact . . . this was his case, his suspect. Fact . . . there are still things we don't know about his actions. Fact . . . because of those actions, Marcus May will no longer murder and skin children for whatever perverted reasons he had. Fact . . . nor will his crazy sister wife or whatever the fuck she was.'

A slight smile appeared on Anderson's face. 'Indeed. There is still a lot to know but, as it stands, I believe I have enough to not just suspend him, but to arrest him.'

AC Morne shook his head. 'Do it then. What's stopping you?'

'As I said, the optics.'

'Oh, yes. The bloody optics. You don't want to look bad? So, what you're saying is, you have enough evidence to arrest Paterson, yet you're concerned with how it looks, yes?'

Anderson watched his AC. He could see the man was getting riled.

'Seems to me that you've forgotten that once you have sufficient evidence to arrest someone for a crime — and God knows you've been trying to arrest him for a long time now — you're duty-bound to do so. Looking bad shouldn't be an issue, should it?'

'You seem a little upset, Sam.'

'To be honest, I am. Your obsession with "catching out" these two officers is bordering on the unhealthy. There's no doubt they sail close to the wind, but there is no evidence against them to say they've done anything criminal. Suspicion and speculation, yes, but no evidence. Now, you can have them nicked, sure. But if you want to know how it looks then I'll tell you . . . fucking disgraceful. The majority of people love these two because they do what very few others could, or would, do. The court of public opinion will bury us alive if you take any kind of action against them without rock-solid evidence.'

'And because the people and press love them they get a free pass, do they?' Anderson's own anger was rising. 'Because if that's what you're saying then maybe you shouldn't be a policeman. We're here to uphold the law. To ensure that our officers always uphold the highest standards of integrity and decency. Not to run around the streets of London like a couple of wild west cowboys.'

'In an ideal world, you'd be right,' said AC Morne. 'But we're not in an ideal world. Not even fucking close to one. I'm not prepared to stand around and let you ruin the careers of two men who have more guts, decency and integrity than any of us sitting around in this cosy little office just because you're fucking jealous of them.'

'Jealous?' Anderson looked taken aback.

'Jealous. They're everything you're not and never could be.'

'All right. That's enough.'

AC Morne stood. 'You're right. It is enough. If you insist on going after these men for whatever petty grudge you're harbouring, I won't be supporting you.'

'Very well,' said Anderson. 'I'll expect your resignation on my desk by the end of the day.'

AC Morne pulled his warrant card out of his back pocket and slung it on Anderson's desk. 'Have it now. I'm going to use the rest of the day to write up my full report into your constant vindictiveness, harassment and threatening behaviour toward these two men and send it with my resignation to the Home Secretary. Arsehole.' He stormed out of the office.

'Anyone else?' said Anderson.

Deputy Commissioner Richard Johnson and Assistant Commissioner Judy Levenworth, in charge of the Met's crime unit, both stood. 'Yeah,' said Levenworth. 'I can't work with you anymore. You're a bloody fool.' She turned on her heels and walked out.

Deputy Commissioner Johnson shook his head in disgust and fished out his own warrant card. 'See you at the enquiry,' he said.

CHAPTER THIRTY-NINE

Three days later, Detective Chief Inspector Len Grimes had gathered together what was left of Paterson's team, ready to brief them on events. With the deaths of two more colleagues and Paterson and Clocks still in hospital, they were all in a sombre mood. Some sat around with cups of coffee and a few, including Monkey Harris, openly drank scotch. Ordinarily, this would have bought them a severe bollocking from Grimes, a man not known for his sense of humour, but today was different.

'Good evening, everyone. For those of you who don't know me, I'm Detective Chief Inspector Grimes. I'm currently in charge of Two Area Serious Crime. I've been asked to brief you all on today's events and bring you up to speed with Mr Paterson and Mr Clocks. I know you're aware of some things already, but there may be a few of which you're not.

'As you know, both are still in hospital. DI Clocks is in a severe state of shock and depression and has received both medical and psychological care. We're hoping he can be released in the next day or two. Rest assured he'll receive the best of care and will be well supported by his colleagues. Superintendent Paterson suffered severe facial injuries at the hands of a man we know to be Marcus May. I am informed that, as bad as it looked, and it looked bloody bad, he will be able to have some form of plastic surgery. He will be scarred, of course, but a beard will remedy that. As for Inspector Clocks, the mental scars will be the longest and hardest to heal.

'DC Hartnett's wound to the throat is a life-changer. Surgeons fought for hours to keep her alive and thank God they did so. However, it's too early to say what effect the stab wound to the throat will do to her ability to speak in the future. She'll be off sick for a considerable time with the injury and rehabilitation but there will also come the depression. She may never come back, Time will tell.

'So, moving on . . . We've managed to piece together what the situation was with the May family. It seems there were three of them. Two females, Elizabeth and Beverley and one male, Marcus. They all suffered from some form of mental illness and to varying degrees. Whatever those degrees were, it's safe to assume they were high on the charts of the testing standards used. All three were the product of an incestuous relationship. Their mother and father were brother and sister and a pair of seriously violent bastards. These acts of violence were perpetrated on the kids in the form of beatings and rape.

'I guess because they had their problems and were something of a tight-knit group, they carried on the family tradition and were all having sex with each other.'

A few of the team wrinkled their brows and noses.

'Elizabeth, the youngest, was the weakest mentally and she was infatuated with her sister, Beverley. Worshipped the ground she walked on and desperately wanted to be her. Literally *be* her. At seventeen though, Beverley and Marcus fled the family home and set up together. Beverley changed her name by deed poll to Karen Long, but at twenty-one married her brother, Marcus, and became Karen May. The name change was important because anyone taking an interest would likely not have seen the deed poll papers, just the new name.'

'Sir?' said Dusty.

DCI Grimes pointed to him. 'Go on.'

'Didn't Elizabeth say that she had a child with Marcus and that both she and Marcus murdered and cut up that child?'

'She did, yes. When she was twenty-three, she lost a baby. A second — a girl — was born a few years later. She lived until the age of eight, at which point she disappeared. She is still on the missing list to this day. Tests are being run on the bodies of the children found in the basement to see if one of them is a DNA match. I suspect one will be.

'For the moment, we can find no concrete evidence to support that assertion. But, as I said, Elizabeth believed in her mind that she *was* Beverley and we think that it is likely because she would have known of Beverley's missing child and, getting the past and present mixed up in her mind, believed that she and Marcus had the child together and cut it up. Confusion reigns, I'm afraid.

'From there, things get a little patchy. We believe that Beverley used to visit her sister at Lynton Road and we think she always took one of the kidnapped children with her. Why, we're not sure of yet but the most likely answer is that each child she took with her was already dead and stitched together and she was showing Elizabeth what she had done. She filled her head with stories of making her own children with Marcus, hence Elizabeth's use of the term "Childmaker" and we also believe that she was using her as a form of defence should anybody cotton on. Who better to pin the blame on than a disturbed woman with severe mental issues, and what better way to frame someone than to hide the bodies in the walls of that person's house?

'What she and Marcus never counted on was Elizabeth killing a burglar and then the police officer. That basically threw a spanner in the works. When Paterson went out to visit Marcus, they must have assumed that the end was just a matter of time and, instead of running, they decided to double down and go out in a blaze of glory, so to speak.'

‘Where is Elizabeth now, sir?’ said Monkey Harris.

‘Psychiatric lock-up. She won’t be coming out for a long time.’

‘Did the search of Marcus’s house turn up anything else? Any more kids?’

DCI Grimes shook his head. ‘Only the one. The little girl that had been stitched together from others. Their “daughter”. Marcus ran off with her and left her in the house of Mr and Mrs Angel. We’re running tests to see if any parts of her match the bodies found in the Lynton Road address. I’d be shocked if they didn’t.’

He looked around the room. ‘Any more questions, anyone? No? Well, thank you all for your time and well done on a good job.’ DCI Grimes gave a slight nod and walked out of the room leaving the team alone.

‘Well done on a good job?’ said Monkey Harris. ‘We didn’t do fuck all. It’s on Ray and John again and I bet they don’t dish out medals to those two poor bastards.’

CHAPTER FORTY

Lyndsey walked out of the small hospital shop carrying a couple of bags of sweets and a copy of *The Times* for Paterson. She looked a bit sheepish.

'D'you get 'im any flowers, then?' said Clocks.

She kept walking. 'No. Got him some sweets instead. Come on.'

Clocks glanced inside the shop. 'What d'you mean? I asked you to get 'im some flowers, a porn mag and a bottle of voddy.'

'Yeah, I know. Didn't have any of that, though.'

'What? None of it?'

'No. None of it.'

Clocks pulled a face and frowned. 'Not even flowers?'

'No.'

'But it's a flower shop innit?'

'No. It's a sweetie cum paper shop. Hence the sweeties and paper.'

'Yeah, but they normally sell flowers too. All little shops in 'ospitals do.'

'Not in this one they don't.'

He eyed her suspiciously then walked into the shop himself. Lyndsey sighed. ''Scuse me, love,' he said to the old woman behind the till. 'Where'd you keep the flowers, please? I want some for me mate. Someone tried to cut his face off and he's a bit upset about it. I thought a bunch of flowers might cheer him up seein' as how he can't chew properly.'

She smiled at him, showing an uneven row of broken teeth. He noticed she smelled of mothballs, but he said nothing. 'He would be upset, wouldn't he?' the old lady said.

'I know I would be. Give me a right 'ump, that would.'

'I'm sorry, sir, but we don't keep flowers anymore. We're not allowed to sell them now.'

Clocks looked outside the shop at Lyndsey, whose face told him to get his arse out of there now and not make a fuss. He turned back to the old woman. 'Come again? Not allowed to sell flowers? Why's that then?'

The old lady shrugged. 'Health and safety. Not sold them for ages now.'

For a second, he thought she might be winding him up. 'You're 'avin' a laugh ain't ya, love? Health 'n' safety. Fuck's that all about?'

'John! Don't swear. It's not her fault.'

'Sorry, love. Didn't mean to swear but seriously, what the fuck?'

The old lady just smiled at him.

'You're serious, aren't you?'

'Yes, sir. Someone decided that they were an infection risk.'

Clocks wasn't sure if he was hearing her right. 'What? Infection risk? A bunch of flowers? 'Ow are they a bleedin' infection risk? I mean, seriously. When was the last time someone turned their toes up at getting a bunch of bleedin' flowers as a present?'

'My mate Elsie did,' said the old woman.

'What? What 'appened to her?'

'Her boyfriend sent a bouquet to her. Beautiful, it was. Interflora. Must have cost him a few bob.'

'And?'

'And her husband got the nark about it. Stabbed her in the guts, he did. Got ten years for that.'

Clocks shook his head. 'But she didn't die from an infection, did she?'

'Yeah, she did. She got septicaemia.'

'Christ . . .' Clocks muttered to himself.

'You can complain if you want, but this is an *all hospitals* policy. No hospitals sell them these days.'

'Jesus Christ. Fuckin' world's lost the plot.'

'John. I said not to swear.'

'Yeah, I know, Lynds, but . . . come on. No flowers. Everyone in 'ospital 'ad flowers when I was a kid. I mean, I've never seen a death certificate that said the victim snuffed it because they 'ad an 'ooterful of sniffin' a bunch of daisies, did they? Who's ever had an infection from a daisy? I'll tell you . . . *no one*. No one in the history of the world ever, ever died from a flower infection. I'll bet no one ever even *'ad* an infection from a daisy, either. That's like peanut allergies. That's all made-up that is. No one ever died from a peanut when I was a kid.' He stopped for a moment. 'Scratch that. Kid in my class did but that was 'cause he got about a dozen of 'em lodged in 'is throat, the greedy little bastard.'

Clocks stopped his ramble for a moment and pulled a face. 'Oh, 'ang on a minute. I know what's happened. Some little Jesse probably sniffed one, sneezed and ran off cryin' and the fuckin' government pissed their pants and whacked a ban on 'em. I bet that's what 'appened.'

'Can I get you anything else, sir?' said the old woman.

'Yeah. You can get me back to anytime before the late eighties when the world made bleedin' sense, love.' He pointed behind the counter. 'If you can't do that, give us some of them painkillers, will ya, gel?' He rubbed his forehead. 'I've got one of me 'eadaches coming on.'

He complained all the way along the corridors, in the lift and on the way along the corridors. Lyndsey ignored him, checking her phone as she walked. They found Paterson's ward and announced themselves at the reception desk. A middle-aged man pointed them to a ward further down another corridor.

CHAPTER FORTY-ONE

Ten minutes' wait later, they were allowed in to see Paterson. He was sitting up in bed and staring into space. He didn't see them come in.

'Oi, oi, saveloy!' Clocks marched up to Paterson's bed. 'Johnny Clocks's mobile make-up service has arrived. How can I 'elp you today?'

Paterson's head jerked up as he snapped out of his reverie. Then he turned and gave them a little wave. 'Hiya. How you doing, both of you? It's good to see you.'

'Good gawd,' said Clocks. 'Fuck all I can do for you, mate. Way too late for my 'elp.'

Paterson shook his head. He adjusted his position and made himself more comfortable. Lyndsey kissed him on the forehead and gave him his sweets. He put them on the bedside table.

'We're better than you, mate, by the looks of it,' said Clocks. He nodded his head towards Paterson's dressings. 'They've made a good job of that, ain't they? No bunny ears this time. I liked them though. They were cute. Suited you.'

'Yeah, I'll bet they did?'

'No flowers?'

Lyndsey shot Clocks a look. 'No, Ray,' she said. 'Sold out.'

Clocks grinned.

'What's the plan for the face long-term then, Ray?' she asked him.

'Bandages stay on for another couple of nights then I'm shipping out.'

'Shipping out?' said Lyndsey. 'What d'you mean?'

'I've booked myself into a top plastic surgeon in London. He's already been in to see me a couple of times. Said he can put my face back together with minimal scarring. Lucky, it seems.'

'How so?'

'The scalpel was extremely sharp. It made very fine cuts along the jawbone. The doctor says he can fix it in such a way that the scarring will be easy to hide. I'll have to grow a bit of the old designer stubble but at least I won't look like Frankenstein's monster.'

'I'd sack him now if I was you,' said Clocks.

'Why's that?' said Paterson.

'Well, he's obviously blowin' smoke up yer arse so he can rob you of a few quid. You've been an ugly bastard all yer life so I doubt he can do much for you. Save yer money, mate.'

Paterson gave him the finger.

'Oh, that's nice, innit? There's me thinkin' only of you.'

'I know,' said Paterson. 'You're all heart.'

'He reckons I'll probably lose a lot of feeling in the face too. Fair bit of nerve damage where the bastard ripped it away.'

'So, you'll be a bit like one of those supermodel birds with shitloads of Botox in their faces? They can't feel much either, can they?'

Paterson ignored him and turned to Lyndsey. 'Really, Lynds. No flowers? They'd have brightened it up in here a treat.'

Her shoulders fell.

'Turns out you can't buy 'em in 'ospitals anywhere now.' Clocks seized the opportunity for a moan.

Paterson looked doubtful.

'Not shittin' yer, mate. Straight up. The ol' bird in the shop downstairs said they're a serious infection risk so that's that. Stopped. I reckon some full-time *Guardian*-readin' nonce got a stick up his arse about summin'. Probably got hay fever, I dunno, and 'ad a little cry before firing off a letter. "Dear sir. We need to stop selling flowers in 'ospitals a bit lively. I went in to see my mate Tarquin Fafflebaff and I bought him a bunch of daisies. Havin' taken a big ol' snifter of daisy pollen, poor Tarquin sneezed his delicate little 'ead off until the curls fell out of his golden locks. Please start a campaign banning all flowers in 'ospitals immediately and forthwith. Yours. Angry of Knightsbridge."'

Paterson and Lyndsey said nothing. They just looked at him.

'Is he broken again, Lynds?'

'Oh, yeah. I'm not sure he can be fixed this time, though.'

'Leave off. You know I'm right. Lynds. Am I lyin' to him?'

She shook her head. 'It's true. He's been moaning about it all the way up here.'

'I'm not surprised. To be fair though, that's not on at all. Who's ever had an infection from a bunch of flowers?' Paterson was genuinely mystified.

'Thank you,' said Clocks. 'Exactly what I said.'

'Jesus,' said Lyndsey. 'I think you two ought to get married.'

'Yeah, I've thought about that, Lynds,' said Clocks. 'But he's not as good a bunk up as you. An' his tits are way too little for me, too.'

'John! For God's sake, grow up.'

'Just sayin'.'

'How's Jackie?' Paterson felt it best to change the subject before Lyndsey punched Clocks out. 'She making progress?'

Lyndsey nodded. 'She's getting there. But she's not out of the woods yet by a long way. She's still in intensive care and in a coma. Good news is, it's an induced coma. Bad news is, the doctors are still not sure yet whether she'll be able to speak again and they won't know for sure until she's had operations on her throat. Lots of them apparently. Poor cow's got a lot of grief and pain coming her way.'

'Make sure she gets everything she needs, Lynds. You know the score. My bill, okay.'

Lyndsey nodded.

Paterson's eyes widened as he looked between Lyndsey and Clocks. A familiar face had come to visit.

Ex-Commissioner of Police Wallace Young strolled into the ward and beamed his biggest smile toward the threesome. It had been some time since they'd all last met up and this wasn't the best of circumstances.

'Wol!' said Clocks.

'Hello, John. How the devil are you?'

'Yeah, good to see you.' They hugged each other briefly, patted each other on the back and quickly separated ways. Neither man was comfortable with public displays of affection. The big hug was reserved for Lyndsey. The two had grown close since their escapades in America and were genuinely fond of each other. He kissed her on the cheek as they held each other.

'And how are you?' he said to her. 'You look so well. You still going to marry him?'

She shrugged. 'I was. But now you're back up on the scene I may have to have a rethink.' The two of them made a point of flirting like a couple of kids in front of Clocks. It usually drove him mad but today he wasn't going to bite.

Wallace let her go and moved toward the bed. Paterson's face had lit up at seeing Wallace. The man was a genuine ally who had gone to bat for him and Clocks so many times. It hadn't always been that way of course. When Paterson had been suspended and investigated for the shooting of Adam Walker, Wallace was originally after his guts but he felt there was something in the man that warranted attention. He made sure Paterson got all the help he needed and was instrumental in getting him posted with Johnny Clocks on his return to work. He knew the pair together could, and would, make a difference. And they did. So much so that he argued and covered for them even when he shouldn't have and, on his retirement, went with them to America to bring back the escaped criminal Albert Tanner.

That trip had nearly cost him his life when he was stabbed in the chest. He would have died but for Paterson paying for the very best of care that was available.

'Ray, I'd hug you too, son,' he said, 'but you're half-undressed and in your bed. Given your reputation, I won't chance it.'

'I bloody well will,' said Lyndsey. 'Move yourselves.' She pretended to push Clocks and Wallace out of the way and pulled the covers back.

'Still a torment, then Lynds?' Wallace said.

She raised her eyebrows. 'Who's tormenting? I'm bloody serious.'

Clocks shook his head.

'So,' said Wallace. 'Seems you two have been in the thick of it again. You know you don't have to take every shitty case that comes along, don't you? There are plenty of husband-and-wife domestic murders you could look at. Way less risky.'

Paterson smiled. 'Yeah, you're right. Fools to ourselves, really. Still, someone's gotta do the nasty stuff. Might as well be us.'

'Indeed. Well, from what I've seen of it, you two did a brilliant job again, so this ex-Commissioner thanks you.'

Paterson's eyes suddenly welled up and he turned his head toward the window.

Clocks frowned. 'Ray. You all right, mate?'

Without turning to look at him, Paterson said, 'Yeah, I'm all right. It's okay.' He dabbed at his eyes with the knuckle of his hand and turned back around. 'John . . . Lynds . . . Listen, would you mind if I had a word with Wol? Alone? I'm sorry.'

They both looked a bit surprised but were happy to agree. Clocks in particular. He wasn't a fan of hospitals at the best of times. 'Yeah, no worries. Tell you what . . . we're gonna bugger off. Lyndsey's gotta go into the office today — a few things to do. I'll pop back in later tonight. That all right?'

'Yeah, of course. Course it is.'

Lyndsey bent down and kissed him on the head. 'You take it easy, Ray. I'll come and see you tomorrow. And comb your hair, you scruffy bastard.'

Paterson laughed and grimaced at the same time. A good sign that not all of his facial nerves were damaged.

When they'd gone, Wallace gave Paterson a serious look. 'What's the matter, Ray? Out with it.'

Paterson gave a weak smile. 'Sit down.'

Wallace pulled over a big heavy faux leather chair and sat himself down next to Paterson.

'It's so good to see you, Wol. Sorry I'm not at my best.'

Wallace shook his head. 'Don't be silly, son. You've been through the wringer this time. Wouldn't expect you to be in top-top shape today.'

The room fell silent for a moment or two. Both men with plenty to say, neither knowing where or how to start. Paterson swung his legs up and onto the bed and pushed himself back into his pillows.

'You said earlier that me and John don't have to take every shitty case that comes our way. You're right. But . . . someone has to deal with the shitty stuff, the *real* shitty stuff. Might as well be us as anyone, eh?'

'Well, you two did an outstanding job on this one. I doubt many other people could have put this to bed so quickly.'

Paterson looked Wallace Young in the eye. 'Outstanding? I got Carrie killed and Jackie seriously injured. How the fuck is that *outstanding*?'

'It wasn't your fault.'

'Wasn't it? I was the one who was taken in by Marcus. I was the one who took Carrie along. I was the one who let her go upstairs alone. I was the one who got jumped from behind and . . . and . . .' He turned his face to the window. 'I couldn't save her. I couldn't save her.'

'I know . . .'

'And Jackie. I put that crazy bitch Karen flat on her back and in reach of that knife. If I hadn't done that . . .'

'That was . . . unfortunate. Bad luck.'

'Bad luck? Bad luck? Bad luck is one number away from winning the EuroMillions jackpot. This is on me. They're both on me. Like the others. All the others and . . . I can't keep doing this, Wol. I can't.'

'Doing what?' said Wallace. A look of concern spread across his face.

'Can't keep killing people. Fuck! Even you nearly died because of me.'

Wallace sat forward in his chair and stared at Paterson. 'All right, Ray. I get it. I do. I know you're feeling pretty crappy at the moment, but that's enough. You need to get out of your own head and stop taking the blame for a series of tragically unfortunate events. That's what they were. That's all they will ever be. Unfortunate. Yes, people died. But not by your hand.'

Paterson ignored that remark. He had long suspected Wallace knew exactly what he did to Adam Walker on the top of Tower Bridge to avenge his wife.

'They died because you and John do a godawful dirty job. You chase down the worst dregs of society and sometimes, *sometimes*, it goes wrong. That's the nature of the beast, Ray. You've got to stop this or you'll drive yourself insane.'

Paterson pulled his knees up to his chest and hugged them tight. 'No more, Wol. I can't keep doing this. No more.'

Wallace said nothing.

'It's just too much. Every night when I sleep, if I sleep, every time it goes quiet, every time I go home to an empty house, I see them. Dead people. Not the people who deserved to die, but the people who didn't, who wouldn't have died if it wasn't for me being in their lives. Lisa, Dave, the girls, the Angels, poor bastards. If it wasn't for me, they'd all still be alive. I can't handle the fucking guilt anymore.'

'Do you have a plan then? How to deal with this guilt?'

'Quitting.'

Wallace shook his head. 'You've said that before. You keep saying that you've had enough and you're packing it in but you never do, do you? God knows, with your resources you could walk away and not bat an eyelid but, again, you never do. So, why? What's stopping you?'

Paterson gently touched at his bandages, followed the line from ear to chin. 'I swear to God, I don't know.'

'I do. Look, Ray, I don't want to pile into you but here's the way I see it. You two will never stop. You can't. There's something in the pair of you that drives you on so you just have to accept it. Acceptance is the key to this life of ours. If you learn to accept it, that you're destined to have a hard life, see and do some tough stuff, you'll be okay. You will. Stop fighting against it, son. Life will get easier if you do. You make decisions in a split second. You have to. Do you make mistakes? Yes. We all do but that's the nature of this particular job I'm afraid. Don't keep analysing it. Accept it. Trust me.'

Paterson looked at him. He knew the man was right. He needed to get himself together. 'How's John? Really? Underneath all the Jack-the-Lad persona and silly jokes. How is he?'

'In pain.'

Paterson nodded. 'Will he be all right?'

'In time.'

'Yeah.'

'You both will. Trust me.'

'You know Commissioner Anderson is after me? Us?'

Wallace smiled. 'You can scratch that.'

Paterson sat up a bit. 'Scratch that? How'd you mean?'

'He's about to be put on gardening leave. Seems a few of his senior team have had a severe crisis of confidence in his ability to remain impartial and carry out the duties of his office with a clear and level head. The Home Secretary is drawing up a suspension notice pending a full investigation into his behaviour not only toward you two but also into his bullying of junior and civilian members of staff. Should be suspended by the end of the day.'

For the second time that day, Paterson smiled. 'Would I be right in thinking you may have had something to do with that happening, Wol?'

'Me?' Wol looked surprised. 'Do you honestly think I would encourage a bunch of my old colleagues to stand against my successor and bring his career to an ignominious end?'

'You might, you crafty old sod.'

'And you'd be bloody well right, you young whipper-snapper. C'mon Ray. He'll not give you any more grief. Think about what I said. Get out of your own head and look toward the future. Things can only get better for the two of you.'

CHAPTER FORTY-TWO

It was just after 4 p.m. and DC Toni Bell was getting ready to knock off for the day. Since the incident with the Childmaker she, like most of Paterson's team, had been placed on restricted duties until she was deemed fit enough mentally to resume normal working. But before she went home, she had the unenviable task of going through a dead woman's locker. Carrie had been gone for a week now and her locker had to be emptied of all its contents and anything that wasn't police issue had to be returned to the family. She'd been dreading this since she was asked to do the job by Carrie's mother. Though they didn't know each other too well, they were on chatting terms and so she seemed the best choice to collect her daughter's belongings given that Lyndsey had reported sick with stress. She could hardly say no. She didn't feel that comfortable about snooping around in Carrie's possessions.

She really hoped there wasn't a diary. She'd already told herself if there was, she wouldn't read it but, in reality, she knew she would. She'd have to. She didn't want anything coming out about Carrie that was unflattering and that was a risk if someone got hold of it. It wasn't unknown for photocopies of people's diary pages to end up on the canteen notice board.

It still didn't make her feel good about it.

She wandered across to Carrie's locker pulling out the little silver key for the padlock from her jeans. She stopped for a moment, a wave of sadness overtaking her knowing that she'd never see her again. The lock made a small click as it opened. She lifted off the storage box that had been left on top for her and dropped it to the floor. It rattled about with a hollow plastic sound until it settled down.

Inside she saw the usual stuff: a couple of suits that she wore for court appearances; skirts, shirts and blouses and two pairs of jeans hung from the rack in the middle. Neatly stacked on the top shelf was a pile of books: a job notebook, three A5 Black 'n' Red ruled notebooks, a battered paperback and a stack of pens and pencils in a china cup. There was also a small Olympus digital recorder. She pressed the power-on button and a little red LED glowed. She turned it off and put it in the storage box. She then took everything from the top shelf and placed it all carefully and neatly into the box. Next, she took out all of Carrie's blouses and shirts, folded them up and dropped them on top of everything else. The suits, skirts and jeans she left on the hangers and hung them on the back of the door for the time being. They could be laid out flat on the back seat of her car.

In the bottom of the locker was a small kit bag and two pairs of shoes. One pair for working in, the other for dancing in. She knelt down, took the shoes and dropped them into the box. She pulled out the bag, which was heavier than she expected.

Pulling back the zip, she saw that it was full of A4-sized notebooks, loose sheets of paper with writing on, mostly in red, and a couple of photo albums. She sat herself down on the floor. Going through this lot was going to take a bit of time but it had to be sorted through. For whatever reason, more than a few coppers had taken and hidden files or bits of information relating to criminal cases and stuffed them in their lockers. She hoped that Carrie hadn't been that stupid.

She picked up the first notebook and skimmed through its pages. Nothing struck her as being out of the ordinary, just some notes on various aspects of the law. She knew Carrie had talked about taking a promotion at some point. Maybe these were her study notes.

The next one was more of the same, so she tried a photo album after that. As she flicked through the pages, she shook her head. Mostly photos of her and Paterson on days out. She remembered once asking Carrie why she still kept prints when everything was digital these days and she'd replied that she liked to keep copies of the special ones. The digital ones tend to get buried along with the hundreds of others that get taken day after day after day. Toni understood that. She had more than a few prints of memorable times from her life hung on the walls at home.

She pulled out another notebook and flicked through its pages. This one was full of writing again, but it also had a few drawings in it. She stopped flicking and looked at the drawings more carefully. She read the notes on the opposite page and her jaw dropped.

'Dear God, no . . . Oh, no!'

Toni began to sob as she worked her way through the book, unable to comprehend what she was looking at. At the end of the book, she closed it up, sniffed and wiped at her nose with the back of her free hand.

She needed to tell someone. *Had* to tell someone. And they had to be high up in the chain of command.

CHAPTER FORTY-THREE

Johnny Clocks sat himself in the chair that Wallace Young had vacated earlier in the day. Paterson could see the pain etched deep into his friend's face and he wondered if, for all of his bluff and bravado, he would ever get over this. He doubted it.

'Hello, John. Thanks for coming to see me.'

Clocks was peering at Paterson's face. 'S'all right, mate. I don't have anything much else to do, to be honest.'

Paterson gave him a small smile. 'How are you?'

'Shattered, to tell the truth.'

Paterson's shoulders dropped. He knew what Clocks was going through and he knew also that there was nothing he could do to help him. For all his bullshit, Clocks cared, and he cared deeply about his friends. Time would be the only healer — so they had told him when he lost his wife. Time. The trouble with that was, no one ever said how much time.

'The whole thing was a fuckin' mess, Ray. One big colossal clusterfuck of a mess.'

'I know. I'm sorry.'

Clocks bristled. 'So you should be. What the fuck were you thinkin' going out there without proper backup?'

'I . . . didn't suspect, not for a second, that it would end like that. Not for a second. I just went to get the papers he said he had.'

'Papers. For a set of fuckin' imaginary papers, all this happened. All those people died. Jackie's proper fucked. She'll never be the same. Not ever.' He shook his head.

'John . . . I don't know what to s—'

'Nothin' *to* say, is there? What's done is done. End of.'

As quickly as he reared up, Clocks calmed back down. Paterson knew the behaviour pattern well. Clocks's moods would be all over the place for months until acceptance set in.

'I'm sorry,' said Clocks. 'Didn't mean to snap. Sorry.'

'It's all right, mate. I get it.'

Clocks stared out of the window. 'Nice view, you've got. Is that a statue out there in the garden?'

'Yeah. Some old doctor. Think he was the Chief Surgeon or something. Haven't really looked to tell the truth.'

Clocks sniffed and quickly cuffed his nose with the back of his hand. Paterson could see that he was fighting back tears.

'John.'

Clocks ignored him and bit his bottom lip in an effort to stop it from wobbling.

'John. It's okay, mate. Let it go.'

Clocks took a sudden, sharp inhalation and turned back to Paterson.

'How the fuck do you live with it?'

Paterson's stomach tightened, unsure of exactly what he meant. He prepared himself for an onslaught of anger. It never came.

'The pain. God, the fuckin' pain. It's killin' me, mate. It's killin' me.' He buried his head in his hands, rubbed his face and looked at Paterson for an answer. 'So many people. You know I loved your Lisa too, don't you? She was a diamond.'

Paterson looked slightly embarrassed. There was no good answer to this.

That was a time when he and Clocks despised the sight of each other. Worlds apart until Lisa was torn apart by a serial killer and Clocks allowed Paterson to take his revenge. That night changed everything and set them on their path. A path that brought them here with more dead bodies behind them than they could have ever imagined.

'I know you did, mate. I know. Have you been holding that in as well?'

Clocks scuffed his nose with the back of his hand. 'Yeah, course I 'ave. I can't get the image of when I found her out of my mind. I can't. It haunts me day 'n' night. Nothing 'elps me. Therapy . . . booze . . . fightin'. Nothin'.'

'Why haven't you told me this before?'

'What? Not gonna tell you that am I? You've got enough on yer plate as it is. It's 'ard for me but's it's a damn sight 'arder for you. Must be. Besides, what good's whining about it gonna do?'

'It's gonna let you get it out. To talk to me can only help.'

Clocks rubbed the back of his neck. 'Nah, you know me. I just get on with it, don't I?'

'Apparently not if you're still struggling with it.'

'Yeah, well, change the subject.'

Paterson sighed. He knew Clocks would clam up now. No point pushing him on it. He stared off out through the window and into the courtyard. It was dark outside now but he could still see the statue of the man he thought might have been a surgeon. He didn't know quite what to say to Clocks. Certainly not now, not at this time when emotions were so raw and the wounds so deep. 'Just give it time.'

Clocks snorted. 'Time. Oh, yeah. That's the secret is it? I'm gonna feel like I've 'ad me bollocks kicked all the way up into me throat for . . . gawd knows 'ow long, an' then one day I'll wake up an' it's all gone away, yeah?'

Paterson said nothing.

'Hasn't gone away for you though, 'as it?'

'I'm getting there. All you can do is go one day at time. I'm not gonna lie . . . it's a bastard of a battle sometimes.

Most times. It's hard to drag yourself up and out of bed. To shower. To shave. To shop. To do anything. But you have to.'

'It's my fault. If I hadn't taken Jackie with—'

'Don't go there, John. Don't do that to yourself. It wasn't your fault. You couldn't have known the outcome. None of us could.'

Clocks rubbed his eyes with the heel of his hands and took in a deep breath. 'So, what do we do now?'

Paterson sighed. 'Honestly? I really dunno. To be honest, I've had a gutful of this. I don't — *we* don't need any more. Seems the more good we do the worse it gets for us. Wol's had that prick Anderson dealt with but I can't see it being over. Anderson'll never let up until we either quit or go to prison. And prison isn't high on my list of places to visit.'

'You'll be all right. Should fit right in now you're an ugly bastard like the rest of us. They won't be after you in the showers so much now.' He gave Paterson a weak smile. Right then, Paterson knew that although Clocks had a long climb back, he'd make it. They both would.

'So, what do we do, then? You sayin' we should break up the band? Do a Simon and Garfunkel?'

'Who?' said Paterson.

'Don't matter. Before your time.'

'Packing it in seems sensible.'

'Well, if we pack it all in, then what? I can't do anythin' other than this job. I've got no other skills, have I? I mean, who's gonna wanna take on an obnoxious fucker like me? An' I can't see meself working on a checkout somewhere. First one who gets stroppy with me is going 'ome with his teeth in one of those Bags for Life.'

'Don't worry about a job. You'll be all right money-wise. I'll make sure you're all right.'

Clocks sat quietly for a moment, then shook his head. 'I dunno. We can't give in, son. That's not us. Carrie wouldn't want us to. She always said we were supposed to be together and gettin' into all sorts of scrapes. Fuck, she was always a bit surprised no one had made us into action figures with the bendy arms that kids could play with. I can imagine that.'

Paterson laughed. 'Me too.'

'Besides, I wanna make the bad people's lives' a fuckin' misery for as long as I possibly can.'

'Then we're both gonna have to get ourselves some serious help before we have a total breakdown.'

CHAPTER FORTY-FOUR

DI Marcus Goodwin of Beckenham CID stood at the back of the room and allowed the family of DCI Chris Lambert to be with him when he died. His wife sat in shock and his daughter held his hand, shaking it, between great heaving sobs, begging him to come back, to stay with them.

The nurse in the room, Sylvia Lord, spoke gently to Lambert's dazed wife, telling her that the family could stay with him for as long as they liked. No rush. Donna Lambert, eyes glazed over, her mind struggling for reason and still unable to grasp that her husband was about to die, gave Nurse Lord a small smile and quickly retreated back into her own head.

Things had not been good between her and her husband for some time. They still loved and cared for each other, but they just couldn't seem to work things out. Divorce had been spoken about several times but it wasn't something either of them really wanted. And now, none of that mattered anymore. The decision was no longer theirs to make.

A few hours before he died, Chris Lambert found moments of lucidity in between bouts of consciousness and sleep. When awake, he was staring up toward the ceiling and began mumbling the same thing over and over again.

His daughter, Katie, tried to calm him and he would drift off before waking again, repeating the same muffled incantation. But, just once, he said something that was clear. Katie Lambert's eyes had widened.

'Nurse,' she'd said.

'Yes, my love. What is it?' Nurse Lord had been writing something on a clipboard.

'Can you get that policeman outside to come in here, please? It's urgent.'

'Of course, One second.'

'Now, please. It really is urgent.'

Nurse Lord recognised the tone and walked outside holding the door open.

'What is it, miss?' The guard, PC Flag, had poked his head into the room.

'Can you get a senior officer here, please? My dad's saying something. It's important.'

The guard looked over at DCI Lambert lying in his bed muttering to himself.

'Come and listen.'

'I can't leave my post, miss. I have to stand on the door.'

'You're not leaving your post, are you? Not really. Just come and listen.'

He had looked hesitant but did as she asked. 'What's he saying?' He bent down and placed his head near to Lambert's. Then he stood up and pressed the record button on his video body cam.

Within the hour, DCI Goodwin from Southward CID arrived and listened carefully to what Lambert said. He made a careful note of his words and got Donna and Katie Lambert, Nurse Lord and PC Flag to sign his notes as being a true and accurate record of what was said. Six minutes after he did that, DCI Lambert died and the notes were to become his dying declaration.

The signing of the notes was done to prevent any rigorous questioning in a court of law, should the person who shot him ever be brought to justice.

Without the signatures, it would be attacked in court as the ramblings of a man in his dying moments and with no real grasp of what he was saying. This statement would never be challenged. But, the ace in the hole was PC Flag's bodycam footage.

DCI Goodwin slipped quietly out of the room and left the family to their grief before walking out into the corridor. When he was far enough away, he took out his mobile phone and checked the time on his watch: 11:38 p.m. He scrolled through his contacts before making a call.

CHAPTER FORTY-FIVE

Sir Scott Anderson couldn't get back to sleep. His mind was racing from the brief conversation he'd just had with DCI Goodwin. He sat up, pulled off the duvet cover and swung his legs out of bed. His wife stirred and rolled over onto her side. Anderson covered her up gently before stepping into his slippers and slipping on his dressing gown.

He picked up the notebook he kept by his bed and went downstairs to the kitchen. He made himself a cup of tea and sat himself down at the table. As he sipped at his tea, his mind ran over the conversation he'd had with Goodwin.

When he'd got the call, it had taken him a few seconds to realise what was going on. When Goodwin got to the important part, he wondered if he was actually dreaming.

If what Lambert had said before he died was indeed verified by all in the room, then he knew that his day had just taken a dramatic turn for the better. At around midday, he'd been visited at home by Commander Jackson of Southwark division and DC Toni Bell. From the outside, people would wonder why, when he was on suspension, he'd received a visit from them. But those people didn't know that DC Toni Bell had been working for Anderson since before she joined Paterson's team with explicit instructions to get as much dirt on the two of them as possible. And now her patience had paid off in an unexpected way and it might even see him reinstated.

She had handed him the books she'd taken from Carrie Gedmine's locker and he'd skimmed through them while she told him what was in them in more detail.

He shook his head as he looked at the notes and drawings of Carrie Gedmine's total obsession with Superintendent Ray Paterson. There were pages of poems and draft love letters she had written but never sent. There were little pictures she had drawn of his face with the words *my darling husband* written neatly underneath. In all, it looked like the writings of a lovestruck twelve-year-old girl.

'And these were in her locker, yes?' he'd said to Toni.

'Yes, sir. These were bad enough, but this is the one you really need to see.'

She'd handed him a small notebook and he'd read through the entries more carefully on this one. There were no poems, no drawings, no hints of the twelve-year-old girl. The language had changed. The tone had changed. These were plans. Detailed plans. Different scenarios had been catered for. *Many* different scenarios.

'Next page, sir,' Toni had said.

Anderson had flipped the page and, as he read, his heart had skipped a beat. In black and white Carrie Gedmine had laid out how she had shot and killed DCI Chris Lambert and killed the girls in the Beckenham and Bromley area in a demented homage to Paterson.

That was a huge blow, a police officer being responsible for killing innocent women. In the back of his mind, though, he felt hope begin to rise and he couldn't help but wonder if Paterson knew or was involved. He tried to dismiss the thought but the more he read, the more his hopes rose.

And then, this evening, DCI Goodwin had phoned. He had told him about Lambert's declaration, about the body cam footage the armed police guard had taken. Anderson dunked a biscuit in his tea, fired up his laptop and clicked on the link in the email that DCI Goodwin had sent him. He popped in a small pair of earphones and turned the volume up a touch. He took a swig of his tea as he watched DCI Lambert struggling to sit up. He watched intently as Lambert pointed his fingers like a gun to no one in particular. He heard him speak, slurred. He backed up the video, turned the volume up and pressed one of the earphones further in. Same again, still unsure of what Lambert had said. Rewind. Play again.

And then all his Christmases came at once.

Lambert's last words as he mimicked his attacker's action with his pretend gun fingers. '*A message. From Paterson . . . and Clocks. From Paterson . . . From Paterson . . . Clocks . . . Not personal. Not perso . . . No . . . Fuck off and die. Fuck off and die. Fuck off . . . and . . .*'

Anderson's hands shook as he set the cup down next to his laptop.

'And there it is. You've finally slipped up, boys. Now you're fucked.'

THE END

ALSO BY STEVE PARKER

DETECTIVE RAY PATERSON BOOKS

Book 1: THEIR LAST WORDS
Book 2: THE LOST CHILDREN
Book 3: THE BURNING MEN
Book 4: YOU CAN'T HIDE
Book 5: THEIR DYING BREATH
Book 6: CHILD BEHIND THE WALL

FREE KINDLE BOOKS

Do you love mysteries, historical fiction and romance? Join thousands of readers enjoying great books through our mailing list. You'll get new releases and great deals every week from one of the UK's leading independent publishers.

Join today, and you'll get your first bargain book this month!

www.joffebooks.com/contact

Follow us on Facebook, Twitter and Instagram

@joffebooks

Thank you for reading this book.

If you enjoyed it please leave feedback on Amazon or Goodreads, and if there is anything we missed or you have a question about, then please get in touch. The author and publishing team appreciate your feedback and time reading this book.

We're very grateful to eagle-eyed readers who take the time to contact us. Please send any errors you find to corrections@joffebooks.com. We'll get them fixed ASAP.

Manufactured by Amazon.ca
Bolton, ON